Praise for SUE HENRY's
ALASKA MYSTERIES

DEADFALL

"Wonderfully evocative."
Baltimore Sun

"Riveting suspense."
Publishers Weekly

"Real thrills set against
the wild beauty of Alaska."
Minneapolis Star Tribune

DEATH TAKES PASSAGE

"Spectacular."
Oklahoma City Oklahoman

"Her best outing yet . . . Henry keeps the intrigue
swirling and the tension mounting."
Kirkus Reviews

SLEEPING LADY

"Twice as vivid as Michener's natural Alaska
at about a thousandth the length."
Washington Post Book World

Books by Sue Henry

MURDER ON THE IDITAROD TRAIL
TERMINATION DUST
SLEEPING LADY
DEATH TAKES PASSAGE
DEADFALL
MURDER ON THE YUKON QUEST

SUE HENRY

MURDER ON THE IDITAROD TRAIL

AN ALASKA MYSTERY

AVON BOOKS, INC.
An Imprint of Harper Collins*Publishers*
10 East 53rd Street
New York, New York 10022-5299

Map by Vanessa Summers; for further information write Artmaps, P.O. Box 221030, Anchorage, Alaska 99522

Published by arrangement with The Atlantic Monthly Press
Library of Congress Catalog Card Number: 90-20925
ISBN: 0-380-71758-1
www.harpercollins.com

First Avon Books Printing: March 1993

Printed in the U.S.A.

WCD 20 19 18 17 16 15 14 13 12

In memory of my father,
C. A. "JACK" HALL

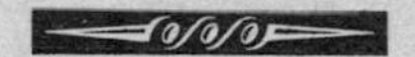

The Iditarod Trail follows the checkpoints along the southern route every other year, as I have described. Aside from artistic license in creating the story, every attempt has been made to keep the details about the Iditarod as accurate as possible. There may be minor errors, for which I apologize. Special thanks are due to the Alaska State Troopers, the Scientific Crime Detection Laboratory, and the Iditarod Trail Committee, without whose assistance I wouldn't have been able to write the book. I wish it were possible to mention all the people who helped me in the research and the writing of this book, as well as each of the hundreds of dedicated people who keep the race in motion each year. They all deserve recognition and gratitude.

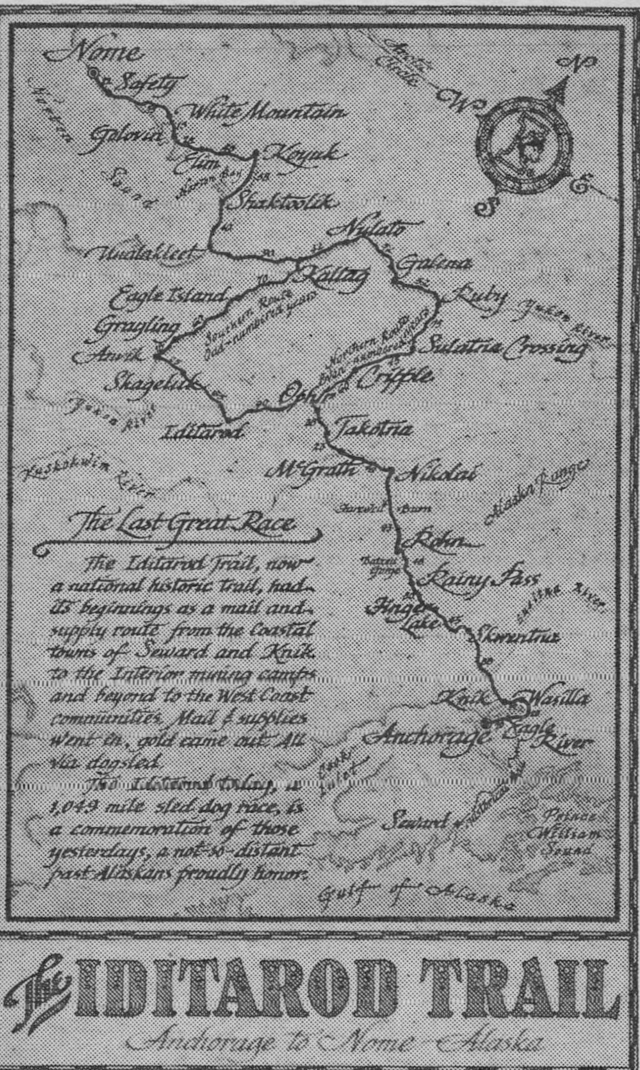
Nome
Safety
White Mountain
Golovin
Elim
Koyuk
Shaktoolik
Unalakleet
Nulato
Kaltag
Galena
Ruby
Eagle Island
Grayling
Anvik
Southern Route
Odd-numbered years
Northern Route
Even-numbered years
Sulatna Crossing
Shageluk
Ophir
Cripple
Iditarod
Takotna
McGrath
Nikolai
Alaska Range
Rohn
Rainy Pass
Finger Lake
Skwentna
Knik
Wasilla
Anchorage
Eagle River
Seward
Prince William Sound
Gulf of Alaska
Yukon River
Kuskokwim River
N
W
E
S
The Last Great Race
The Iditarod Trail, now a national historic trail, had its beginnings as a mail and supply route from the coastal towns of Seward and Knik to the Interior mining camps and beyond to the West Coast communities. Mail & supplies went in, gold came out. All via dogsled.
The Iditarod today, a 1,049 mile sled dog race, is a commemoration of those yesterdays, a not-so-distant past Alaskans proudly honor.
The IDITAROD TRAIL
Anchorage to Nome Alaska

1

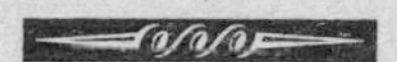

Date: Sunday, March 3
Race Day: Two
Place: Between Skwentna and Finger Lake
checkpoints (forty-five miles)
Weather: Clear skies, light to no wind
Temperature: High 8°F, low 4°F
Time: Late afternoon

THE IDITAROD TRAIL OUT OF SKWENTNA, ALASKA, ran easy and level, bending its way northwest for miles through snow-covered muskeg. Without strong winds to erase them, the tracks of sled runners were still visible in the late afternoon light. The musher watched them flow beneath his sled. A day and a half into the thousand-mile sled-dog race to Nome, he was among the leaders in a field of sixty-eight participants. His sixteen dogs were eager to run, well rested from a four-hour stop in Skwentna. But, riding the runners behind his sled, George Koptak fought fatigue. An hour of poor sleep at the last checkpoint had not been enough. His body demanded more. He'd spent thirty-one hours on the trail, most of it standing up, pushing the sled or pumping behind it.

Checkpoints in a long-distance race offer little rest for competitors. Once fed, tired dogs almost immediately curl into tight tail-to-nose balls in the snow and sleep. The musher must haul water, cook another batch of dog food for a trail feeding, repack equipment, find something to eat (though his hunger often seems inconsequential compared to his need for rest), and, finally, lie down for a ragged hour's sleep.

Excitement, anticipation, and nerves left over from yesterday's start had continued to feed a certain amount of adrenaline into Koptak's system, as had the knowledge that some of the most difficult challenges in the race must soon be met and overcome.

Now the tired musher leaned forward over the handlebars of his sled, trying to find a semicomfortable way to rest on top of his sled bag. Although the trail was level, it was not smooth, and the bow caught him under the ribs, gouging with every bump. He straightened, stretched his shoulders to relieve the ache between them, pumped for a while with one foot, then the other, and talked to his dogs to keep awake.

At the site of the old, abandoned Skwentna Roadhouse, the trail plunged down onto ice and followed the frozen river for a while before climbing the opposite bank to enter the spruce and alder forest surrounding Shell Lake. Though the sun had set, light lingered on the snow. Knowing it would soon be dark, he stopped his team on the riverbank before going onto the ice.

He snacked his dogs, tossing them frozen whitefish. After munching a few handfuls of trail mix, heavy with nuts and chocolate, he drank half the hot coffee in his metal thermos, filled at the checkpoint. Locating his headlamp, he checked the batteries and fastened it in place. Twenty minutes later he was heading upriver.

For half an hour, the coffee kept him awake. Then, as he came up off the ice and into the trees, fatigue caught him again. He drifted in and out, catching a few seconds of sleep at a time, as the team snaked its way along the trail between the trees with a steady, almost hypnotic rhythm.

When he jerked awake to the dangerous reality of the narrow, winding trail, he was afraid. Dark had fallen quickly among the trees. He switched on his headlamp, losing his perspective and night vision in the process. The trail became a tunnel, closing in around him.

The dogs, stretched out for almost forty feet in front of the sled, were rarely all visible at the same time along the twists and turns of the trail. Like fireflies, strips of reflector tape on their harness winked back at him when hit by his light. Low-hanging tree limbs flashed by overhead, making him duck, though most were beyond reach. He knew the agony of having wood lash cold flesh and had seen mushers come into checkpoints with swollen, battered faces—the result of a moment's inattention.

The trail curved perilously close to trees as it swung back and forth through the forest. The sled, responding to the centrifugal pull, slid toward these as if attracted by a magnet. If he didn't quickly throw his weight to control the slide, he risked slamming into the trunks, which bristled with small limbs and sharp broken branches that could scratch and tear at face, clothing, and sled.

One brush against a tree trunk ripped a hole in the sled bag. In the next small clearing, he stopped, knowing he must repair that hole or risk having essential gear fall through and be lost. He searched through his supplies for a needle and dental floss, standard temporary repair material, and squatted beside the sled to attempt the chore.

Trees closed off most of the sky. Only the circle of light from his headlamp, focused on the needle and the tear, was real. Everything else disappeared, even the dogs, the trail. He nodded drowsily, then jerked awake, forcing himself to attention, opening his eyes wide.

After a few minutes of working without mittens his fingers grew numb with cold and he could no longer feel the large needle. He stopped and put his hands under his parka, wool shirt, and long underwear, directly on the warm flesh of his belly. Waiting for feeling to return, he leaned his head against the side of the sled bag and closed his eyes.

He threw his head back with a start, the headlamp casting a narrow arc of light over the sled and trees beyond it. His hands were warm, but more than anything he wanted to lay his face back against the sled. Refusing to give in, he stood up. His back and legs had cramped slightly, and he stomped around the sled to stretch them. The dogs raised their heads, waiting for his word, but he still had to complete the repair. Slowly he finished the stitching and repacked the needle with care so as not to lose it in the snow.

He did not understand why he was so exhausted and wondered vaguely if he was ill. Dulled reflexes and reactions were more common at the end of the long trail. He had always been able to adjust to the early pace, shake off sleepiness. Coffee usually helped, but this time it was not working.

Coffee. Pulling out the thermos, he drank all but a few swallows of the still warm brew, determined to wake up. Whistling up the dogs, he continued down the trail.

Within minutes his eyes were closing again. His head lolled against one shoulder, then the other. The world turned to fog. He could hardly hold on to the sled. Summoning a gigantic effort, he took the thermos from the bag on the back of the sled, uncapped it, stuffed the cap into the bag, and finished the coffee. Before he could put it away, it slipped from his hand and bounced behind him to lie forgotten in the trail.

The dogs followed an abrupt turn to the right. A large tree loomed ahead, so close to the trail that the swing dog on the left brushed her flank against it as she passed. Koptak fell forward across the drive bow, aware of nothing. As the sled, out of control, whipped into the turn, it slid solidly into the tree, mashing a stanchion and cracking the left runner. The musher, body limp, mercifully unconscious, was thrown directly against the trunk, face first.

His headlamp shattered as it hit. So did his nose and cheek. A wicked, foot-long limb projected from the side of the trunk. Cold and sharp, it entered his closed right eye and pushed through his brain until it hit the back of his skull. There it stopped. His body hung against the trunk of the spruce until his weight broke the limb and he fell slowly onto the trail.

A half-hour later, the corpse was starting to stiffen. The next driver, curious about a thermos picked up three turns back, swung into the curve. Horrified but unable to stop, he felt the lurch as his runners passed over the heap he recognized as his friend.

2

Date: Sunday, March 3
Race Day: Two
Place: Between Skwentna and Finger Lake
checkpoints (forty-five miles)
Weather: Clear skies, light to no wind
Temperature: High 8°F, low 4°F
Time: Midevening

FORTY-FIVE-YEAR-OLD DALE SCHULLER HAD NOT set out from Skwentna with any premonition of impending tragedy. If anything, his expectations for the rest of the Iditarod ran high. He had every reason to suppose he had as good a chance of winning as anyone in the race.

The start in Anchorage the day before had been clean for everyone, though soft snow had slowed the pace somewhat. Warm temperatures had brought enough snow so the city had not had to truck it in to Fourth Avenue. Schuller had drawn number nine in the starting lineup, and the trail to Eagle River, fifteen miles away, had still been in good shape when he hit it, not yet churned up by the feet of over a thousand sled dogs from the sixty-eight teams. He sympathized with the last forty mushers. The year before he had been number thirty-two. Now, though he had passed and been passed by mushers as they jockeyed for position, he was moving consistently and well.

In Eagle River the teams had been loaded onto trucks and transported twenty-five miles to Settler's Bay for restart. This avoided crossing the Knik and Matanuska rivers, which sometimes weren't frozen on the first Saturday in March.

After restart, the run across the Knik Flats to Rabbit Lake and Skwentna had been uneventful. It had felt good to step off the sled for a couple of hours' rest, but the ground had seemed to go on moving slightly as Schuller fed and watered his dogs and completed the necessary chores.

This was his seventh year of mushing, his third attempt at this greatest of all dog-racing challenges. His team was well seasoned, just at their peak, with over fifteen hundred training miles behind them. He had won the Knik 200 and come in third in the Kuskokwim 300, both good mid-distance races. The prize money was security. But with two local sponsors solidly behind him, money was not the problem it had been in earlier years. The huge cost of running a kennel, obtaining the best equipment, and paying entry fees would not put him in debt this year.

All of his dogs were running well and eagerly. Comet, his veteran lead dog, was behaving like the lady she was, keeping to the trail and ignoring distractions with dignity. She had a good head, was here to do a job, and knew it. Pepper, her three-year-old son, was running for the first time this year and, so far, had managed to hold his own. The sixteen other dogs were healthy and strong, the pick of his kennel.

When they pulled up off the river ice, Schuller had

tensed slightly as the trees closed in around them, but he soon relaxed into the rhythm of the curves, enjoying his driving skill and the response of his team. It caught him off guard when Comet made a seemingly senseless error.

For no apparent reason she missed a sharp right turn and led the first half of his dogs off the trail to tangle themselves in the trees. Schuller thought he saw a light on the trail ahead but dismissed it in his surprise and frustration. Swearing, he stepped hard on the brake and dug in the snow hook before leaping forward to assess the situation, concerned with the danger of strangulation for a dog snarled in its harness.

The dogs yelped and struggled, trying to free themselves from branches and brush. "Whoa. Easy there. Down, Comet. Easy girl." From what he could see, they were tangled but safe and not going anywhere without help. Reaching the turn they had missed, he stopped. The light from a headlamp flashed across his face.

Bill Turner, who had left Skwentna only a few minutes ahead of him, sat in the trail. Another musher lay across his knees. There was little left of the musher's face. Blood covered the front of his parka, and a great splash of it stained the snow under the bloodstained tree trunk.

"What the hell happened?" Schuller asked, striding forward quickly and dropping to his knees in the snow beside them. Removing his headlamp, he directed its beam more closely as he stripped off his mitten and laid his fingers along the soft hollow beneath the musher's jaw. There was no pulse.

"It's George," Turner said stiffly. His pale face reflected the light, his eyes huge with shock. "He m-must have lost it on the corner and hit the tree. God, Dale. I r-ran over him."

Schuller could hear Turner's teeth click together as he tried to talk. "I can't find his team. Wh-where's his dogs?"

"You looked?"

"Yeah. But I c-couldn't let him just . . . lay here in the snow. I knew you'd be along pretty close behind me, so I waited."

"Sit still. I'll be right back." Schuller rose and returned to his sled. Unzipping the sled bag, he removed his sleeping bag and a pint of brandy he carried with his personal gear.

Critical accidents were not common. No musher had ever died on the trail in a race. Bones were broken, skin lacerated, joints dislocated occasionally, and a few dogs died as a result of accident or illness, but traumatic human death was not a serious concern for racers. Their largest fear was of injury or damage to equipment that would make it impossible to continue and isolate them in the emptiness of the Alaskan winter. Food for the team and musher could run short before they could be located and a rescue accomplished. That sort of close call was possible in this sport, where blizzards could blow up in hours, last for days, and force the Iditarod's flying support into idleness.

Schuller drew a deep breath, marshaling his strength, knowing he would have to make the decisions. Turner was, justifiably, in shock. George Koptak had been a friend and mentor to the younger man; they'd both been obsessed with sleds and distance. For over two years they had raised and trained dogs together in Teller, an Eskimo village outside Nome. George had run the Iditarod many times, but this was

Bill's first try and, Schuller hoped, not his last. It was like losing family for the twenty-six-year-old rookie to lose George. To be the one to find him dead in the trail had to be devastating.

Taking his sleeping bag and brandy, Schuller walked back to the bloody tree.

"Here, take a hit of this." He forced Turner's cold fingers around the bottle and raised it to his lips. The younger man choked down a swallow or two, coughed before he took a third, and handed the brandy back.

"What are we gonna do?"

Schuller looked down again at George's body. "We're gonna get him to Finger Lake, Bill. We can't leave him here." He thought of the wolves that periodically stole dog food during the race. "We'll put him on my sled in my bag, since we don't have his. But you'll have to help me get him on. Maybe we'll find his team on the way in."

He took a long pull of the brandy and shoved it into his parka pocket. Hell, I'm in shock myself, he thought.

They worked the body into Schuller's sleeping bag and lashed it to his sled. It took over twenty minutes to untangle the traces and straighten out both teams.

Before they left, Schuller tied his red bandana to the trunk of the tree as a marker. After the race, he promised himself, I'm coming back to cut down this damn tree.

3

Date: Monday, March 4
Race Day: Three
Place: Finger Lake checkpoint
Weather: Clear, light to no wind, snow predicted
Temperature: High 5°F, low −3°F
Time: Early morning

STATE TROOPER SERGEANT ALEX JENSEN WASN'T INterested in hunting. The first autumn or two after he had moved to Alaska he had gone out after moose and caribou, but the allure of big game soon palled. Carrying a rifle was part of the attraction of the hunt for those who kept their guns in the rack most of the year. He wore a .357 Magnum as a part of his uniform. His off-duty choice was a Colt .45, the semiautomatic side arm he had learned to prefer as squad leader of a Marine airborne team. He qualified as an expert with both. Shooting moose held no excitement; working homicide was blood sport enough. He felt no hesitation in using firepower when appropriate, but it was identifying a killer that challenged him, patiently putting details together until an unmistakable profile emerged.

Alex worked out of Palmer, center of the Matanuska Valley farms and dairies. It was surrounded by the majestic peaks of the Chugach and Talkeetna mountains, forty miles from Anchorage, a morning's drive from Mount McKinley, and three hours from the fine fishing of the Kenai Peninsula.

He had moved there eight years before from Idaho, soon after the death of his fiancée. A month before the wedding, a shadow had appeared on an X ray. Seven months later Sally was gone, leaving him more thoughtful and less inclined to laughter

Jensen was tall, rawboned, clean-shaven except for a reddish-blond mustache as full as regulations would allow. There was a gleam of ironical humor in his clear blue eyes. He was pleased to be out of uniform for the assignment he was beginning in the predawn glow of this Monday morning. Under his jeans and wool shirt he wore a layer of thermal underwear; over them, a heavy sweater and bibbed snow-machine pants. Insulated boots covered two pairs of wool socks, and behind him in the rear seat of the helicopter were a down parka, double mittens, and a fur hat with flaps to protect his ears. A ski mask and thick wool scarf lay in the parka pocket, in case a snow-machine trip was necessary.

Reaching forward with his right foot, he pressed the communication switch on the floor of the helicopter and spoke through the microphone to the pilot over the roar of the spinning blades. "How much farther, Bob?"

"Fifteen minutes. Maybe a little more." The pilot's disembodied voice came back through the headphones against the constant rush of static. He thumbed at the right window. "There's Skwentna."

In the half-dark, Alex could just make out lights

against the horizon and the shape of a few buildings. Closer, a wide bend of the Skwentna River swung north toward Finger Lake. He turned as far as his double shoulder harness and seat belt would allow to see if Trooper Philip Becker had heard the exchange, then back to watch the frozen river unwind under them.

The midnight call from Iditarod headquarters had gone to the Anchorage dispatcher, relayed down the trail from Finger Lake by the ham-radio operators who volunteered to handle race communications each year. The report of a death, first ever in the famous sled-dog race, had set wheels spinning rapidly. The story would undoubtedly hit newspaper headlines and national television news. Local law enforcement had better be quick to answer the inevitable rush of questions about the unattended death. Since the incident fell along the western edge of Trooper Detachment G's territory, Jensen found himself aloft well before sunrise, anticipated arrival at seven-forty. This time of year each twenty-four hours gained about four minutes of daylight.

As they came down onto the ice of Finger Lake, the rising sun cast its glow over the mountains of the Alaska Range, turning each peak the color of rose quartz. The small lake was divided down the northeast end by a narrow peninsular. Several teams rested in the snow around a small cabin at the top of a steep bank. At the sound of the rotors the dogs all lifted their heads. Some tested their restraints, barking and lunging. As Alex watched, a dozen or more people came out of the cabin and stood waiting on the hillside. Two of them started down through the restless dogs toward the helicopter on the ice.

Alex removed his headphones. "Let's get the gear

out," he said, stepping down to the ice's snowy crust. From a rear compartment they unloaded food for two or three days, heavy sleeping bags, a two-man tent, a camera, and other miscellaneous detection and survival gear. A couple of lightweight over-and-under rifles in compact cases were last onto the pile.

The two figures from the cabin reached them, and the taller one held out a mittened hand. "Tom Farnell," he said as Alex awkwardly shook the bulky paw. "This is Roy Hamilton, the race checker. Glad you're here. We've had quite a night."

"So I hear," Alex responded. "We should take a look at the site. Can we get there by chopper?"

"Doubt it," Farnell said. "Schuller said it was around fifteen miles. That area's covered pretty thick with spruce and alder. You'd have to land so far away it'd be easier to take a snow machine."

Alex turned to Bob. "Guess you might as well go on back. We'll load the body so you can get it to the Anchorage lab and then do our bit here."

Bob began to rearrange the left-hand seats in the helicopter. Minus their cushions, they folded flat to accommodate a collapsible metal stretcher, which he took from its compartment and handed to Jensen. The four other men headed off across the lake toward the cabin.

Roy Hamilton, a round ball of a man, spoke as they went up the hill. "Why the lab?"

"We need to know how and why it happened, verify accidents. It's standard procedure for any unwitnessed death. An autopsy's part of the process."

"That's going to go hard with Turner," Hamilton said to Farnell.

"Turner the guy who found him?" Alex asked as they went around the cabin to a small woodshed.

"Yeah, one of them. He's pretty shook up. They trained together."

"Who were the others?"

"Just one. Dale Schuller. He's gone on to Rainy Pass."

"Didn't someone tell him to stay put till we got here?"

"Yeah, but we got a race going on and Schuller has a shot at it this year. He marked the tree with a red bandana. He'll be easy to find if you need him. Every checkpoint clocks him in and out."

They fell silent as they stepped into the shed. George Koptak's body, still in Schuller's sleeping bag, lay on a piece of plywood across two heavy log chunks. The drawstring at the top of the bag had been pulled tight and knotted. Alex untied it and, unzipping the bag, lowered the fabric to search the body for injury. "Good God. A tree did all this?"

Farnell answered. "Dale said there was a sharp limb that he went into face first."

Alex nodded and examined the rest of the body. Finding nothing further, he reclosed the bag.

They had brought a regulation body bag with them from Palmer. With Koptak's body already in the sleeping bag, Jensen elected to forgo the inner liner. They placed the body in the heavy outer cover, zipped it up, and sealed it. "Let's get him on the stretcher."

It wasn't difficult. The body was frozen stiff. As they brought it around the cabin, five of the mushers who waited by the door stepped forward. "We'd like to do that," one of them said. They raised the stretcher to their shoulders. Although they didn't walk in step as they went down the hill and crossed the ice to the plane, it occurred to Alex that he had seldom seen anyone accorded more respect.

"When and where were his dogs and sled found?"

"About two this morning. Ron Cross brought them in behind his team. We'll make sure they're sent back to Anchorage with Turner's dogs when the support plane comes in. Bill's decided to give it up."

Jensen nodded. "I need to go through the gear before it leaves and see Turner. Then I can release it. We'll have somebody meet the plane in Anchorage."

Bob took off in the helicopter, initiating another round of sound effects from the dogs.

For the next hour, Jensen and Becker carefully went through everything in Koptak's sled. Jensen's expertise was in sifting through physical evidence. If there was anything to be found outside a laboratory analysis, he would find it. He had a reputation for picking out the most minute detail and proving it significant. Becker often accused him of witchcraft and swore it was mental alchemy, but he was learning to apply the same painstaking thoroughness to his own investigations. Though the twenty-eight-year-old had been with the post for over three years, he was new to the investigation unit. Becker's fascination with crime detection had caught Alex's attention. He encouraged the younger man, sharing cases when possible, and Becker jumped at opportunities to work with him.

With the assistance of Roy Hamilton, they sorted Koptak's gear. It included what every musher was required to carry and have verified at each checkpoint: cold-weather sleeping bag, hand ax, snowshoes, one day's food for each dog, a day's food for the musher, dog booties, and a carefully packaged handful of envelopes with Anchorage postmarks, which would be postmarked again when they reached Nome. One of the ways the Iditarod race committee made money was by selling the trail mail, while acknowledging mushers of the past who had carried mail to small communities during the winter.

Also in the sled were a Coleman stove, fuel, a large square cooking pot for dog food, George's extra clothes and boots, dog medicines, an assortment of tools, lines, bungee cords, harness, and a small pack containing personal things: a razor, soap, toothbrush, aspirin, Alka-Seltzer Plus, and a plastic quart bottle of seal oil. Instant energy for the musher.

In the smaller sack hung on the back of the sled they found plastic bags of trail mix, vitamins, chocolate bars, and beef jerky, extra mittens and gloves, and George's wallet containing forty-six dollars and his driver's license. Under this, at the bottom of the bag, was a Smith and Wesson .44 in a leather holster.

The gun was not unusual, Alex knew. Many mushers carried them as protection against the moose they often met on the trail. Deep snow made walking difficult for the rangy animals, and they stubbornly refused to give way, sometimes fighting for their right to the packed snow, kicking and stomping dogs and sleds. If they couldn't be avoided, they sometimes had to be shot, although the musher was required to gut the carcass before continuing his run, losing precious time. Mushers usually preferred to drive a wide arc around any moose claiming right of way.

Also in the bag was the cap from a thermos. The thermos itself was nowhere to be found. Jensen frowned as he turned and studied the cap.

Otherwise, neither Alex nor Phil could find anything odd or unnecessary. They photographed the gear, along with the smashed stanchion and runner, repacked it all in the sled bag, which they sealed securely so it could not be opened, and headed for the cabin to talk to Bill Turner.

The cabin on the remote lake shore was home to Tom and Nancy Farnell, who each year welcomed the Iditarod racers with hot food and a place for a brief rest. The only stipulation was that they not park their teams on the lake ice. "We've got to drink that water in the spring, you know," Farnell was quick to remind them.

The cabin seemed smaller inside than out, and its damp heat was oppressive. Clothing, dog harness, and booties hung everywhere, drying. Eight or nine mushers filled most of the open space. Their conversation stopped as the two troopers came through the door. One by one they put on their warm clothes and went out, one carrying a bowl of stew, which he refused to surrender. The last, a tall woman in a red parka and headband, stopped momentarily beside a seated figure. "I'll be back, Bill," she said and left, giving them privacy of a sort.

Turner, a blanket around his shoulders, was sitting on a bench pulled close to the barrel stove. The hot chocolate in the cup he clutched in both hands sloshed over the edge as Alex introduced himself and sat down.

The young man's face was drawn, and dark circles defined his eyes. Though he must have had little, if any, sleep, he seemed alert and answered the troopers' first few questions clearly in a flat, quiet voice. Giving Turner time to grow more at ease, Alex moved slowly into the questions he needed to ask. He and Becker had, gratefully, accepted steaming cups of coffee from Nancy Farnell. Becker sat quietly, staring into the small square of flame visible through the window in the stove door, and listened intently to the conversation. Turner's story closely matched what they had been told by Farnell.

"I understand you're giving up the race," Jensen said at last. "Sure you want to do that?"

"Yeah. It doesn't matter much now. I want to make sure George gets taken care of right. He doesn't have any family. I guess I'm about it."

"We're going back out on the trail to check it out. Is there anything else we should know?"

"No. He was just lying there in the trail. I ran over him before I could stop." An involuntary shudder racked Turner's hunched shoulders. "I can't shake the feeling of the sled going over him."

"Isn't it strange for an experienced musher to hit a tree like that?"

"I guess. But it was a pretty sharp corner. He hit it funny, though. Lower than he should have if he was standing up on the runners. He may have leaned forward, trying to miss it."

"Could he have been asleep?"

"Maybe, but I don't think so. We're all tired. It takes awhile to get into the race. He kept telling me that. 'Give it time and be careful when you start to get tired.' But he was a pro. He wouldn't rest while he drove through the trees. It had to be some kind of crazy accident."

He shook his head and set down the empty mug on the end of the bench. Alex could hear Nancy Farnell across the room, talking quietly to her husband, who had come in from outside. Two mushers lay on sleeping bags on the floor beyond the stove, heads pillowed on their parkas. One had a yellow stocking cap pulled down over his eyes to shut out the light, leaving only his full beard and slightly open mouth visible. In place of the well known CAT logo, this cap read DOG. The man nearest the stove shifted in his sleep and flung an arm out. The other lay on his back, motionless.

How, Alex wondered, did these guys stand it, love it, come back year after year? Close to two weeks on the trail with little sleep and grueling physical exertion. By the time they reached Nome they must be burned out.

"We found a thermos cap in his sled bag, but no thermos," said Becker.

Turner straightened suddenly, remembering. "I got it," he exclaimed. "Picked it up in the trail just before I found him. I put it in my bag and meant to give it to him. He always carried coffee. Filled his thermos at every checkpoint."

"How do you know it's his?"

"It's got his initials on it. I'll get it for you."

Alex stood up and put a hand on Turner's shoulder. "I'll go. I'm already booted up. Where's your rig?"

Outside, he paused to fire up his pipe, relishing the warm taste of good tobacco. He found the thermos in the bag on the back of Turner's sled, as he had described, with the initials G.K. in black paint. It was empty, missing its cap, and ice crystals, faintly brown, showed in the neck. Handling it carefully, he took a plastic evidence bag from his pocket, put the thermos inside, and sealed the top. Back in the shed he also bagged the cap. He stood for a moment with both bags in his hands before he put them into Koptak's sled and resealed it.

Something bothered him about the thermos. He made a mental note to ask the lab to run a test on the traces of frozen coffee and check the container for fingerprints. There was nothing to indicate this death was not an accident. Still, it was odd that an experienced musher would simply fall off his sled and into a tree. Especially one who knew enough about trail hazards to warn his younger friend to stay alert. George Koptak had run this part of the trail before, was aware of its dangers, and took coffee along from every checkpoint.

That was it. If George had carried coffee consistently, why hadn't he stopped to retrieve his only thermos when it fell? Two days into the race, he would not have ignored it when it dropped from his hand. He had tucked the cap into his bag, but left the thermos in the trail.

Heading back toward the cabin, Jensen passed a sled and team camped around a small fire. On the sled sat the woman who had spoken to Turner. She was straightening out a tangled mass of harness that was spread over her knees. Alex nodded to her, then paused as she spoke.

"Bill okay?"

Her voice, low-pitched and resonant, caught his attention. Her face was tanned from sunshine and wind. She looked fit, attractive, and concerned.

"Seems to be, considering," he said.

"Let me know when you're through, will you? I don't like him sitting there alone. We'll make sure he gets some support until they fly him out."

"Sure," Jensen promised. "Get some food down him too, if you can. Bet he hasn't eaten much."

Preoccupied with the thermos, he went on up the hill. Not, until reaching the cabin did he realize he had neglected to ask her name.

Jessie Arnold watched him disappear into the cabin. He seemed to her more like a race official or reporter than a trooper. Even under his heavy winter clothing, she could tell he was well built and strong.

He reminded her of a Viking, especially with the mustache.

For two years, since she had bought land near Knik and, with the help of a few friends, built a sturdy two-room cabin, she had lived alone, four miles from her nearest neighbor. She liked it that way. The healthy noise of her kennel bothered no one, and training the dogs kept her so busy she seldom felt a lack of human companionship. She didn't spend much time in town, preferring her own small log cabin and the company of her forty-three dogs.

Once in a long while, an evening would come along when restlessness infected her, and she would drop into the small local tavern for a beer or two and an hour of conversation or a game of pool. Since it was a place mushers frequented, she felt comfortable. Usually this happened in midwinter, when the daylight lasted less than six hours and she grew tired of driving her teams in the dark. It was nice to be answered in words instead of barks or whines.

The man she watched walk away was interesting, but she shrugged her shoulders and turned back to the snarled harness. Right now she didn't have time to find out.

Back in the cabin, Alex was just sitting down with Turner when the ham radio in the corner crackled to life. The operator, a girl with an Iditarod identification button on one of her red suspenders, stretched the headphones over her braids to answer the call. Something in the straightening of her shoulders caught his attention before she swung around to call to him across the room. "I think you better take this," she said, her eyes wide. "There's been another accident. In Happy Valley."

4

Date: Monday, March 4
Race Day: Three
Place: Between Finger Lake and Rainy Pass checkpoints (thirty miles)
Weather: Increasingly cloudy, light to no wind, snow predicted
Temperature: High 5°F, low −4°F
Time: Midmorning

ANCHORAGE, WHERE THE IDITAROD RACE BEGINS each year, stands at sea level, facing west over Cook Inlet. In the first two hundred miles to Finger Lake, the trail gains only a thousand feet in elevation. In the succeeding thirty miles, the track rises to thirty-four hundred feet at Rainy Pass, the highest point on the trip to Nome.

Gently undulating flats turn into rolling hills and, finally, become an awesome, majestic sweep of mountains overwhelming in their enormous silence. It is almost unimaginable that a route could be found through them in the warmest months of the northern year, let alone in winter. That the Iditarod is able to thread its way through Rainy Pass is due to the coordinated effort of a virtual army of volunteers. The only other possible route bears the name Hell's Gate and is used only when ice makes the canyons of Rainy impossible to cross.

Trailbreakers on snow machines, or "iron dogs," wrestle their way through ahead of the sled-dog racers, carving out the suggestion of a track, which may remain only a few hours before it is obliterated by new snow or blown away by the shrill winds that haunt the heights. At times the trail must be broken more than once to allow the front-runners to pass through. But the race committee has no obligation to maintain the trailbreaking effort, making the trip through the mountains a far greater test of endurance for those mushers following even a day or two behind the leaders.

The snow machine drivers, dressed in layers of outerwear to repel the worst the Arctic can deliver, may cover the full thousand miles without a good night's sleep and with few hot meals. A bed becomes something they dreamed of once; a hot shower, only a memory. They develop shoulders the envy of linebackers. But when they try to explain the pale, empty nights on the ice of Norton Sound, or the northern lights so bright they reflect off the snow in the Farewell Burn, wistful looks come over their wind- and sunburned faces and they drift into silence or stammering attempts at description. Many come back year after year, addicted to the trail.

Leaving Finger Lake, heading into the mountain pass, Virginia Kline drove the winding, tree-lined trail that rose gently until it broke out into the clearing on the cliffs above the ill-named Happy River Valley. Hundreds of feet below she caught glimpses of the curving pattern of its small river, a white, snow-covered ribbon winding through the brush that lined its banks.

In the summer, river water roiled through the twisting valley, fed by the glaciers of some of the highest mountains in North America. In winter it froze slowly, treacherous with overflow, creating deep crust-covered holes and unstable ice bridges that might collapse under a single dog or bear the weight of a two-hundred-pound sled, remaining deceptively solid for the next musher in line. The abrupt and unexpected collapse of such a bridge could dump a whole team into the icy water, drenching musher and gear, sometimes drowning or strangling dogs tangled in their harness.

Happy Valley was not the favorite ground of veteran mushers, and it was the terror of those on their first trip over the Iditarod Trail.

Although she had driven this trail twice before, it was heart-stopping for Ginny to look down, knowing that in a few short minutes she would have to take sled and team not only down into it, but up the other side, to reach the next checkpoint.

Everything was deeply covered with snow carried in by Saturday's storm. The trail had been packed by those traveling ahead of her, but off to the side it was chest-deep. The day was overcast, but it wasn't snowing, though the weather forecast predicted snow before nightfall. Flat light made irregularities in the trail difficult to make out. The few trees she passed cast no shadows, and the ruts left by sled runners frequently threw her off balance.

As the sled gradually followed the hillside it began to sideslip, requiring Kline to lean heavily uphill to keep it on the trail. Earlier in the day she had fallen while carrying a bucket of water to the dogs and had pulled a muscle in her right shoulder. With every jolt of the heavy sled she was reminded of the accident by twinges of pain.

The trail continued on along the cliff for approximately a quarter of a mile, then swung far enough away to alleviate some of her tension. The dogs were running well, though a little faster than she might have liked.

Relaxing a bit, she thought again of Bill Turner as she had seen him come into the Finger Lake cabin last night, sick and shaken. Seeing him so devastated and hearing his story had frightened her enough to make her consider scratching from the race. She had leaned against the wall near the stove and watched the other mushers as they discussed the accident, shadows of tension in their faces. That all the experienced mushers intended to continue encouraged her to go on to Rainy Pass as well. Then, after an overnight rest, if she could make it down the Dalzell Gorge and into Rohn, she thought she could probably finish. One checkpoint at a time; for now, just to make it through Happy Valley would make her day.

With no more than the flutter of pink survey tape as a warning, the trail made a sudden left turn and they were headed down. Kline stood hard on the brake, hoping it would hold, and shouted at her dogs. "Whoa! Whoa! Sally, Bones! Stop, you mutts." The team reacted to her voice, but the snowbank on her right was a blur. Two trees came up fast on the downhill side of the trail. They flashed by as she struggled to keep the sled upright.

Savagely she jammed in the brake and dragged her left foot, trying to slow the sled. There was no time for fright, only for strength and control. Her shoulder ached with the strain of supporting the sled. Rambo, the left wheel dog, tucked his tail between his legs and leaped forward as the brush bow grazed his flank.

Just as she began to feel more solid on the runners, she was astonished to see dogs coming back at her on an oblique angle from the right. After an incredulous moment, she realized they were her own. She passed them and the trail began a steep swing uphill to the right. The trailbreakers, having no room for a regular switchback, had looped the trail around a couple of trees and back over itself to make a turn. Frantically, she worked to ride it through, feeling the centrifugal force pulling her and the sled like a carnival ride. The sled straightened out to another traverse as steep as the first. She had no breath to shout at the dogs; she could only wrestle the sled and hang on.

Some mushers, she knew, turned their dogs loose and rode the sled down without them. It was tempting but technically illegal. Others dragged chains and weights to slow the sled.

A quarter of a mile later, she was ready for a second loop turn. Alert this time, she saw the lead dogs disappear to the left and rode the brake into the tight curve.

Between the dogs and the heavy sled, the gang line, holding the team to the load, suddenly snapped with a report that rang in the air like a shot, sending vibrations back through the sled to the handlebars. The dogs, abruptly relieved of weight, ran faster down the steep slope. The sled was flung out and over the edge of the cliff by the violence of the parting. Kline had only a breath to realize she was airborne as the sled left the trail and fell, tumbling down the side of the hill, toward the icy river six hundred feet below.

The deep new snow made an unstable covering for the steep grade and concealed the huge outcroppings of rock that formed the shoulders of the canyon. Over and over rolled the musher, still accompanied by two hundred pounds of sled and gear. She made no sound as she fell, the breath beaten from her lungs as the sled crushed her against the rocks. A thin tree broke off as the sled careered into it. The frozen trunk swept around to catch Kline hard under the chin. When the sled crashed into the last rock at the base of the cliff, she was under it. There was only a dull thump as both rebounded into the deep snow.

The sound barely caught the attention of another racer, who was working hard to keep his team from sliding into a series of holes in the river ice. He looked up in time to see the sled disappear below the surface of the snow and to watch in disbelief as a small avalanche filled in the depression.

Two other mushers, pausing to rest and melt snow to water their dogs, caught Ginny's sledless team as it ran through the lower part of the canyon.

5

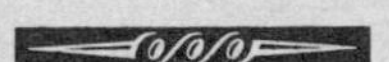

Date: Monday, March 4
Race Day: Three
Place: Between Finger Lake and Rainy Pass checkpoints (thirty miles)
Weather: Overcast, light to no wind, snow predicted
Temperature: High 5°F, low −4°F
Time: Midafternoon

THE WHINE AND GROWL OF SNOW-MACHINE ENGINES rose and fell over the uneven features of the trail between Finger Lake and the Happy Valley gorge. Though the sun had broken through briefly before noon, clouds now covered it, erasing trail-defining shadows.

Sergeant Jensen drove fast but cautiously as he followed Tom Farnell, making time toward the new accident site. He was glad to have a guide, for half his concentration was focused on the unlikely odds of two fatalities within less than a day in a race that had had none in the almost twenty years of its existence.

Between crackling bursts of static, the excited ham operator in Rainy Pass had been able to tell him little except that there had been a second death. Virginia

Kline had fallen with her sled from a switchback about halfway down. She had hit the rocks, rebounded into deep snow, and now lay partially buried under the sled and a small avalanche. A musher had reached her and uncovered enough snow to ascertain her death, then had gone back to the trail for help. A second racer had carried the news to the Rainy Pass Lodge.

Before leaving Finger Lake, Jensen had sent Becker back along the trail to inspect the site of the Koptak death and had radioed for the helicopter to return from Anchorage. With a storm due to blow in from the coast in the late afternoon, he knew they must recover the body and sled as quickly as possible, before wind and weather conspired to cover it. He glanced uneasily at the sky and almost ran into Farnell's snow machine as it slowed ahead of him.

"The trail goes down here," Tom shouted back over the sound of his engine. "Keep close and take it easy. It's a devil of a pitch."

Slowly he advanced, then suddenly he disappeared from view. Creeping up, Alex found an abrupt plunge as the trail went over the edge. With a rush of adrenaline he saw the gorge yawn open below him. The heavy machine slid forward against all the braking power at his disposal. Ahead he glimpsed Farnell wrestling his way around a curve, one booted foot braced against a tree on the downhill side.

They fought their way down the trail, negotiating a couple of looping turns. Then the marks of the sled runners they followed veered off to the outer edge and stopped where air began. At this point Jensen paused for a moment, but he couldn't leave the heavy machine without it leaving him. He could see nothing that might have caused the musher to lose contact with the trail. Down the slope the snow showed deep marks of disturbance, and a small tree had been broken off. The snow-covered rocks and shrubbery made it impossible to see the bottom of the gorge, but Jensen swallowed hard at the thought of leaving the trail to crash down what he estimated to be over five hundred feet of slope. He allowed the snow machine to continue its gravity-encouraged trip down the trail.

He found Farnell waiting at the foot of the steep switchbacks and stopped beside him to take a few deep breaths of relief.

"You take a look at the marks on that second turn?" Farnell questioned. "Damn. What the hell do you think happened?"

"Don't know," Jensen answered. "It doesn't look like she even slowed down. Let's take a look at her rig. It can't be far now."

They continued along the track, Farnell again in the lead. The small frozen river twisted and roped its way in the narrow channel. They drove over and around holes and open spaces of water and overflow until a musher in a blue parka and snow pack boots rose from beside a small fire to flag them down.

"Hey," he called. "You the trooper?"

Jensen pulled off to the side and walked to the fire. "That's right. Sergeant Alex Jensen. You the guy who saw her fall?"

"Bomber Cranshaw, McGrath." The musher was a couple of inches under six feet tall and compactly built. From under a beaver hat, his hair stuck out in spikes over his eyes, and his full brown beard and mustache were rimmed with ice. He nodded and gnawed on his lower lip, then began his account of the accident in a loud, booming voice.

"Hell, I didn't see all of it. She didn't scream, just

fell. I heard a crash and looked up as the sled bounced off that hump of rock." He pointed out the location about fifty feet up the side of the cliff. Alex could see where the snow had been removed, creating a long depression. "She fell the rest of the way, and there was a sort of thump when she hit with the sled on top of her. You can see where the snow came off to bury it. I tied my dogs off, dug out the snowshoes, and hopped on over there to see if I could help.

"There wasn't much to dig out. I did it with my hands, but she was dead when I got down to her. Her head's turned funny. I figured she broke her neck when she hit the rock, or the sled did it landing on her. She wasn't breathing, and I knew I couldn't do much. She's pretty broke up. That's a damn lot of weight to be under. You see anything when you came down?"

Jensen silently assessed the man before him. The musher seemed to have had time to stop reacting and start thinking. His brows were drawn together in a frown, and he gestured widely as he spoke. Bomber was perhaps in his midthirties and, from the look of his sled and gear, not a newcomer to sled-dog racing. Patches from past Iditarod races were stitched to his parka. His memory was keen and his information seemed to be given freely, but there was a watchfulness about him.

"Who went up to tell them at Rainy?" Farnell asked.

"Susan Pilch came through just as I got back to the gang here," he said, waving at his dogs. "Since I was already stopped and they were having a rest, I figured I might as well feed 'em and wait. She went on up to let 'em know."

"You cut yourself a pretty big chunk of time, waiting."

"Well, some things are more important, although I'd probably get an argument on that from some. I'll make it up somewhere. These guys are the best I've had in years." He thumbed toward his resting dogs. "It's still early."

"I appreciate your staying," Alex told him. Then he turned to Farnell. "Let's go take a look. The chopper should be along any time now, and I'd like to have this wrapped up. We're going to catch snow before dark; we'd better get her out of here while we can."

He and Farnell put on the snowshoes they had carried. The other equipment and supplies would be on the helicopter with Becker.

Bomber led the way toward the cliff. His dogs were curled into tight balls in the snow, snoozing, but several raised their heads as he left. He had broken a rough trail on his first trip to the site, but they still found it heavy going.

Ginny Kline lay where Bomber had indicated, partially buried in snow beneath the heavy sled, her neck broken. Her head, one arm, and the upper part of her chest were all they could reach until they moved her rig. In the deep snow it took all three of them working together.

She was, as Bomber had put it, pretty broke up. One side of her face was badly scraped, and her body felt strangely flexible as they lifted it out of the snow and onto the sleeping bag they found in her sled. Although her shoulders were muscular beneath the heavy parka, Jensen thought she looked too small and fragile to be an Iditarod racer. Her knitted cap had come off, and her hair, braided into one long plait, had pulled out in childish wisps that curled slightly around her ears. He tucked the hat into her parka pocket, where he found a penlight, a half-eaten Snickers bar, extra clips for the harness, and several hairpins. Zipped into the opposite pocket were a coin purse with a few dollars, her driver's and fishing licenses, and school pictures of two little boys, aged perhaps six and eight.

As they wrestled the broken sled out toward the trail, the thump of rotors suddenly extinguished the silence. They looked up to see Becker waving from the passenger seat. He had been out to the site of Koptak's death and had caught a lift with the helicopter. Slowly, conscious of the narrow sides of the gorge, Lehrman allowed the machine to settle into a section of the trail flat enough to accommodate the landing. Carefully he tested the stability of the snow before committing to more than a hover. Finding it solid enough support, he set down, but only eased off on the power.

With little time to go through the contents of the sled bag, Alex made a cursory search for anything unusual. He fashioned a cradle from strong line to support the sled so the helicopter could lift it from the gorge. Stepping around, he examined the section of gang line still attached. It was too even a break. It had been cut most of the way through with something very sharp; only a small part of the rope was frayed from the tension that had pulled it apart. He taped an evidence bag over this end and marked it for attention in the lab. It didn't make sense for Ginny to have cut her own line, but an accident of some kind couldn't be ruled out completely. If, as he suspected, the line had been cut by someone else, it couldn't have guaranteed her death. Whoever cut it had not cared when or where it would break—they just hoped for a serious accident. With the added strain of the sharp turns in the gorge, chances had been good it would happen there. It could have put her out of the race whatever the result.

He looked up to find Cranshaw watching.

When the sled had been rigged and hooked up to the helicopter's cable, they bagged and carried the body to the already reconfigured passenger seat.

"Can you take Becker to Rainy Pass and still have enough fuel to get back to Anchorage with the extra weight?" Alex asked Lehrman.

"Sure. Give me your pack, too. It'll make it easier on that snow-go you're riding."

Becker climbed into the seat directly behind the pilot. The sled described circles in the air as the chopper lifted it, but it soon stabilized. In a few short minutes it vanished from sight over the rim of the canyon.

Farnell turned to Bomber. "Is that coffee you've got on? We could use a cup before we get going, if you can spare it."

Sharing the musher's metal cup full of coffee and a welcome slug of bourbon, they stood close enough to the fire to remove their gloves and warm their fingers. Alex puffed his briar and stared into the flames.

"What do you think?" Bomber asked him.

"About what?"

"I saw you looking at that line. It was cut, wasn't it?"

"Can you think of a reason it might have been?" A mild question.

The musher's head came up sharply as he looked very directly at Jensen.

"Hell, no. But I know Ginny pays attention to her gear. She's no rookie."

Farnell's eyes narrowed. "You're saying this was no accident," he said.

"That's right," replied Bomber,

"Then what about George's accident?"

They both looked at Jensen expectantly.

"We'll see," he said. "By the time I get to the pass I should have a lab report."

Bomber kicked snow over the fire and began to pack his gear. "We better get this show on the road. It's gonna snow."

But the snow held off as far as Rainy Pass. Farnell took the trail back to Finger Lake. Jensen drove off in the other direction, breaking trail for Bomber. Though the trail was soft and punchy in places from paws and runners, the climb through the trees and over the rolling hills toward the Alaska Range went smoothly.

They arrived at the Rainy Pass Lodge shortly after dark to find Becker in conference with Matt Holman, the race marshall, who had come in on a supply plane. With him was an *Anchorage Daily News* reporter and a two-man team from KTUU, Channel 2, all of whom were lying in wait for the trooper sergeant. The media assault had begun.

The lodge was full of people: mushers, race officials, support staff, and a few friends and family. A hush fell over the room when they noticed Alex, and everyone watched him cross the room to join Becker and greet Holman. The conversations resumed, but most eyes in the room remained on the trio until Bomber Cranshaw appeared half an hour later, after caring for his team. He was instantly surrounded by a crowd of mushers, all asking questions.

As he removed his parka, he looked questioningly across the lodge at Jensen. Alex shrugged and nodded slightly. Better questions answered than rumors started. The troopers continued to set out the facts for Holman, who had been an organizer of the first running of the Iditarod, in 1973.

As they talked, Alex looked out over the room full of mushers and those who supported or reported the race. How it had grown since its inception. He wondered how he could have lived in Alaska for eight years, so close to this remarkable event, and known so little about it. He focused his attention on Holman and began to ask questions with more than detection in mind.

6

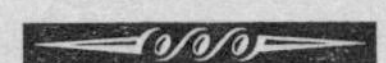

Date: Monday, March 4
Race Day: Three
Place: Rainy Pass checkpoint
Weather: Overcast, light to no wind, snow predicted
Temperature: High 5°F, low −6°F
Time: Early evening

EXHAUSTED FROM THE RUN THROUGH HAPPY Valley, Steve Smith, the twenty-first musher, was relieved to arrive at the Rainy Pass Lodge. After the climb out of the gorge, the trail had maintained a steady climb into the Alaska Range toward the wide saddle of the pass. At last, he reached the tree line, from where the towering, snowlocked mountains rose into the gathering darkness.

Through blue dusk, the glow of campfires ahead told the musher he was nearing the checkpoint. Two official race checkers waited by the steep banks of Puntilla Lake. As they recorded his time of arrival and the presence of required gear, fatigue washed over him. For a minute he wished he could let someone else take care of the dogs while he stumbled into the warmth of the big frame lodge above the lake, found an unoccupied spot on the floor, and slept.

His team had done remarkably well, considering that four of them had fallen through a hole in the ice of the meandering Happy River and been soaked before he could get them out. Lying on the ice, Smith had struggled to pull them up, one by one, while the hook held back the sled and the remainder of the team. The dogs had come out shaking water, which immediately froze on their coats, but had seemed uninjured.

Beneath a sled dog's heavy winter hair lies a thick undercoat that forms a barrier between skin and cold air. In sub-zero temperatures, if the dog gets wet, the insulating properties of the undercoat are destroyed. It's important to dry the animal quickly before it freezes.

Relieved that none had been pulled under and drowned, Smith had not minded kindling a quick fire and carefully rubbing down each drenched dog. He had massaged ointment into their feet, especially between the toes, and replaced their frozen booties with dry ones, taking care not to fasten the Velcro so tight it cut off their circulation.

He had snacked the whole team on high-energy balls of honey, fat, ground meat, and mineral powders and gotten them back on the trail. They would continue to dry out on the run. He had also replaced his heavy insulated mittens. They were a soggy mess, frozen stiff, and would have to be hung to dry in the lodge, along with the harness.

Mitsie, his smallest dog, was one of those dunked in the icy water. Halfway up the steep incline she had begun to lay back her ears and struggle in her harness. By the time they were out of the valley and onto the hillside, she was shivering and dragging against the line. Taking her off, he had bundled her into the sled bag, where she curled nose to tail, licking his hand apologetically.

Every dog carried in the basket adds weight for the others to pull, slowing the whole team. If there was any question of a dog's fitness to pull the heavy sled, Smith decided in favor of the animal. He would have the race veterinarian examine Mitsie at the checkpoint. She would probably be dropped and flown back to Anchorage, where he would claim her after the race. He would miss her; the small dog was a positive influence on the others.

Large white snowflakes began to float through the dark as the checkers finished with the sled. One of them offered to take Mitsie to the vet for immediate attention. Deprived of the warmth of the sled bag she shivered, head drooping, tail tucked under.

With one longing glance at the lighted windows of the lodge, Steve drove past it to the limited shelter of a few sparse trees. He wanted his team away from those already occupying the space around the building, so they could rest comfortably. It meant a longer hike for water and supplies, but it seemed worth the trouble.

Off the trail the snow was deep. He struggled through it to tie the sled to the largest of the trees, then to stretch out the gang line and fasten it to a second tree. It didn't quite reach, so he threw a couple of loops over a lower branch for the moment. The dogs were tired and hungry; several were already down in the snow, snuggling noses into bushy tails. He would find another piece of line and secure the gang line later.

Digging into the sled bag he retrieved his big cooker and a child's red plastic sled and walked down to the lake. A hole had been chopped in the ice, and he filled the cooker and a bucket with water, then hauled them on the incongruously small sled back up the hill.

From the sled bag he took a bag of charcoal briquets and a small amount of kindling for starter. Stomping a level spot, he put down a square metal firebox and grill over chunks of firewood. Many mushers used pressurized gas stoves, replacing their cans of fuel at each checkpoint from supplies provided by the race committee. Smith preferred the long-lasting heat of charcoal, since it did not need constant pumping to maintain fuel pressure.

Using Blazo to soak the kindling and briquets, he started a roaring fire and put the cooker of water on to heat. With an ax he chopped frozen chunks of salmon, beef, and boned chicken combination into a more manageable size and, as the water came to a near boil, dumped in the meat. When it thawed, he would mix in additional fat and some dry dog food.

To run a thousand miles, food, water, and rest are important considerations for both musher and dogs. Dehydration is a demon to be avoided at all costs. Some mushers actually pump water down their dogs' throats with turkey basters if necessary. The best food for dogs running this distance must be high in fat, low in bulk, consistent in its balance of vitamins and minerals, and, most important, appealing to hungry dogs.

Leaving the stew to cook, he headed down the hill to the lake once more. He walked out to where the flat ice allowed for a makeshift runway.

Many small planes fly between Anchorage and the Iditarod checkpoints during a race. Two or three weeks before the start, each musher packs and marks plastic or burlap bags of dog food, human food, and other necessary equipment and supplies, up to seventy pounds per bag, to be flown out to the checkpoints.

Smith found his sacks with the large orange markings in the pile of bags. For this stop, along with food, charcoal, and a dry sleeping bag, he had included straw for his dogs. Because of its altitude, Rainy Pass was often one of the coldest checkpoints. In addition, wind frequently blew away dry snow, leaving little for the dogs to bury themselves in to form body-sized pockets of heat. He was convinced that sleeping on the snow made dogs burn energy to keep warm. Laying down the straw would make a warmer bed for each animal.

Heading back to his team, he paused for a few minutes to greet Mike Solomon, a native Athabaskan musher from Kaltag, whose dogs were already bedded down.

"Better get up to the lodge," Mike told him. "There's more food than you've seen since Christmas and still a few sleeping spots."

"What's the story on Ginny Kline? I saw a helicopter take her sled out of Happy Valley on my way in."

"Yeah. There's a couple of troopers asking a lot of questions. They think someone cut her gang line."

"Jesus. Who would do a thing like that?"

They looked at each other in silence, the idea of it setting them both on edge.

"How far'd she fall?"

"Far enough. Whole load landed on top of her, according to Bomber. Broke her neck."

Another long pause.

"Go on up to the lodge. It's all they're talking about."

"I'll do that. Got to bed the dogs down first."

Smith went back to his team and completed mixing the dog food. He floundered through the snow to feed the dogs, leaders first, and was pleased to see them all eating well. Metal bowls of warm food sank into the snow and provided their own stability as the dogs lapped up food and water. Each animal had its own character and way of eating, some delicately licking at the protein-rich dish, others gulping it down. He grinned at the sight of a team dog, Jake, always the first to finish and look around for more. "Hey, Jake. One day you're gonna choke, fella."

The dogs that had fallen through the ice seemed no worse for the experience. Straw spread, he put more water and frozen meat on to cook for a later meal, taking advantage of the still glowing charcoal. Noticing a dog working its tongue at a left front foot, he stopped and leaned to check for cuts in the pad. With only a low growl of warning the dog snapped at his extended hand, barely missing his fingers.

"Hey!" This dog never snapped, not even at other dogs. "What's the problem, Spook? Let me take a look here."

At the sound of his voice the dog whined, aware of its transgression. Its tail was wagging now.

"Foot. Foot." The dog offered the paw for inspection, but there was nothing the musher could see that would cause a problem. He wondered if this dog might be incubating some virus, as frequently happened in races where dogs from many kennels came in contact. Collecting his frozen mittens and other gear to be dried, he headed for the warmth of the building, and some food and rest of his own. On the way he checked with the vet about Mitsie and they agreed she should be dropped. The vet had already injected her with antibiotics, fearful of pneumonia.

The lodge was filled with mushers, race officials, and reporters, all concerned by the second death on the trail. The troopers were hard to spot in the crowd. Standing to one side of the room, they were in a serious conversation with one of the checkers and the race marshall. Bomber Cranshaw was surrounded by other racers.

A woman racer in one corner looked shocked and frightened. Her companion, a photographer, from the camera hung around his neck, was talking seriously to her as he awkwardly patted her shoulder. A small group of rookies glanced suspiciously around, obviously discussing who might cut a gang line. Beyond the stove, under several lines of steaming harness and clothing, the winner of last year's race slept as soundly as if the place were empty.

A huge table of food occupied one corner of the room: stew, roast beef, rolls, green salad, ham, macaroni and cheese, pies, cookies, coffee, milk, beer. Heaping a plate with food and filling a mug with heavily sugared coffee, Steve sat down cross-legged near the stove to listen to the speculation going on around him. The heat was stifling after the cold, but welcome.

Mike Solomon's compact form soon folded itself down beside him. "See what I mean?" He nodded toward Bomber. "He drove in behind one trooper, just before you came in. The other one came on the chopper. Bomber helped get Ginny out. Cost him some time, I guess. Johnson and Talburgen caught her dogs in the valley. They say the line had been cut twice besides the place it broke."

Scraping the last of the macaroni into his mouth, Smith tossed the paper plate into a black plastic garbage bag behind him. He wolfed the remains of his roast beef and bread between sips of coffee. "Why the hell would anyone cut her gang line?" he asked through the mouthful. "How do they know someone cut it?"

"It was a new line. She wouldn't have cut it herself. Talburgen says he remembers her going over the whole rig last night before she went to sleep. She was worried because last year she dumped about halfway down and cracked a rib or two. The line was cut pretty slick, close to knots so she couldn't see."

Solomon faded into thought. For a few minutes he looked speculatively at the serious faces of those gathered in the lodge. "Well, I guess I'd better have a last look at the mutts and catch some bag time. There's no way to sleep in here with this going on. Think I'll hit my sled."

"I'll stay and soak up some more of this heat, but I think you're right. See you later." Smith rose to get a refill on coffee.

Forty minutes later he left, well fed but a bit dazed from the damp heat of the lodge, stumbling before his vision adjusted to the dark. Too little rest in the last four days, and the warmth and hot food of the last hour, conspired to make his feet feel like lead in his heavy boots. His eyelids drooped and he yawned widely. As he approached his camp in the trees, he remembered that he still needed to extend the gang line to the second tree.

He could see that a few of the dogs were on their feet, rather than in their usual heat-preserving curls. He was headed for the cooker, ten feet from the first pile of straw, when he heard a low growl from the nearest dog. Concerned with transferring the food to an insulated container, he ignored it.

Reaching the fire, he tossed a handful of straw and kindling under the cooker for some light. As he turned to the sled, another dog growled suddenly. The sound of teeth snapping was accompanied by a yelp from a third. Smith whirled to face his team.

He was confronted by Rabbit, one of his largest dogs. His lips were pulled back from his teeth in a savage snarl, and the hair on his neck stood up in an angry ruff. His body was crouched near the snow, ready to spring at the astonished musher. Behind him, three other dogs emitted deep-throated growls. They crept forward, primitive, hostile, pinning him against the fire.

"Rabbit, Jake." He spoke sharply. "Down. What's wrong with you? Down, damn it."

The dogs crawled closer, snarling, drooling, and he realized they had pulled the line from its temporary anchor. He yelled, looking for something to swing. Suddenly, for the first time in his life, he was terrified of his own dogs. Nothing was within reach except the simmering dog food on the fire. As he grabbed for the handle, Rabbit, so named because of his speed and agility, charged. Hitting Smith high on the chest with both front feet, the dog buried his teeth in the man's parka and shoulder, knocking him back over the fire into the snow. The cooker spilled over the musher's legs.

The rest of the team went crazy. Though he fought with fists and flying boots, they tore his parka and insulated pants to shreds. Sharp teeth, well honed on frozen food and bones, slashed into flesh. Smith screamed. Rabbit sank his teeth into his master's exposed neck. The musher screamed again as the animal tore his throat, opening the jugular. Two fingers were ripped from his right hand by Chunk, a dog he had raised from a pup. His blood stained the snow around him.

The sound of the frenzy drew mushers from their camps and out of the lodge. Every dog in the area barked and howled, on their feet, straining toward the fight. A checker reached the camp first and was immediately attacked by three dogs that turned at the sound of his shout. He retreated, beating them off as he stumbled back, but not before he was deeply bitten on the forearm he'd flung up to protect his face. One dog held on ferociously until the man flung it against the sled in desperation.

"Son of a bitch!" he shouted. "Get a gun, somebody. They've got Steve."

Another man attempted to pound the dogs with a piece of firewood. He stunned one, but quit when he realized the rest were completely beyond control. He backed out of range, unbitten. The troopers arrived from the lodge and were confronted by a mass of snarling, slashing dogs. Leaving their master unconscious, bleeding to death in the snow, they swung the entire gang line toward the crowd, ready to renew the attack.

Astounded, the mushers stood facing the team, which, just hours before, had been composed of well-behaved, friendly dogs. They were scarcely recognizable now. A pack of wolves would have been less threatening.

"Shoot them," a voice said loudly but firmly from within the group, "before they tear that line loose."

Jensen slowly unholstered and raised his revolver and began to drop dogs one after another. After six shots he ejected the shells and clipped on a speed loader for six more. When he had shot these he turned to his partner, but one of the older mushers stepped forward with a .44 from his sled. With tears running down his face, he fired three shots to complete the grisly chore. "Shit," he said with each one. "Shit. Shit."

The last dog died still throwing himself repeatedly against the line tethering him to his fallen teammates. In silence they stood staring at the carnage for a long minute as the trooper approached the dead musher.

Down the hill, Mitsie, tied near a fire in front of the vet's tent, raised her muzzle and howled. Every other dog wailed in response, the sound floating in the frosty air and echoing from the surrounding hills.

7

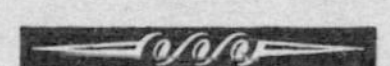

Date: Monday, March 4
Race Day: Three
Place: Rainy Pass checkpoint
Weather: Overcast and snowing, clearing and lower temperatures predicted for Tuesday
Temperature: High 5°F, low −6°F
Time: Midevening

"WHAT A BITCH," SAID BECKER.

He and Jensen paused to survey the site in the light of a spotlight, borrowed from the lodge and equipped with a small gas generator. The dead dogs were now wrapped in individual plastic garbage bags, and had been moved to the ice of the lake, ready for pickup the next day. The body of Steve Smith, the savaged musher, more heavily bagged, lay near his dogs and sled, which had been repacked and sealed for lab inspection.

"They're going to have enough sleds and equipment in the crime lab to start their own race," Becker said. The young trooper looked tired, his brows knit in a frown of concentration as he made sure they hadn't missed any vital piece of evidence. Even he was growing quiet.

The cooker, filled with chunks of frozen dog food dug out of the snow, had been separately bagged. Jensen doubted there would be much to find when these rations were analyzed, considering it had been the first batch that had fed the dogs. There might be traces, but any significant clue would be retrieved from the bellies of the dogs. Their individual bowls, which might reveal something however well licked, had been sealed and marked for evidence.

Matt Holman, a checkpoint official, and Bill Pete, the musher who had shot the last three dogs, had volunteered to stand guard over the whole collection, leaving the troopers free to complete their job at the site.

Now they stood looking at what little was left. Before moving anything to the lake, they had staked off the area and run pink survey tape to close it off. Then they had gone over it, foot by foot, sifting through the trampled snow for clues. Thoroughly churned by the attack of the dogs, the site offered little.

The straw had been bagged and marked. On one clump of it they had found a smaller dog, apparently dead from something besides a bullet. There were vomit and feces in the straw, and the animal lay in an odd, convulsed position. Jensen marked the bag for this dog as a priority and included the straw and excretions, the only known connection between a specific dog and its meal.

"What the hell you think this is all about?" Becker asked as they began to break down the spotlight equipment. It had begun to snow again, gradually erasing what remained of the bloody battle.

Alex paused, rested one booted foot on the generator, removed his mittens, and pulled his pipe and tobacco from a jacket pocket. He packed the pipe and lit it. Puffing a cloud of richly scented smoke into the snowflakes, he considered the facts he had to back up his answer.

Time and experience had taught him to rely on his intuition to a cautious and calculated extent. His subconscious gathering of many bits of information created a total impression that was often accurate, but difficult to defend.

"I think someone is either trying to stop this race or is heavily invested in its outcome," he said slowly. "These are not random accidents. The traces of coffee left in Koptak's thermos and the tests on his stomach contents and blood showed secobarbital. Someone had doped his coffee in Skwentna. Probably the same someone who came on to Finger Lake and cut Kline's gang line, then found a chance to dump whatever it was into the food Smith gave his dogs.

"What I can't decide is if these mushers were picked specifically, or if the setups were made as opportunity presented itself, with no particular target in mind. The secobarbital that went into the coffee is not the same substance that turned these dogs into a killer pack. However they were selected, these incidents were premeditated."

Becker nodded his agreement. "What do you want to do now?"

"Just now," said Alex, tapping his pipe on the generator to remove the dottle, "I want a quart of hot coffee and something to eat. Then I want to talk to a number of people. The first thing is to find out who was at Skwentna, Finger Lake, and here—who had the opportunity to cause all three incidents. Then, who had a reason and what that reason was. After that I want three or four hours of sleep, if I can get it. I have a bad feeling about this one, Phil. Most of this race is still ahead. For now let's haul this thing back to the lodge."

Minutes later, Jensen started down the hill to see Matt Holman. Between the lodge and the frozen lake several mushers had started a communal fire, and he could see figures silhouetted against the flames. Concentrating on the rough path, he almost ran into someone who had stopped on the way up and stood facing him. In the dark he did not realize it was a woman until, lifting his flashlight to her face, he recognized her from Finger Lake.

Her eyes were wide and gray, her hair a short honey-blond tumble of waves and curls. The cold air had brought a blush to her cheeks and nose. She looked at him directly and did not flinch as the light passed over her face, but she waited until it dropped before she moved.

"Jessie Arnold," she said, pulling a hand from her parka pocket. It was warm and strong in his. "Can we talk for a minute?"

He hesitated. "Sure. Let's walk."

They moved off toward the lake, along a side path.

"You were in the cabin at Finger Lake," he said. "A friend of Turner's?"

"More of an acquaintance. Most of us know each other. He's just a kid, and he seemed so broken. George was a friend of mine from a long time back. He helped me get started. It was like doing something for him to be there for Bill."

He said nothing, waiting for her to go on.

She stopped abruptly and turned to face him. The glow from the fire by the lake barely touched her serious face. He could see tiny reflections of the light in her eyes. She looked at him for a long moment, seeming to assess him as a person as well as a trooper.

He wondered briefly what influenced her judgment.

"Look," she said. "Let's be up-front. What the hell is going on? There's a lot of talk, and folks are more worried than they will admit. These aren't really accidents, are they? One I could buy. George. It's possible for anyone to run off the trail for some reason. This race has never killed anyone, but it's crazy sometimes. They say Ginny's line was cut, more than once, and now Steve's dead in a way that just doesn't make sense. Dogs don't do that. I've seen sick or nasty ones. A few people still mistreat their dogs, enough to make them vicious, but not a whole team."

She didn't take her eyes off his face. "There was something in the food, wasn't there?"

He didn't answer immediately, but stood looking down at her, considering. She was asking a lot of questions, but so, he supposed, were most of them at this point. She was asking straight, important questions, anticipating the same kind of answers, and he had a hunch she could probably handle them.

Most people were wary of the law. They automatically hedged or told you only what they thought you wanted to know. A basic fear or resentment of authority made them pseudorespectful. You wondered what they really thought and said about you behind your back. Sometimes you knew because they said it to your face.

This woman stood her ground, said what she thought, and asked what she wanted to know. She was treating him as an equal, not awed by his authority, but not disrespectful either. It made him want to answer her candidly. The impulse was tempting, but it conflicted with his training.

"Wasn't there?" she asked again.

Throwing his head back and taking a deep breath,

he reached into his pocket for his pipe. She watched him fill and light it, waiting.

"I don't know," he said finally, puffing smoke. "It will have to go to the lab for tests."

An amused expression took the edge from her next comment. "That's some smoke screen you've got."

He shrugged and smiled, admitting it.

"But you know there was something. And there was something wrong with George too, wasn't there?"

"Why do you think so?"

"Oh, questions with questions." A bit of exasperation showed now. "Because it makes sense. I'm not a trooper, but I'm not stupid, and neither are the others. I guess what I'm thinking is there will probably be someone else, won't there? If this race goes on there could be several someone elses. Somebody is killing mushers.

"What I want to know is what we're going to do about it. It scares the hell out of me. I've never been around anything like this and I don't like it. But we have a race to run. There's a lot at stake: money, time, reputations. But none of it's worth lives. What are we going to do?"

We. She kept saying "we" as if she were a part of finding out who was responsible. And maybe she was. Maybe they all were.

"How many times have you run this race?" he asked.

"Five."

"How have you finished?"

"My best was last year. Sixth."

"What makes you suspect there will be more?"

"Because there doesn't seem to be anything but the race as a connection. None of the people who've died were particularly close. None trained together or had borrowed or rented dogs from each other. Is someone trying to shut it down? Has one of those humane-society nuts finally gone too far, trying to make us stop what they think is cruelty to dogs? What is it?"

Alex looked at her, surprised. Vaguely he remembered a controversy a few years back involving the humane society. Some of its members refused to believe that a dog might be run in a racing team without damage or trauma to the animal. They had generated enough negative publicity to make race officials, vets, and mushers generally uncomfortable and resentful. He recalled thinking the whole thing a little ridiculous, but also wondering if a thousand-mile race wasn't pushing the dogs too far. Now he was beginning to realize that the main stress lay on the musher. Some of the dogs, he was told, actually gained weight during the race and loved to run, as they did in training every winter day. Abused dogs would never win a race and the mushers knew it. Reason, however, would not change the mind of an obsessed animal-rights advocate.

Another possibility he had toyed with was that someone had a big bet going. There had to be thousands of dollars riding on this race in illegal wagers. He wondered how much and where. All sports were subjects for gambling and vulnerable to attempts to influence their outcomes. Greed as a motive might make more sense.

These options opened up the case to include things that could not be investigated from an Iditarod checkpoint, but he was convinced that the solution was to be found here on the trail. Only someone familiar with the race could have known Koptak's habits, the stress on a line in Happy Valley, Smith's probable feeding schedule. Since he wasn't a musher, he knew he couldn't anticipate the killer's thinking, didn't know enough firsthand.

"Miss . . . ," he started.

"Jessie," she said.

"Jessie."

He went on, thinking out loud. "I have several problems here. First, I have to find out what's going on. Second, I don't know enough about dogs, racing, mushers, equipment, attitudes, or any of it to know what I don't know. You just mentioned a possibility that would have taken me days to dig out. There are a few troopers who have helped with this race off and on, and I'm going to get one of them up here in a hurry. But even that won't give us the inside story. You and other mushers know each other and the sport as we never will. Would you be willing to share some of that? To work with me, give me the benefit of your experience?"

She waited a minute or two, assessing him again.

"You," she said, "are not what I expected in a trooper."

"What were you expecting?"

"I don't know." She shook her head slightly, silent for a while before she spoke. "I hope you're not asking me to spy on other people. I won't do that."

"Don't get me wrong. I'm not looking for a snitch. I'm interested in a coach. And I don't mean to depend on just you. That's not how this sort of thing is handled. But there are a lot of things you could help me with. For instance, was Ginny Kline married? There were pictures in her wallet of two little boys, maybe six or eight years old. Are they hers?"

"She wasn't married and didn't have any kids. They're probably her nephews. Her sister from Fairbanks was at last year's finish, and I heard them talk about her children."

Jensen was about to ask another question when he heard Becker's shout. "Anyone seen Sergeant Jensen?"

"Here," Alex called.

"Anchorage," Becker yelled. "On the radio."

"I have to take that call," he told her. "Can we talk later?"

"What's your first name?" she asked him.

"Alex."

"Good." She smiled. "I like to know the people I work with."

8

Date: Monday, March 4
Race Day: Three
Place: Rainy Pass checkpoint
Weather: Overcast and snowing, clearing and lower temperatures predicted for Tuesday
Temperature: High 5°F, low −6°F
Time: Late evening

IT WAS MORE THAN AN HOUR BEFORE ALEX HAD A chance to sit down. The radio call from Anchorage, patched through two ham operators and full of weather-induced static, relayed information that confirmed his suspicions concerning the death of Ginny Kline. The gang line on her sled had definitely been cut, and whatever had sliced it had been exceptionally sharp.

The autopsy revealed no chemical substances, only many broken bones, a ruptured spleen, and an artery severed by the jagged end of a rib. Internal bleeding would have killed her had it not been for the broken neck, which the coroner had determined was the principal cause of death.

From the radio, Jensen had gone directly down to

the lake to speak with Matt Holman. Reviewing the situation as clearly as he could, Jensen got to the crux of the problem as he saw it.

"I have the authority to stop this race right here, and I'm tempted to do it. Though I have no report on these dogs," he motioned to the black bags near his feet on the ice, I think something in the food, or at least something ingested, caused the attack on Smith. Do you agree?"

Holman nodded. "Yeah. Dogs don't act like that. Sure the hell can't understand what would make anyone do this kind of stuff. And we don't know this is all, do we? If the race goes on, there may be other attacks. Right?"

"I think we should assume that."

"Now, a lot of mushers'll be pretty pissed off if it's canceled. Besides, how do we get them all out of here? Equipment, supplies, dogs, and all the rest. Need an airlift to pull out checkers, vets, radio operators, officials, volunteers—hundreds of people, tons of stuff. And if it stops we may never find out who's responsible, right? They'll scatter all over the state, the lower forty-eight, and even other countries. There are five internationals—two from France and one each from Japan, Switzerland, and Sweden. Even some of the vets and radio operators come from out of state."

Holman had obviously been thinking. He had also talked it over with the musher and checkpoint officials who stood watch with him, for they backed him up with nods of agreement.

"There's some who wouldn't quit," the musher said slowly. "These guys are pretty damn stubborn and competitive. Ego has a lot to do with this race, not just money. They train all year and come determined to finish. Some would just harness up their teams and take off. Then what could you do?"

Jensen knew if it came to that, there was little he could do, except feel somehow responsible if any of them died. Officially stopping the race would mean that those who went on to Nome would not be competing for money, which would take some pressure off the situation, but only if greed was the motive.

"Well," he said, "I guess it isn't a decision to be made without the mushers. I think we should hold a meeting and find out how they feel. What do you say?"

"Good idea," Matt agreed. "I'll put out the word. In the lodge? Half an hour?"

"Yeah. I'll send Becker down here to relieve the three of you. Especially you, Matt, because they'll listen to you. In fact, I'd like you to run the meeting. Okay?"

In a short time almost everyone in Rainy Pass was gathered in the lodge. As Holman climbed onto a chair by the stove and raised a hand for silence, the mumble of voices subsided, and only the shuffling of feet could be heard.

"We got a problem." His deep growl filled the room.

"More than one damn problem," someone commented from the back.

"Yeah. More than one. This race has never been stopped. Suspended a couple of times in bad weather when the supply planes couldn't fly, but never canceled. We may have to do that now."

A mutter of negative response rose from the group. Jensen noticed a few heads nodding, however. The group seemed split about in thirds: those opposed, those in favor, and those still reserving judgment. Few mushers were among the ones in favor. Most of those seemed to be officials and support people.

In the rear he saw the DOG stocking cap shaking back and forth.

"Hey," called one of the men. "What the hell is going on? I've heard three different versions of these . . . *accidents,* and I don't know what to believe. How about some information?"

Holman turned to Jensen. "You better do this," he said. "You've got the info from the lab."

He stepped down from the chair and Jensen climbed up.

"I'm Sergeant Jensen, State Troopers, Homicide," he said. "I'm going to be straight with you. I'll tell you everything I can, but I also need your help. Decisions have to be made here.

"At least two of these mushers were murdered," he went on, wanting to shock them. "We are assuming Smith is the third.

"It has been called to my attention that a whole team of dogs does not go mad without reason. What makes most sense is that something was put in their food earlier this evening, but until I have confirmation from the lab in Anchorage, I can only say that this is probable.

"The other two deaths were definitely homicide. George Koptak went to sleep on his sled because his coffee was drugged, probably in Skwentna. Virginia Kline's gang line was cut, causing her to fall into the worst part of Happy Valley.

"Murder is what's going on. I can't say it plainer. Someone is killing mushers. We don't know why, or who. But we will. I just don't want any more of you to die. If we stop the race now, the deaths will probably stop too. You had all better think about that carefully."

He started to step down from the chair but was held by a question from a musher in the front row. "What do we do then, just sit and be targets here? There are over forty other mushers out there, some in Rohn, but most on their way up. What about them? How do you know whoever is doing this isn't out there picking them off right now? I'd rather be out running, where I feel in control, than sitting here like a duck in a shooting gallery."

"There is that, of course, I can't guarantee anything. We don't know about the mushers in other locations except that we haven't heard of problems from anywhere else. I also have to be honest and say that I believe if Smith's dog food was poisoned here, it only stands to reason that whoever did it may still be here. Unless any of you know of someone who left after Smith fed his dogs."

Negative response. Two mushers had left for Rohn early in the evening, but no one had gone into the Dalzell Gorge beyond Rainy Pass since before seven-thirty in the evening, and none were likely to now. It was a section of the trail as tough on mushers and teams as Happy Valley. With new snow falling, these drivers would wait to attempt it in daylight.

On clear nights, with luck, under the best conditions, the run could be successfully completed in as little as eight hours. On others, when wind howled through the canyon, blowing snow obscured the trail and made a treacherous maze of the descent. Mushers could wear themselves and their dogs out trying to work their way through unbroken drifts. The soft, feathery snow that was now falling was deceptive in its loveliness. Even the trailbreaking snow machines had come back up from Rohn early in the evening and waited in Rainy. They would pack down the new snow in the morning as soon as it was light.

"Look," said a tall veteran musher, "I think you should let those who want to go on, go. I agree with Jim that I'll feel like a rat in a trap if I have to stay here. It's a long way to Nome, but I'll feel better out on the trail. I can watch myself if I only have whoever's in front and in back of me to deal with. Let those who want to scratch and wait for transportation out. I don't intend to be careless, but I've got a race to run. I've got too much invested to shut 'er down."

A woman whose face even Jensen knew from the news coverage of her victory two years back stepped forward and turned to face the group. "What if we agree to travel in twos or threes? A lot of us do that anyway. Until we get closer to the finish, we could keep track of each other."

She turned back to Jensen. "Each of these mushers was alone when he or she died, right?"

He nodded thoughtfully. "That's a good idea, if you really want to keep going." He stepped off the chair and motioned Holman back onto it. "Ask for a vote," he suggested. "I want to know how many think the race should continue."

Holman did, and almost half those in attendance immediately voted to continue the race. Slowly, as Holman counted, more hands were raised until he had to start over. "Damn it. Only mushers vote. Put 'em up and keep 'em up," he demanded finally. "Can't tell how many of you there are." The final count indicated that all but three of the mushers were in favor of continuing.

"You agree to travel together?" he asked. "If you

do, and you report anything suspicious right away, I'll let the race go on for now."

They agreed.

"I've gotta tell you I can't promise to let it keep on if anything else happens," he told them. "And for God's sake, don't cover up anything just to keep this damn thing going. Keep track of each other. I mean it. This scares the hell out of me and it should you, too."

He hopped off the chair and the meeting broke up. Within minutes mushers had chosen traveling partners and were headed off to rest until morning, either in the warmth of the lodge or out on their sleds where they could keep an eye on their dogs. Through the window, Jensen watched as some of them moved their teams closer together. While one partner stayed awake to watch, the others returned to the lodge or bedded down on their sleds.

With a sigh he sat on a bench near the stove. He knew he needed sleep too, but he couldn't quite make himself go to arrange the watch with Becker. What he really wanted was information he couldn't get until morning. He needed to know which mushers had been in the three checkpoints at the critical times and enough about them to establish possible motives.

He dug his pipe out of his pocket but found the ritual of filling and lighting it too much of an effort. So he sat with the bowl cupped in the palm of his hand until he saw Jessie Arnold crossing the room toward him with two steaming mugs of coffee.

Gratefully, he accepted the one she gave him, sliding over to make room for her on the bench. For a long moment they sat, sipping the coffee while they watched the bedding down of those who were not headed back for more food. A couple of them gave

Jessie a questioning look, obviously wondering about her proximity to the law. Though he was sure she noticed, it did not seem to make her uncomfortable.

"Well, what do you think?" she asked finally.

"I think it's the best we can hope for now. Holman's satisfied and they sound like they trust him."

"They should. He's run the race nine times, been marshall for three years, and knows as much about it as anyone alive."

"Do you think they'll keep together?"

"For now. As we get closer to Nome it'll spread out and become more of a dash for the finish. There'll be lots of psyching each other out, slipping out of checkpoints, running with headlamps off in the dark, stuff like that. They'll be less inclined to stay together, but they'll also be more aware of exactly where everybody is. The ones who aren't aimed at the top twenty usually travel together and just enjoy the trip."

"Sounds like you aren't going to stop here."

"No, I'm going on with a couple of guys I've run with before. Bomber you met. Jim Ryan is the other. Bomber and I both have moose guns, and we'll keep them handy. I'll be okay."

"There's always another race next year," Jensen suggested.

"Maybe, but I already started this one. I don't quit easy. Besides, there might not be another one for me for a couple of years. I've put everything I have into this one, including some of my dad's money for the entry fee." She hesitated, then went on. "The Iditarod's an expensive business. Just raising enough dogs to put together a good team takes twenty thousand a year. I can't go on doing this unless I'm in good financial shape."

Alex calculated rapidly, adding the thousand-dollar entry fee to the cost of air transportation, food and supplies, plus sleds, harness, clothing, and a lot more. He hadn't thought running this race meant much more than standing behind a sled from Anchorage to Nome. Now he was surprised so many had entered.

He got his pipe going. "How many do you think will pull out?"

"A few, but most will go on in the morning. Daylight will cure some of the tension. Some who're having a bad time will scratch. Wilbur Close wrecked his sled in the trees before Finger Lake, and coming down through Happy Valley he smashed up the one he borrowed. He's already said he's had it. One or two others, probably."

The door of the lodge opened and two mushers came in carrying sleeping bags. One was the bearded musher with the DOG cap. They found a place on the floor as close to the stove as they could get, removed their heavy boots, hung their socks over a line to dry, and crawled into their bags. The wooden floor was beginning to look comfortable to Jensen, and he realized again how tired he was. He was glad he and Becker had already pitched their tent on the lake and that he had plenty of insulating pad to put under his down bag.

"Who's the guy with the hat?" he asked. "I keep seeing him."

She grinned. "Paul Banks from Bethel. I think they're all slightly mad down there. Maybe that's what happens when the river eats the ground under your town year after year. He says you have to be nuts to live on that particular curve of the Kuskokwim. Caterpillar's his biggest sponsor. The mechanics gave him the hat."

They fell silent and Alex looked at her, surprised that this woman was putting herself through punishment many larger, stronger men found difficult.

"Is it tough being a woman on the trail?" he asked suddenly.

Jessie smiled a little self-consciously. "We don't talk much about our problems, or how tough it is," she said, "except to each other once in a while, when there're no men around."

"Why not?"

She looked thoughtfully at the floor for a minute, then turned slightly to face him on the bench.

"You have to understand that some male mushers still think there's no place on the trail for women, especially on the Iditarod Trail. Some of them still see things in terms of male and female, rather than the expertise required to make it. You can't exactly blame them. This state's a macho place, and we scare them. Some of them will do almost anything to keep from getting beat by a woman. Coming in behind one of us threatens most of them.

"I've had guys do the damnedest things. One year I ran with two of them for almost half the race. The minute we hit the coast and the push to Nome was on, they said they were going to water their dogs, but when I went out fifteen minutes later, they were gone. They sneaked out and left me, after I'd broken more than my share of trail, including the last ten miles into Unalakleet. I was so mad I chased them all the way across the ice, passed one in Elim and the other eight miles out of Nome. One of them still isn't speaking to me. The other has come to laugh about it." She nodded toward Bomber Cranshaw, who was finishing up a last piece of apple pie across the room, and smiled. "He figured out that I probably wouldn't have been so determined to beat him if he hadn't pulled that stunt.

"So, we women have a sort of unspoken pact. We try not to whine about anything in mixed company. You may hear the men complain, even some of the best. It's part of the hype. But we don't say a word that will give them the idea we can't cut it. But when a few of us get together, we bitch to each other, let some of the tension out."

Jensen nodded. "Seems a little silly," he said. "With women winning, you wouldn't think there would be anything to question."

She smiled again and shook her head. "When have men—well, people—ever been rational? It's how things seem and feel, isn't it? Not how they are."

He turned to her with a question that had been growing in his mind as she spoke of prejudice on the trail. "How deep does this feeling go in the guys who are threatened?"

She turned her head in a quick motion to look at him for a minute before she answered. He could see on her face the connections her mind was making.

"You mean is anyone mad enough to do something about it?" she said. "That's a pretty serious thought."

"Off target?"

"I think so," she said slowly, but he could see the idea wasn't one she could dismiss with total conviction. "I can't think of anyone I would accuse, and I know a few who are pretty bitter. But a couple are also bitter about not winning the last few races. Does that help?"

He waited, feeling she had more to say.

"In the last part of the race almost every year, people are so tired they get a little weird and lose their tempers easily. Last year I heard one musher say he was sick of nursing women through the race who just got in his way and saved their energy, letting the men break trail, then walked off to Nome. I shrugged it off. We're all unreasonable toward the end, driven by emotion, not intellect. Some of them hold back, forcing any woman to break more than her share of trail. Others go out of their way trying to take care of you, which is worse. And there are other things.

"They say we haven't the upper body strength they have, and that's true, but they ignore the fact that we don't need as much, just enough to do the job. Where they can muscle through a bad spot, we have to compensate, think and move a little faster, keep our sleds lighter, choose our dogs with that in mind. But it can work to our advantage sometimes. Lighter women and sleds may not break through ice that will dunk an extra hundred pounds of man and sled."

She grinned. "It equals out, or we wouldn't win, would we?"

He nodded, slowly, pulling on his pipe as he considered the pleasant, confident look of her. She had something, this unusual woman. She seemed so alive and filled with pleasure in what she was doing. It was refreshing. He thought he might ask Holman about her later, if he could do it casually.

As he reminded himself he was in the middle of a homicide investigation, he realized he was staring. His ears burning self-consciously, he glanced at the floor. Looking back he saw her watching him.

"Makes you think about women a little differently, doesn't it?" She stood up. "I've got to get some rest, if not some actual sleep. If you don't have any more questions, I'll see you in the morning."

Alex watched her cross to the door and go out, thinking of the thousand miles plus between Anchorage and Nome. He realized his ideas were changing. Jessie Arnold was not what he had expected to find driving a team in the toughest race of the year. He had imagined most women mushers were less serious about the whole thing than the men. Thinking back on the women who had won this race over the last few years, he knew this wasn't the case. Winners were made of long, hard training and experience, and gender had little to do with it. Intelligent, well-conditioned, dedicated people, who planned ahead and could cope with all kinds of weather and trail conditions, won races.

From the far corner of the lodge he could hear the quiet voice of the ham operator and the distorted response from the radio, still full of static, but better than it had been earlier. The storm was weakening and he hoped it would clear by morning.

He took his empty coffee mug back to the table and headed down the hill toward the lake with its silent population. Passing the dead musher's campsite, he thought of Smith. What a way to die.

As he walked, the cold, which had intensified since he went inside, reached in around the neck of his heavy parka with icy fingers. At least it helped open his sleepy eyes. He knew he would keep close track of Jessie in the next few days, and the knowledge made him vaguely uneasy. It was a feeling he had closed out of his life since his move to Alaska. He doubted he would act on it, but the interest was there. He kicked a lump of snow in the trail, defensively, feeling ridiculously like a teenager.

9

Date: Monday, March 4
Race Day: Three
Place: Rohn Roadhouse checkpoint
Weather: Overcast with snow flurries, clearing and lowering temperatures predicted for Tuesday
Temperature: High 5°F, low −4°F
Time: Late evening

ALMOST FIFTY MILES NORTH OF RAINY PASS STOOD an old log cabin, the Rohn Roadhouse checkpoint. Inside, a group of six men and one woman listened incredulously as the news of the three deaths and the conditions established for continuing the race came in over the radio from Rainy Pass. The checkpoint official, a vet from Soldotna, stood beside the operator and glanced at his clipboard to see checkout times of the two mushers still on the trail between the two points. He estimated they should reach Rohn within the next six hours, unless they elected to overnight somewhere below Dalzell Gorge. That was unlikely. Most drivers tried to make the run without major stops. Overnighting would only be the choice of a musher completely worn out from struggling through the unusually heavy new snow.

On clear nights the run through the Alaska Range between these two checkpoints is one of the most beautiful of the trip. Coming through the pass, a musher is flanked by deep blue shadows in the folds of snow-covered mountains, slopes rising into the clouds that cover the summits. Northern lights weave across the sky in sweeps and pulses of pale green, red, and blue, swaying like curtains blown by atmospheric winds. At times they're so bright a musher and his team cast shadows on the snow.

Following a branch of Pass Fork, the trail winds its way sharply around rocks and holes in the ice. Finally, it runs into Dalzell Creek, snaking through the narrow canyon of the same name, until the creek empties into the Tatina River.

Here, and on the South Fork of the Kuskokwim, some of the worst overflow on the Iditarod Trail can be found. In the heart of the Alaskan winter, a river may freeze all the way to its bed. In early March, Iditarod time, snow begins to melt and water trickles, flowing over the top of the old ice, creating wide, shallow ponds that freeze to sled runners and dogs' and mushers' feet. At times the ponds conceal holes deep enough to swallow a whole sled.

The overflow often refreezes, forming perfectly smooth glare ice, which is quickly swept clean of falling snow by the wind that whistles through the gorge. With little traction, dogs and mushers scramble for footing, slithering along. The scratch of toenails and scrape of runners can be heard far down the canyon, as can the tense commands and profanities of the drivers.

Turning off the river ice into deep woods, a musher hears the sound of dogs barking among the trees as he heads toward the Rohn checkpoint.

Though maintained as necessary, the small checkpoint cabin at Rohn is uninhabited during the rest of the year. Its shallow, pitched roof is protected by five-gallon gasoline cans, flattened and nailed down. Over the door is a rack of moose antlers. A supply of dry firewood is always available.

Just before each race a vet, a checker, and a radio operator are flown in, to remain until the last Iditarod musher has passed through. Everything is then packed up and the cabin closed. From a narrow airstrip hacked out of thick forest, unused dog food, the radio, and other necessary items are flown out, leaving the cabin ready for next year. The long narrow checkpoint cabin and another nearby, probably the original Rohn Roadhouse from the days when the trail from the Kenai Peninsula to Nome was used regularly to haul freight and mail, remain deserted and waiting.

This checkpoint has an atmosphere different from any other. The relief of successfully negotiating the pass makes exhausted mushers a little giddy, while the prospect of crossing the Farewell Burn, the longest stretch in the race, looms before them. There is a feeling among some that if they have made it this far they can make it anywhere. A sense of camaraderie develops in the small cramped cabin. Songs are sung around campfires and special snacks broken out for the dogs. Everyone sleeps better.

Sometime during the race, each musher is required to take a mandatory twenty-four-hour layover at a checkpoint. Many veterans take it at Rohn. The pass and the following stretch of Farewell Burn are the longest, most physically demanding sections of the trail. Rest between the two makes sense and works well for those who stop there annually.

This year most of the front-runners were staying in

Rohn, although two mushers had checked out for Nikolai without declaring a layover.

Dale Schuller, who had reached Rohn early in the evening, was among those gathered around the radio. He sat on an upended wooden crate near the stove and listened as talk flowed around him after the transmission from Rainy. In the light of a Coleman lantern, clothing and harness hung to dry cast dark shadows. The generator for the radio had been shut down to conserve fuel.

After a time, the others either moved out to their sleds for the night or settled down in the cabin, still discussing the unbelievable situation. Schuller, deep in thought, stayed out of the conversation.

When the group around the radio had thinned to the two officials, he crossed the room and put a hand on the checker's shoulder.

"Harv," he said, frowning, "they said something was put into the food for Smith's dogs. Right?"

"Unofficially, yeah. They think so."

"Do they know what it was?"

"No. The dogs have to be checked in Anchorage at some lab, and they won't get a plane until morning. Why?"

"Wait a second. I'll be right back."

Outside, he went directly to his team, removed his mittens, and dug into the bag on the back of his sled until he found what he was looking for. Carefully he lifted it out, holding it by the top, between thumb and first finger. Pulling a clean bandana from his personal gear, he wrapped the object loosely before returning to the cabin.

He displayed the bundle on the palm of his hand to the checker and unfolded it. On the bandana lay a clear plastic pill bottle from a pharmacy. There were no pills, but it contained traces of white powder.

"I don't like trash left on the trail," he said. "Sometimes I pick it up if it's not too bulky. I found this when I stopped to snack the dogs. Somebody else had stopped there before me."

Harv examined it closely. "No label," he said, reaching to turn it over.

Schuller pulled it back before he could touch it.

"I know fingerprints sound ridiculous, and it may not have anything to do with this at all, but I think I'd better talk to that trooper in Rainy, don't you?"

"Yeah. I guess we'd better find a safe place to keep that thing for the time being." The checker shook his head. "Damn. I can't believe this is happening."

10

Date: Tuesday, March 5
Race Day: Four
Place: Between Rainy Pass and Rohn Roadhouse checkpoints (forty-eight miles)
Weather: Clear, light wind
Temperature: High 1°F, low −10°F
Time: Early morning

BEFORE IT WAS LIGHT ON TUESDAY, MUSHERS WERE ready to leave Rainy Pass. Snow had stopped falling and the sky was clear, promising a morning filled with sunshine, although the temperature remained below zero. Pearly light brightened the snow-covered peaks that towered above the broad bowl of the pass.

Everyone not in the process of repacking sleds or feeding and harnessing dogs was finding their own breakfast. Racers took turns going for water or returning to the lodge, where food and coffee were available. They didn't leave their cookers unattended.

Two trailbreakers pulled away from Puntilla Lake and, snow-machine engines whining, headed for the north pass and the Dalzell Gorge beyond it. Immediately teams began to swing in, one behind the other, leaving little space between.

Jensen stood by a lodge window nursing a third cup of steaming coffee while he watched them go.

Headed across the flat saddle of the pass toward the Dalzell Gorge, Jessie kept her team moving with the others in the long line of sleds and dogs. They went slowly as they followed the snow machines, giving them time to break through the new snow. But the sky was clear, and at least they were moving.

The sweep of slopes and broad curve of the pass reminded her of pictures she had seen of the mountains of Afghanistan, so massive it was hard to believe them real. They commanded the landscape, dwarfing everything in sight.

The drop into the canyon would be five miles of a wild roller-coaster ride. The other forty-two should be easier though wrestling the sled around holes and overflow along the Dalzell Creek was always a struggle. In some narrow sections the only way to cross the gorge was to tilt the sled onto one runner. Ice bridges would fall, hopefully behind the team, but sometimes right under the dogs, slamming the sled into the opposite bank, stopping the team with a jerk. The musher then had to lift and work it loose, up and over, back onto the trail.

This early in the morning, colder temperatures would keep the trail through the Dalzell and the Tatina River overflow more solidly frozen. Once on the river the group would spread out and make better time into Rohn.

Comfortable with the rhythm of her sled, Jessie let her thoughts wander. After her conversation with Alex the night before, she had gone back to her team to find Jim Ryan awake and watchful. Bomber snored in his sled. Dogs and gear were grouped close together, and Ryan sat on a pile of straw near the fire, drinking hot water—silver tea.

Mushers are always drinking something. Dehydration is a threat to humans as well as dogs. Humans lose moisture faster, having their whole body surface through which to perspire. Dogs only sweat through the pads of their feet and their noses and lose water through the air they exhale.

At temperatures below freezing, moisture freezes from the air, drying it. The colder it gets, the faster it freezes and dries. Though breathing cold air doesn't damage throat and lung tissue, because it is warmed and moisturized by the body before it reaches these sensitive areas, it is uncomfortably drying to the skin.

The night before, Jessie had been applying Chap Stick liberally to her lips and nose when she caught sight of Jensen going down the trail to the lake. He had lifted his face to the falling snow, then shrugged his coat up around his neck and hurried on, looking tired, concerned, and strangely vulnerable. She had intended to mull over their conversations a bit, but when she got into her down sleeping bag, spread on the sled over an insulated pad, she had dropped into sleep like a stone tossed into a still pool.

Now, as she rode the runners, automatically calling signals to the dogs, she thought of Jensen and smiled to herself. He was interesting. She wondered what it would feel like to be kissed by a man with such a mustache. She had not been kissed lately, except for sloppy licks from her dogs. Alex was definitely more appealing. It had been a long time since a stranger had attracted her. Too long.

The last two years had been satisfying. She liked breeding dogs, training them, establishing her own kennel, and doing well in competition. Doing it alone had been a relief after the struggle to maintain a personal and professional relationship with a man whose ideas on training dogs had turned out to be remarkably similar to his views of women. He had manipulated both with frustrating swings from affection to rejection, offering rewards only when things went his way.

Meeting Alex Jensen had caught her off guard. His attention was flattering and—

Abruptly, her reverie was interrupted as the ice chute of the gorge opened in front of them. With his rebel yell echoing from the canyon walls, Bomber plunged over the first downward slope. Quickly checking her dogs, she followed, foot ready on the brake, hoping Jim wasn't too close behind her.

11

Date: Tuesday, March 5
Race Day: Four
Place: Between Rainy Pass and Rohn Roadhouse checkpoints (forty-eight miles)
Weather: Clear, light wind
Temperature: High 1°F, low −10°F
Time: Midmorning

THE GLARE OF SUNLIGHT ON SNOW DREW JENSEN'S eyes into a squint as the small plane gathered speed and lifted away from the ice of Puntilla Lake. Glancing to his left at the tinted glasses worn by the pilot, Trooper Ben Caswell, he wished he hadn't left his own in his pack.

His stomach lurched as the plane wobbled slightly in a mild wind shear. Rainy Pass was the point of confluence for the gusts flowing from the mountains around it.

As they gained altitude, the brightness diffused until he could took down without discomfort at the ridges, deep valleys, and canyons of the rugged terrain. Peaks of the Alaska and Teocalli mountains rose enormous around them. Caswell dipped the left wing to swing their course a bit more to the west, following the Dalzell Gorge. Watching it unfold, Jensen was glad he was not among those threading their way out of the pass at ground level.

Just after nine o'clock a plane had arrived from Anchorage. Half an hour later, they had been loading the black plastic bags and their grisly contents when Caswell landed his Maule M-4 and taxied across the ice. Headquarters had agreed they needed their own transportation. Jensen and Becker loaded their gear and headed for Rohn and their interview with Schuller. The evidence plane would also make a quick stop in Rohn to pick up the plastic pill container.

At Alex's request, Caswell flew fairly low over the gorge toward the Tatina River. It was easy to see teams coming through; one behind the other. From the air, the lines of dogs stretched out in front of the sleds like centipedes. Most had come through the steep parts of the canyon and were beginning to space themselves out. Traveling quickly over trail still solid from the night's lower temperature, several of the leaders had pulled away and were nearing the halfway point. Alex looked carefully as they passed over the eight or ten mushers at the head of the pack but couldn't locate Jessie Arnold's bright red parka.

"Take it around once more, would you, Ben?" he asked.

On the second run he used the binoculars and spotted Jessie, Bomber, and Ryan not too far from the river, with about a dozen teams between them and the leader. They had stopped for a break beside the trail, and all three waved at the plane as it flew over. Satisfied, he directed Caswell to go on to Rohn.

The landing strip at Rohn is a narrow swath cut between stands of spruce. It is often plagued with crosswinds, which make incoming pilots pay white-knuckled attention, and passengers hold their breath and brace their feet. Though the air was comparatively still that day, all three troopers were relieved to climb out of the plane after it jounced to a stop on the uneven ground.

"Any real wind and I would have punched a hole in the floor," Jensen told Caswell as they tied the plane securely between trees.

"Yeah. This one's always a shot of adrenaline. I've landed here on probably a dozen occasions, and I swear those trees get closer every time. Once I did three touch-and-go's before I finally made it."

After getting directions from the checker, Jensen found Schuller a short distance from the cabin, replacing the battered plastic runners on his sled.

Schuller had removed the old strips, worn from contact with rocks and ice, and was inserting new ones into the tracks on the runners of his overturned sled. He shook hands with Jensen through a thin working glove.

"Glad you could get down here before I had to take off," he said. "Do you mind if I finish this? It will only be ten minutes or so."

"Hell no, go ahead. Need help?"

"No thanks. Appreciate the offer, but they'd throw me out of the race if you did. No direct help allowed. It's okay. I've got this down, so it won't take long."

"Then I'll watch and ask a few questions. I haven't seen this before. Then you can show me that container you picked up."

"No sweat. We stashed it, and no one's handled it but me, and whoever had it before me, of course."

He turned back to the sled and, with the heel of an ax, continued to drive in a runner. "I knew about

George, of course, but what's the story on Ginny and Steve? How's Turner doing?"

"I haven't heard since we left Finger Lake, but he was holding his own there."

Schuller looked up and frowned. "Think I'll get the ham to call Anchorage and check. Sure hope it doesn't screw up his racing. George expected a lot from him."

"Jessie Arnold said about the same thing."

"Well, she'd know. She's pretty damn good at it herself."

"Yeah?"

"We ran part of the Kusko together this year. She's a good friend and a quality handler."

Alex found himself wondering if the other man meant more than he said.

With a last whack, the runners slid into place. Schuller drove in the screws, flipped over the sled, and the job was complete. Carefully, he repacked his tools and the gear he had piled around.

"Let's get that bottle—and get inside where I can thaw out these wooden fingers. The gloves aren't much, but I can't work in mitts."

In the cabin Jensen held the container up to the light, careful to keep the bandana between his fingers and the serrated edge of the lid. Two scratches marred the surface on opposite sides of the clear, rounded plastic. Gently removing the safety lid, he examined the traces of white powder adhering to the inside.

"What is it?" Harv, the checker, questioned. "Ain't you gonna taste it or something, like they do on TV?" He pushed back a violently purple stocking cap. Along with the fringe of red hair and beard encircling his chubby face, it made him look like a demented gnome.

Jensen shook his head.

"Not a chance. If this was all it took to put away a whole team of dogs, I'm not risking it. Leave it for the lab boys. Some hallucinogens are so potent that an amount the weight of a dime would kill eight people."

"Jesus, man. Put it away."

Alex sealed it into an evidence bag.

"Where'd you pick this up?" he asked Schuller.

"About halfway down the Tatina," he said. "I stopped to snack the dogs in a wide space where another team or two had pulled over earlier. It was maybe three feet off the trail."

"These marks on each side. Did the bottle rub against anything in your pocket or sled?"

"No. It was in my sled bag, but there wasn't anything to mark it but my extra socks. It's like it was when I found it."

"Either of you talk to anyone else about this?"

"People were tight enough after hearing from Rainy last night." Harv frowned. "It didn't seem worth it to rattle 'em any more. We decided to leave it to you."

"Good," Jensen said thoughtfully. "It may be completely unrelated, and we may as well not cause any more rumors. Keep it to yourselves. There'll be a plane here in a while to pick it up."

"Will you tell us what you find out?" Schuller asked.

"If I can. It takes the lab a while to run drug tests. Check with me before you leave, will you, in case I have other questions."

"Sure."

He turned to Harv. "Can you give me the times for everyone who's come in here so far? I need to find out where they were when all this happened."

"Here's the record." The checker handed over a clipboard holding the report begun the day the checkpoint opened. Carefully listed were the checkpoint and checker's names, musher's name, date and time of arrival, number of dogs in harness and carried in the sled, verification of required gear, elapsed time from the start, date and time of departure, and the driver's signature.

Jensen fervently wished for a copy machine when he saw the amount of information.

Harv grinned at the expression on his face. "Here," he chuckled, reaching for his clipboard. "I can do it faster. You gotta have other stuff to do." Scrubbing his head with the purple cap, he turned to the radio table and reached for a pencil.

"Thanks," Alex said gratefully. He went off to find Becker, who was interviewing the drivers of teams in the order they were scheduled to leave Rohn. He added Harv to his mental list of helpful people, which now included Matt Holman, Bill Pete, and several others, including the support crew who had cooked his eggs that morning. And, of course, Jessie.

He pulled on his coat and walked out across the clearing toward a group of people standing around a fire. The sound of an angry voice intruded on his appreciation of people's goodwill.

"Who the fuck do you think you are? You can't push me the hell around. I haven't done anything. I wasn't there when any of this shit happened. I'm leaving here in a couple of hours and I haven't got time for this shit. I don't know *anything*.

As Jensen came up to the fire, he caught Becker's eye, but the younger trooper was too busy with the furious man confronting him to do more than nod.

The angry musher was a formidable four or five inches taller than Becker's five feet ten, with shoulders to match. He stood with one hand on his hip, the other clutching a tangle of harness, which he shook in Becker's direction. Clean-shaven and sharp-featured, he glared at the trooper from under brows so heavy they were, apart from his size, the first thing one noticed about him. Alex recognized him as both a winner and challenger from pictures in the newspapers and remembered also that the man had gained a reputation for being both outspoken and difficult.

"Hey, Tim," cajoled a man from the listening group. "Chill out. He's just asking. Don't take it personal."

The fierce dark eyes turned on the peacemaker. "Oh yeah? I wasn't fucking *there.* Neither were you, John. Where does he get off, thinking any of us here could be responsible? That's what he's doing, man. Can't you see that? Well, I can. And I damned well do intend to take it personal."

Next to Alex, a dark-haired woman driver stared into the fire as if pretending she was elsewhere, anywhere. He'd met her at Rainy Pass. Her name was Gail Murray, and this was not her first Iditarod trip. Nearby a dog began to bark, made uneasy by the angry voice.

"Well, I don't see it that way. Steve was a friend of mine and I'll answer any questions that will help. How the hell can he know where you were unless you tell him?"

Tempted to step in, Alex caught himself. This was Becker's show. Let him handle it. He waited, watching closely.

He was soon glad he had. The younger trooper

stepped forward and offered his hand to the cooperative musher.

"Thanks," he said, "I'd like to talk to you when I finish with Mr. Martinson." Turning back, he continued in a steady, authoritative voice.

"Sir, I understand you're not comfortable with this. But we need help to get to the bottom of it. We have to go through the steps in order and not leave anything out. That's how it's done. I admit it's unlikely you know anything, but maybe you do and don't know it.

"Now. We can get through this painlessly, which means you answer my questions, or . . . I can hold you here until you do. I won't say I'd go as far as an arrest for hindering an officer, 'cause I know you're not going to push it that far. That's not a threat, Mr. Martinson, that's simply an assistance the law allows.

"You want to continue this race? You talk to me."

He stood waiting. Martinson opened his mouth, then shut it again, still glaring. They stared at each other while the musher thought it over. Finally he broke eye contact and tossed the harness down on a sled beside him.

"Okay, damn it. Have it your way," he growled.

"Great. I appreciate it. Let's take a walk."

Alex watched the two of them amble off toward the river, Becker asking questions, the other man answering resentfully. They stopped on the edge of a stand of spruce, and the musher seemed to have found something he considered important. He now dominated the conversation. The trooper nodded and took notes. Satisfied, Alex turned and began to ask a few questions of his own.

12

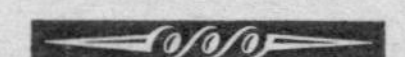

Date: Tuesday, March
Race Day: Four
Place: Between Rainy Pass and Rohn Roadhouse checkpoints (forty-eight miles)
Weather: Clear, light wind
Temperature: High 1°F, low −10°F
Time: Midmorning

BESIDE THE TRAIL AT THE GENTLER NORTHERN END of the Dalzell, Jessie, Bomber, and Jim rested their dogs. Although the sun shone brightly, glistening on a million tiny crystals of fresh snow, the temperature still hovered below zero.

"The gorge from hell," Bomber had announced when they pulled over, waving a sweeping gesture toward the section of trail they had just completed. "Once again survived. Once again a bastard." He flopped back in the snow by his sled and rolled his eyes.

Jessie scooped up a snowball and tossed it, catching him solidly in the face.

"Spare us the melodrama and get a fire going, you fake."

Sputtering, Bomber sat up to paw snow from his eyes.

"Aw, shit, Even adoring fans will turn on you for one small lapse of dignity."

With a grin Bomber dug through his gear to find the coffeepot, a container of coffee, and a handful of straw and small sticks. "Hand over some of your charcoal, Jessie."

She handed him several chunks, along with the can of starter she carried. With these materials he proceeded to kindle a small, efficient blaze, and soon a pot of melted snow was transformed into steaming brew.

When they had snacked the dogs, they rested by the fire and broke out their preferred trail food. Bomber alternated handfuls of chocolate-covered peanuts with bites of a stick of butter.

"How can you eat that stuff straight?" Ryan asked. "Doesn't it give you the runs?"

"It's pure energy, man. But I never get the runs. Think I must be part fuckin' goat. Want some?"

"I'll stick with this, thanks." Ryan waved the salami he was slicing into chunks. He had heaped spoonfuls of cocoa mix into his coffee.

Jessie held up a fried chicken drumstick. "I'll be glad to get my stuff in Rohn. I'm getting tired of this and peanut butter and jelly sandwiches. My mom makes the world's best ham and cheese macaroni, and I've got two or three bags of it waiting for me. I have dreams about that macaroni, even when I'm not on the trail."

"I always get cravings for food during a race," said Ryan. "Last year, about Ophir, I got hung up on the idea of lasagna. By the time I got to Nome I would have traded the team for it. Couldn't get it out of my head. Nothing I had tasted right."

Jessie moaned. "I had it bad for pepperoni pizza two years ago. I've packed it in my supply drops ever since. What do you have in Rohn?"

Ryan grinned. "La-sa-gna!"

Laughing, Jessie sat back against her sled. "I'm pooped and we're only halfway to Rohn."

"Yeah, but the second half's better. We won't have to spend most of our time going sideways," Bomber said.

"Sure hope it doesn't warm up much this afternoon. My mutts don't like running on the ice when there's water. They keep trying to jump up the bank." Ryan dumped out the dregs from the bottom of his cup and refilled it with coffee.

"You know who is . . . was . . . really good at the gorge?" Bomber asked. He sat by his sled on a clump of straw, his feet stretched toward the small fire. "George. He had it worked out. Packed his sled so the weight was distributed right and moved his dogs around so that those with the shortest legs were on the uphill side. He'd stop when he needed to and reshuffle his dogs. He was never fastest through, but none of his dogs ever got stove up. Goddamn, I'm gonna fuckin' miss him."

Jessie looked up and was startled to find him staring at her.

They were all silent for a minute or two.

"You know," Jim said finally, "I think there should be an award or something for him. He gave away more Iditarod know-how than I'll ever learn."

"He and Joe Redington should have been named master coaches years ago," Jessie added. "Everyone would have agreed. No problem. I couldn't begin to count the number of things they taught me."

"Well," Bomber said, "I like the idea, but if it's another damn trophy to be handed out at the banquet in Nome, I can't stand it. The thing was over four hours long last year. I was looking forward to breakfast when they finally got through. If it wasn't required, I'd skip it."

Jessie stood up and went to search through her sled bag. Returning to the fire with a pair of rubberized boots and dry socks, she sat down again and began to change.

Bomber leaned back against his sled, which was closest to the fire.

"Good idea, I'm ready." He held up one foot in a new, well-oiled leather boot. "Last year when it was so cold and we were past the Tatina, for some reason I figured we were through the worst. I put on my mukluks and before I knew it I was asshole deep in water. It looked like solid ice. We drove onto it, and the first warning I had was water splashing me in the face. I had to stop and change all our feet. I fuckin' hate "

"Watch the language, man." Ryan, finally fed up, nodded toward Jessie.

Bomber raised his eyebrows. "Hey, back off. She's heard it before. If she wants to be one of the guys . . ." He shrugged. "Right, Jess?"

She glanced at him but didn't respond.

As she finished lacing up her boots, the sound of a plane filled the air. Looking up, they watched the pilot waggle his wings as he flew over them at low altitude. Ryan stood up and they all waved back. Turning north, the plane disappeared from sight.

Jensen, Jessie thought. "They must be checking on us." It was comforting to know the trooper was there.

But, she considered, maybe it wasn't him. It might be Holman.

"Hey, Jess. What'd the trooper have to say?"

Bomber raised his head, also interested.

"Oh, not much that we don't already know. He wanted to find out about the race, stuff like that."

"Did he say anything more about George or Steve?"

"Not really. He just wanted to know more about how things work out here."

She stopped talking and began fastening the toggles on her sled bag, her back to the men at the fire. She hadn't really thought much about Jensen, or their conversations, since early that morning. Now she found she was reluctant to share any of it with her companions. Bomber's attentiveness bothered her, but she turned when he spoke.

"I don't know, he seemed like a pretty good guy. But didn't all those questions piss you off? Who'd he want to know about?"

What's that to you? she thought. She saw Ryan looking at her expectantly and resented him as well. What's the matter with me? It isn't as though they didn't have a right to be concerned. They aren't accusing me of selling them out, for God's sake. Why should I feel so damn defensive?

"He was easy to talk to. A lot more than I expected. Besides, I'd like to see them get whoever's doing this, and maybe talking to him will help."

"Who do you think it might be?"

"Damn it, I haven't any idea. I don't think he does either, yet. He's afraid someone else'll get hurt. So's Matt."

"Me too," Ryan said.

"Well, let's get this shit on the road." Bomber

stomped snow onto the fire, which sizzled and died. He dumped the last of the coffee and grounds over it, wiped out the pot with a handful of snow, and stowed it in his sled bag. "We can catch a real rest in Rohn for twenty-four."

Ten minutes later they were all repacked and ready to leave, Bomber in the lead.

"Gentlemen," he called to his dogs, "are you ready?"

Like a line of reverse dominos, starting with Junkie, his leader, the dogs came to their feet, shaking themselves into line, ready to run. Cranshaw named all his dogs after drugs or booze. There were Snow, Mary Jane, Stout, Speed, Brandy, Black Jack, Jose, Kahlúa Lou, and several others Jessie couldn't remember.

"Off like a herd of turtles." Bomber pulled the snow hook and let them go.

Jessie and her dogs followed close behind. Bomber looked back and grinned. I'd better watch it with him, she considered, knowing the display was mostly for her benefit. She was glad Ryan was a part of their small group.

13

Date: Tuesday, March 5
Race Day: Four
Place: Rohn Roadhouse checkpoint
Weather: Clear, light wind
Temperature: High 1°F, low −9°F
Time: Noon

THE EVIDENCE PLANE HAD COME AND GONE FROM the Rohn checkpoint, carrying with it the container Schuller had picked up on the trail. Before the pilot left, Alex talked to him about things he couldn't trust to the radio's open frequencies.

The trooper pilot took notes and then assured him there had been no current grumbling by the humane society.

"It's been a long time since they got crazy," he told Alex, "and then it was just for a year or two. During one race a reporter spotted a musher beating his dogs. That set the society off. It kind of hung around, you know, kept filling space in the paper every year."

"Which musher?"

"I don't remember. Somebody from McGrath or Ruby, I think. The guy was fined and suspended or something. But ask the vets. It really doesn't happen much now."

Alex asked him to check it out anyway. There was always the possibility that even one person held a grudge.

The second, and more feasible, possibility was the illegal-gambling angle. He was sure a fair amount of it went on somewhere. It was too good an opportunity for those who would bet big money on a uniquely Alaskan sporting event.

"Have someone lean on the Anchorage bars, the private clubs. There's always something going on down there. Tell Abbott to have a shot at it. That's his turf anyway, with his cousin in the APD. Between them they should be able to get some idea."

"Okay, but it'll take a day or two."

"I know. That's fine. I just don't want to leave anything flapping in the wind."

"Speaking of which, I'd better get my wings out of here and that plastic thing to the lab before it closes. If they can get the tests started tonight, you might have results by morning."

"Thank Farber for giving me Caswell."

The trooper pilot threw him a snappy salute, climbed into his plane, and was gone.

The times that mushers came in and out of checkpoints was Jensen's main concern. From that information he could gather an initial list of possible suspects. The afternoon would be full of interviewing mushers as they came and went from Rohn, but Becker and Caswell could handle it.

He picked up the list of times Harv had compiled and spent an hour comparing it to those from Skwentna, Finger Lake, and Rainy Pass.

When the troopers all got together for lunch at the

campsite, he shook his head at Caswell's questioning look.

"We'll get to it in a minute. What have you guys got from this morning? How about Tim Martinson, Phil? What did he have to say after you masterfully defused his temper?"

Becker grinned at the praise and pulled a notebook from his parka pocket. "He really *didn't* seem to know much," he said, summing up his scribbles. "He's totally involved in the race. But, after some encouragement, he remembered Koptak and three or four other mushers around the same fire in Skwentna. He says they all came in about three in the morning. He thinks they camped together until whenever they took off the next day, because when he drove past them on his way out at five, they were all in their bags. Turner was one of them, and there were two others, Paul Banks and Bill Pete. Couldn't remember the fourth, or if there really was one."

"Banks—Jessie Arnold said he's from Bethel."

"You spent a lot of time with her yesterday, Alex. Anything we should know?" Becker teased.

Jensen felt his face grow warm and took a long swallow of his coffee, burning his tongue in the process. "She knew Ginny Kline," he said, feeling defensive and disliking it. "Also suggested the humane-society crowd might have something to do with this. I sent word to Anchorage to check it out. What else'd you get, Phil?"

"Nothing I could pin down, but I'll go through the notes again. It's not real easy getting these people to talk. Some are scared. Some don't like to say anything about other mushers. Others are concentrating so hard on the race and their teams that they wouldn't notice a train if it ran through here. What've you got, Cas?"

"Well . . . I asked about that bottle Schuller picked up, but nobody knew anything about it. Of course, if it's related, whoever dropped it isn't going to say so."

"There's something about the marks on the sides of that thing that really intrigues me," Alex said. "They were caused by something rubbing on it. If the lab finds it fits into place, I want to know what caused those marks. I think it all goes together somehow. Any amount of money says that stuff went into Smith's dog food."

"You narrow it down any from those times?" Caswell asked.

Alex pulled out the lists and reviewed them in chronological order. "Skwentna was damn crowded," he told them. "It's so near the start they're still running close together. Twenty-six mushers, a vet, two checkers, and a radio operator were there between the times Koptak checked in and out. Two mushers dropped out there, and four others didn't make it to the next two checkpoints in time to be responsible for the other deaths."

"Of course, there's everyone in Skwentna, if we want to include them. Maybe twenty-five residents and all the fans who fly in to watch the race go through," Caswell mused.

"Right," said Alex, "and we don't have any idea when that thermos was doctored."

"But they couldn't have been in Finger Lake to cut Kline's gang line," Becker broke in. "Who was there between the time they say she checked her lines and the time she left in the morning?"

"Who saw her check her lines?" Cas asked.

Alex checked his interview notes. "Talburgen, the

Swedish musher who caught Kline's dogs after her line broke. He says he saw her going over her whole rig after midnight, before she went to get some sleep. He left early the next morning, thirty-five minutes before she did, with Cranshaw between them."

"Okay," Becker nodded enthusiastically. "Now, who else was in Finger Lake and Rainy Pass?"

"One at a time, Phil," Jensen grinned. "And it's not that easy. There weren't as many in Finger Lake. Bill Pete, Dale Schuller, Paul Banks, Bill Tuner, Bomber Cranshaw, Jessie Arnold, Tim Martinson, Jim Ryan, Ron Cross, Rex Johnson, Jules Talburgen, Steve Smith, Wilbur Close, and a few others were there at the right time. Again we had a vet, a checker, and a radio operator, but none of them had been at Skwentna or were in Rainy Pass later.

"I think we can eliminate race officials for lack of opportunity. All of them were only at one location, like Harv here in Rohn and the staff at Rainy Pass."

Caswell considered the idea, then frowned. "That's true on the officials, as long as one person is responsible. Could it be more than one?"

I don't think so, Cas. It doesn't feel like that, but it might be possible, barely. Let's assume it's only one for now. If you find something that says otherwise, let me know."

Caswell nodded, still frowning.

"Okay," Becker galloped on. "Now, can we eliminate anyone who left before Smith arrived in Rainy Pass? We can't, can we. Not until we hear whether the stuff in the bottle was the same as whatever killed the dogs. And if it is, doesn't that mean we have to consider everyone at the front of the race too? If it is . . ."

"Whoa. You can't build a fence without posts,"

Alex cautioned him. "I know what you're getting at, but we don't have the report yet. For now we'll put them all on the tentative list."

As he shuffled the papers to find the one for Rainy Pass, he considered Becker's predictability with amusement. The younger man thought with his mouth. *How do I know what I think till I say it?* His talent lay in his people skills; easy laughter, interest, and enthusiasm. It was hard not to like Phil Becker. People instinctively trusted him, often said things they didn't mean to. Under that bright, greedy-for-facts exterior, however, lay an increasingly efficient detection unit, capable of handling problems like Martinson. Gulping information as fast as he could and wanting more, he could still be counted on not to let a crumb of it get away.

In contrast, Caswell, sparing of words, worked things out carefully in his head before testing his ideas. *Let me kick it around a little.* Mentally, he seemed to walk through the facts of a case like a flea market, picking up treasures others might miss. There was something of the bulldog to him. Alex knew he hadn't heard the last of the more-than-one theory and, also, that he could depend on Cas to keep him straight on details.

"Martinson, Schuller, and five others—Gail Murray, T. J. Harvey, Rick Ellis, John Grasle, and Rod Pollitt—left Rainy before Smith arrived. Now here's the kicker list. Not counting the ones I just mentioned, there are nine who were at all three locations: Bill Pete, Paul Banks, Bomber Cranshaw, Jessie Arnold, Jim Ryan, Rex Johnson, Jules Talburgen, Mike Solomon, and Susan Pilch. I've eliminated Close since he dropped out in the pass."

They all contemplated the names in silence for a while.

"You know," Cas said slowly, "it's interesting. Not one of these deaths has been caused by personal force, like shooting or stabbing. No direct contact. Each has died but could just as easily have only been injured and come out alive. Koptak could have fallen from his sled into the snow and slept it off. Kline's gang line might have broken somewhere besides the gorge and simply let her dogs get away from her. Smith could have noticed the change in his dogs and kept out of their way, or only have been bitten.

"The other interesting things are that none of the methods was used more than once and that the perp could have been male or female, large or small. In fact, poison's more a woman's method."

"Drugs," Becker corrected.

Caswell nodded but pursued his organized line of thought.

"The drugs indicate premeditation. It doesn't seem likely they would have turned up out here if someone hadn't planned in advance to use them. But the cuts in the line could have been done by anyone on the spur of the moment.

"Does that tell us anything? It might support the two-person theory. You got any idea on motive, Alex?"

"Nothing specific," Jensen answered, "except that even without the deaths each incident would probably still have put the musher out of the race. Anchorage is looking into gambling and animal-activist possibilities. A few of these guys would like to see it be an all-men's race, but it isn't just women getting killed. It's too soon to pull anything together. We need more information. We got to talk to the rest as they come in tonight. Harvey and Ellis are on the way to McGrath, so we'll have to catch them there."

He stood up and stretched. "Becker, you're doing great with the interviews. People respond well to your style of questioning. Why don't you start catching the ones coming in from Rainy. They should be here mid-afternoon, according to Harv.

"Cas, you can help me go over these lists again. Maybe two of us can spot something."

"You want to stay here tonight or go to McGrath? I should do a better tie-down on this bird if we stay." Caswell was already moving toward the plane.

"I want to get hold of Holman before I decide, but we'll probably stay here. I like the idea of having him on one side of the burn and us on the other. I'll get back to you as soon as I can raise him on the radio, okay?"

Becker, collecting trash, glanced at Alex with innocently widened eyes. "When's Miss Arnold getting in?" he asked.

"Stuff it, Becker. I'm too busy to take you on. Your ability to deal with the Martinsons of this world doesn't earn you complete immunity. Don't push it."

The guffaw from Caswell was muffled by the door of the plane. He stepped out with a serious face, but his eyes danced.

"I'll find you at the cabin in a few, okay?"

"Sure," said Alex. He started for the checkpoint, after pausing to get his pipe drawing well.

He knew that as soon as he was far enough away, they would talk about his interest in Jessie Arnold. Although he was jealous of his privacy, he really didn't much mind the teasing. Then it occurred to him that he was daydreaming about a woman he had talked to twice. No, three times, if he counted that brief exchange at Finger Lake. Good God. He didn't know her at all. She might, as far as he knew, be seeing someone. Besides, he didn't want to get involved, did he?

He stomped up to the cabin and threw open the door, only to find Dale Schuller talking to Harv over a cup of hot chocolate.

Harv, the gnome, reported that there was nothing out of the ordinary on the trail and set about trying to reach Holman. Alex managed a civil word of greeting for Schuller and didn't even ask about the mushers on their way from the pass.

14

Date: Tuesday, March 5
Race Day: Four
Place: Rohn Roadhouse checkpoint
Weather: Clear, light wind
Temperature: High 1°F, low −9°F
Time: Late afternoon

BY THE TIME JESSIE, RYAN, AND BOMBER ARRIVED in Rohn late that afternoon, Jensen and Caswell were satisfied with their final list of potential suspects, but were no more enlightened.

"It'll be dark in a couple of hours," Alex remarked. "Let's set up camp in the trees by the plane."

Between them they had the tent up in half an hour, with sleeping bags on cots to keep them off the frozen ground. Jensen zipped the flap and looked up to see Becker heading toward them through the trees.

"Guess who got in thirty minutes ago," he said casually to Caswell, ignoring Alex.

"Becker!"

"Oh sorry, boss." He grinned irrepressibly. "Bomber Cranshaw and friends. Just thought you wanted me to keep close track of who was coming and going."

Jensen tossed a piece of firewood at him. "Here, make yourself useful."

Much later, when they had finished dinner and Becker had gone off to the checkpoint cabin, Alex, his pipe clenched in his teeth, headed through the trees to find Jessie. Holman had radioed that he had seen nothing unusual from his spotter plane. Caswell was reviewing Becker's interview notes by the light of a Coleman lantern when Jensen left the campsite.

He found Jessie alone by a fire, around which three teams of dogs slept soundly next to empty bowls. She was scraping macaroni and cheese residue from the sides of a plastic cooking bag. There was a satisfied look on her tired face as she licked the spoon.

"Hi," he said as she looked up. "Glad to see you made it."

He was also glad not to see Schuller around, then remembered that, his twenty-four completed, the musher should now be on the trail for Nikolai. This didn't disappoint him, but he wondered why Schuller hadn't checked with him before leaving.

Jessie had known he was coming before he arrived. The scent of his pipe tobacco had preceded him on the light breeze blowing from the airstrip. She smiled up at him and smoothed a strand of hair back from her face. "Hi, yourself."

Pulling his hand from his pocket, Jensen held out a foil-wrapped package. "Carrot cake. Caswell's wife sent it with a supply plane. We had more than enough for three."

"Hey, thanks." She unwrapped it and scooped up a fingerful of cream-cheese icing. "Mmmmm."

He watched as she ate the cake with obvious relish. Then he sat down on a log to one side of the fire, and accepted her offer of a cup of peppermint tea.

"We waved at a plane this afternoon. Was it you?"

"Yeah." He grinned. "Caught you sitting down on the trail, didn't we?"

"You've got to rest sometime. As Bomber so theatrically puts it, we had just survived 'the gorge from hell.' "

"It looked like a screamer from the air. I was glad to fly over it."

"It wasn't so bad this year because there's lots of snow. But it's some of the worst."

"You look tired. Will you take your twenty-four here?" Alex was proud of himself for the bit of Iditarod jargon.

"I'm pooped and, yes, we'll stay till tomorrow afternoon. I want the pups really rested before we tackle the burn. Even with good snow cover, it can be nasty. Two of them have sore feet from ice between the pads and can use the time."

The conversation felt forced to Jensen, and he struggled to be casual. Self-conscious from Becker's teasing and his own thoughts, he didn't know quite how to change the mood. He looked at Jessie and considered her weary look, knowing she felt it too. She was looking into the fire. Her hair was tousled and needed combing, and there was a charcoal smudge across her right cheek. Still, the lines of her face and the graceful angle of her hand holding the cup were attractive, tired or not. She wasn't beautiful in the ordinary sense, but in the sum of herself she was arresting.

As he studied her in silence, she glanced up and met his gaze, held it for a long moment, then smiled easily. Something warm and slightly electric passed between them, and the tension was gone. He smiled back.

"Jessie," he found himself asking, "do you . . . ?"

"No. I live alone out on the Knik Flats in a two-room log cabin with forty-three dogs—and maybe half a dozen new puppies by the time I get home."

Alex burst into laughter. "Alone? Forty-three dogs, and she says she lives alone?"

She sat back, arms around her knees, and grinned at his mirth. "Well, it's all relative, I guess. Where do you live, Anchorage?"

"Nope. Palmer. Right next door to you, sort of."

"Alone?"

She was direct, and he liked the honesty it implied. He paused, feeling the weight of his simple answer.

"Yes."

They both smiled, comfortably pleased with themselves, then she nodded. "It'll keep," she said. "I've got a race to run and you have . . . all you have to do."

"Right. Would you like me to get out of here so you can get some rest?"

"Mmmmm . . . pretty soon. First tell me what's going on. Did you get anywhere today?"

For the next half-hour he related the activity and revelations of the day while she listened and asked questions. She didn't think that any of the mushers mentioned would have doped Koptak's coffee.

"It just doesn't make any sense. Every one of those guys liked George. They all ran together at one time or another. They traded and loaned dogs to each other. He and Pete go back years."

She laid her chin on her knees and looked thoughtfully into the flames. "You know," she said, "I really can't understand why anyone would want to kill George. He was such a sweet man, quiet, kind."

"Well, they may not have meant to kill him, you

know. Maybe just put him out of the race. But the stuff in his coffee was no mistake. The thermos had his initials painted on it, G.K."

"What?" She straightened up suddenly and swung around to face him. "But I saw Ginny filling that thermos. I thought it was hers."

They stared at each other as the implication sank in. G.K. George Koptak. Ginny Kline.

"God," said Alex. "I never saw it, and we've gone over the list of mushers three or four times."

"You wouldn't have. It's always listed as Virginia Kline."

"And you saw this in Skwentna?"

"Yes."

"When I went through her sled in Happy Valley, the thermos I found was red and didn't have any initials."

"She had a red one, too. She filled both. I was standing right next to her and she poured a cup for me before she put the pot down."

"Where was this?"

"In the checkpoint cabin. They had a big pot going all the time for everybody."

"So . . . she must have filled Koptak's for him when she filled her own."

"That's possible. They were friends, and from where she was camped she would have walked by his team on her way to the cabin. They must have thought the thermos belonged to Ginny, not George."

"And when the wrong person died, they had another try at Ginny in Finger Lake." Alex paused, thinking hard. "Think, Jessie. Who else was in that cabin? Can you remember?"

She shut her eyes and tried. "The ham operator, the checker, Bill Turner . . . Tim, Ron Cross . . . Bill Pete, telling moose stories. No, damn it, that was later. Ryan, I think. Oh, Bomber and Paul . . . or was that before?" She opened her eyes, shaking her head. "Sorry, Alex. I can't swear to anyone but the officials, Ginny, me, and Bill. It was busy—everybody coming and going—and I wasn't paying attention. It could've been anyone."

"That's okay," he told her. "Don't push it. But if you do remember . . ."

"Right."

"One other thing."

"Anything."

"This is serious. Keep it to yourself. Whoever did it won't know we've figured this out. It may be important."

"Sure. Don't worry. There's nobody I'd tell."

"Don't Ryan and Bomber ask questions?"

"Yeah, but I don't have to answer them. They did get a little curious this morning." A frown crossed her face.

"What?"

"Oh, nothing. Bomber was just a little weird."

"Weird how?"

"Oh . . ." She hesitated, self-consciously. "I think he's more concerned about my talking to you than in what we talk about."

She thought for a minute, then turned to look at him straight. "I like you, Alex. I think he knows that and doesn't like it."

"Does he have some right not to like it?" he asked carefully.

"None at all. I had to discourage his interest a year or so ago, but it came out okay."

"How about Ryan?"

"Jim's fine. He's a good friend and I'm glad he's there. But Bomber can be a bit much."

Uncertain whether to ask her, Jensen was quiet for a minute. "Do you remember an incident a few years ago when a musher was caught beating his dogs?"

"Oh God, that again? Won't they ever drop it?"

"Who was it?"

A long, tense silence; then, shaking her head, she told him. "Bomber, but . . . No, Alex. No. It was much further into the race. He was tired. He got off the trail and his dogs quit on him. He just lost it for a minute. It could have happened to anyone."

"Would it have happened to you?"

She considered. "No, I guess not. But . . ."

"Do you mean he doesn't do it now, or he doesn't do it in public?"

"Well, he's a little rough sometimes, but I don't think so."

"Would you like to get out of the threesome?"

She was quiet again for a bit. "No. There's no reason to make an issue of his attention. Part of it's probably because he's more upset about George than he lets on. He thought a lot of George. I think I know Bomber. There won't be a problem I can't handle. And if I need him, Jim's there too."

"Sure?" He waited to make certain she meant what she said, forced to trust her judgment. He wasn't entirely at ease, but it was, of course, her call.

"Yeah . . . Yeah, I'm sure."

"Well, if you get split up for any reason, make sure you wind up with Ryan."

He was on his feet, ready to go back to his own camp, when Bomber and Jim returned.

"Jensen." Bomber nodded and introduced his companion. "You and Jess got it all solved?"

There was a slight bitterness in his tone, but no specific affront.

"I wish I could say yes," Alex replied carefully. "We've just been reviewing your trip through the gorge today."

"We made it. That's all that counts. Saw you fly over, taking it the easy way."

Something in Alex refused to put up with this needling, but he held his irritation in check, not wanting to cause Jessie any trouble.

"Want to trade?" he asked.

"No, thanks. I'll stick with my friends here."

He turned away to his sled and began to unroll a sleeping bag.

Ryan looked questioningly at Jessie. When she shook her head, he too began to get out his sleeping gear. She turned to Alex and shrugged, giving him half a smile.

"I'll see you tomorrow," he said. "Good night."

As he crossed back to the tent, he was glad he had held his temper. Bomber had said nothing that couldn't be taken more than one way. Anger would only have brought instant denial. As opposed to the cooperation he had shown in Happy Valley, he was now subtly confrontational and a touch condescending. That it had to do with his relationship with Jessie, Alex had no doubt, but did it have any other basis? Was the man too clever, or not clever enough? It wouldn't improve his image with the lady he sought to impress.

Maybe he just didn't like cops. Fatigue had probably relaxed his inhibitions and released his hostility, but he was walking a thin line. Alex went to bed and to sleep quickly, knowing he would be watching

Cranshaw from here on. Schuller now seemed a minor annoyance.

Although he woke several times during the night to the sounds of a camp full of people and dogs, and once to the distant howl of a wolf, it was peaceful enough. He quickly slept again, warm in the tent and heavy bag.

15

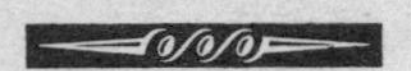

Date: Wednesday, March 6
Race Day: Five
Place: Rohn Roadhouse checkpoint
Weather: Clear, light to no wind
Temperature: High 2°F, low −8°F
Time: Early morning

BEFORE THE RELATIVELY FLAT AREA OF THE FAREwell Burn was a combination of tundra and spruce forest crisscrossed by streams and creeks. In July and August of that year a wilderness wildfire tested the efforts of more than three hundred fire fighters and destroyed over 361,000 acres before burning itself out. All that was left standing were charred stumps and tree trunks.

During years of good weather and deep snowfall, the burn can be crossed carefully by dogsled, although it is an obstacle course of muskeg hillocks, hidden stumps, and potholes. It has been done, from Rohn to McGrath, in less than half a day. During other years the wind, without trees to break its strength, howls across the plains, sweeping the trail down to gravel and fallen trees. Conditions infuriate mushers, who watch with sick fascination as their sleds literally disintegrate under them, or nurse injured dogs along slowly to avoid carrying them in the sled basket. In bad years mushers usually wind up running behind their sleds for a large part of the seventy miles from Rohn to Nikolai, then for forty-eight more to McGrath, arriving in a state of exhaustion. For this reason, some wait for their twenty-four-hour rest until they have crossed the burn.

They stagger wearily into McGrath, sometimes all but carrying their equipment, running on nerve. Some quit, fed up and angry. Some hardly speak until they have slept long enough to discover they're also hungry. Even during years of good snow cover, dogs don't trot into town with their tails wagging, ready to go straight on. If the team and its driver ever need rest, both physical and mental, it's here.

Late Monday evening, two mushers, T. J. Harvey and Rick Ellis, had headed into the Farewell Burn without declaring a twenty-four at Rohn. Feeling their dogs were up to it after several hours of rest, they sought to run rabbit—establish a jump on the rest of the group and take their layover in McGrath, hoping to retain part of their lead and make the others give chase. By running the South Fork of the Kiskokwim River at night, in sub-zero cold, they might make better time than those traveling in the daytime. They could then cross the most difficult part of the burn in daylight.

By the time Dale Schuller left Rohn on Tuesday evening, they had successfully crossed the burn, gone through Nikolai, and were nearing McGrath. Two other racers, Murray and Martinson, checked out ahead of Schuller in the evening, their twenty-fours complete.

The team leaving Rohn directly in front of Schuller was driven by Tim Martinson, which put Dale into fifth place. Two more teams would leave a few hours later. Most would reach McGrath before the rabbits had completed their mandatory rest stop.

All this was explained to Jensen by Harv at six-thirty Wednesday morning as he added new figures to Alex's list of times.

"Everyone has a plan, you see," he chuckled. "They work on them all year, along with their psychological warfare. This isn't just a race from here to there. It's a strategy, with nobody telling anyone else what they're up to."

"I'm beginning to see that," Jensen agreed.

"Just wait till further into it. Some of them will wait till a rival gets his dogs fed and bedded down, then take theirs out of town. It may force the other guy to follow and find 'em bedded down five miles farther on. I love to watch it."

He grabbed a huge bite from a bacon sandwich as the radio crackled to life.

"Hey, Harv. Where's the vet?" someone shouted from the door across the room.

Flapping bacon and bread vaguely southward, his cheeks bulging, Harv finally managed to croak, "Out with Lindholm. He just checked in with sick dogs and a sprained wrist."

"What happened?" asked Alex, watching him wash down the remains of the mouthful with orange juice.

"Caught a bad hole in the Dalzell. Dunked four of his dogs and almost lost one of his wheelers that got hung in the harness between the ice and the bow. He's pouring water out of his boots, I bet." Harv turned to respond to the radio.

Pleased that he could understand what had just been said to him, Alex wrote a large "Thanks for everything. We're off to McGrath" on a piece of scratch paper and laid it in front of Harv, who nodded, waved, and went on telling Anchorage who had checked in and out since his last report. In Rohn at least, it seemed things were getting back to normal.

Before heading for the airstrip, Jensen went by Jessie's camp. There he found Ryan, standing in the middle of what looked like everything he carried in his sled. Near him, three cookers of dog food simmered. While he waited, he was rearranging his belongings.

"Hey," he greeted the trooper with a smile. "This has to be done periodically, or I lose track of essential things, like dogs or toilet paper. Ten minutes ago it was my Buck knife." He held it up triumphantly. "Of course, I found it in my parka pocket, where I had already looked twice. You want Jessie?"

"Yeah," said Alex.

"She and Bomber just went for water. They'll be back in a few minutes."

"I've got to help load the plane. Will you ask her to come over to the strip when she gets back?"

"Sure. You going out?"

"Soon." He paused, not knowing exactly how to phrase the other thing he wanted to communicate to Ryan.

His silence caught the musher's attention.

"You guys going to be okay?" Jensen finally said.

Ryan looked solemn. "I'll make sure of that."

Alex nodded and left.

They had the plane loaded and were having a last cup of coffee when Jessie came through the trees to the fire. Her face, pink-cheeked with cold, was clean and scrubbed, her hair combed. Though her parka and insulated pants showed stains from charcoal and, probably, dog food, to Alex she looked great.

She pulled a hand from a deep pocket to shake hands with Becker and Caswell and gratefully accepted coffee.

"I haven't had time for breakfast yet. The dogs take the first couple of hours."

"How are the sore-footed ones?" Alex asked.

"Better. I greased them up again. They're healing pretty well."

"What's that stuff you put on their feet?" Becker questioned.

"It depends. There's two kinds of salve, an alcohol-based to help keep their feet dry while they're running, and a grease to keep them from getting too dry, for checkpoints or sore feet. We all use different kinds. I mix mine with stuff from my vet. It's good for my cuts and scrapes, too." She held out one hand, marked with several scratches and abrasions.

"Sometimes in the cold you don't feel it when you get pinched in a toggle while you're hurrying to change the dogs around. This one's a burn from the dog-food cooker."

"Bet those sting when they warm up," Becker said.

"Yeah, well, they get a little stiff. I really watch it with an ax or my knife."

Caswell scrubbed out his cup with snow and turned to Becker. "Let's get this fire out and untie the plane." He nodded to Jessie. "Nice to meet you, Miss Arnold."

Alex walked with Jessie into the trees toward her camp.

"Everything okay?" he asked when they were out of earshot.

"Yeah. Bomber was a pain last night, wasn't he?"

"Well . . . I think you're right about him."

"It'll be fine." She stopped and looked up at him. "You're going to McGrath?"

"Yes. Please, be careful."

"Don't worry, we will."

Looking down at her, he wanted to touch her, wanted . . .

Catching his expression, she smiled and, standing on tiptoe, reached around his neck to give him a quick but generous hug, impeded by all their insulated clothing. "Hey, trooper," she said in his ear. "Do good work."

Then she was gone, with a laugh, a wave, and an echo of, "On down the trail."

Alex watched her out of sight.

For a while after they took off, Caswell's route took them up the South Fork of the Kuskokwim River. Because of this years' deep snow, the race would go a long way up this shallow road of ice. They watched for mushers as they flew, but saw none along the river.

Tracing the trail on a map with one stubby finger, Harv had explained to Jensen that in some years it ran up onto the bank through brush and dense spruce forest along the base of a fifty-eight-hundred-foot mountain to the west, part of the Terra Cottas. "There's some of the original Iditarod Trail left there," he said. "Some old blazes on the trees are twenty feet from the ground. Lots of snow back in those early days."

In a few miles the Post River joined the Kuskokwim and the mountains began to recede from the river as the broad open expanse of interior Alaska rolled away to the north.

"What's that?" Becker asked.

Looking down, Jensen spotted several large animals on the flat near the river. "Moose?" he suggested.

Caswell circled the plane to come back over. "Look again."

Through the binoculars, Becker peered at the ground.

"Whoa. Buffalo," he crowed. "Alex, take a look."

Alex could count seven of the shaggy beasts. He would never have associated them with this part of the world. They dug into the snow with their noses and hooves to reach the grass beneath it.

"How the heck . . . ?"

"Sometime in the thirties someone brought them in here," Caswell said. "It didn't work out commercially, but they're still here, in small herds. Once in a while the mushers run into them. The dogs love to chase buffalo."

A little over twenty miles from Rohn, they flew over the expanse of Farewell Lake with its lodge and landing strip. The line of the trail crossing it was visible from above, and they saw one musher, riding comfortably on the runners of his sled. He waved as they passed. Farther to the west Jensen could see radio towers. From the map he knew it was Farewell Station, where the Federal Aviation Administration maintained a weather-reporting and navigation system, an island of technology in a primeval wilderness.

Spreading out to the north, east, and west of the mountains, the interior of Alaska leaves civilization behind. Except for its small, isolated towns and villages, modem culture has made little impression. Fairbanks, a thriving city to the east, is the result of the white man's intrusion, but elsewhere the names given to the Great Land's landmarks remain mostly those of the Athabaskan Indians or Russian fur traders.

The weather in this part of the state changes too. Temperatures are lower and snow more dry. Mushers have good running through clear days and nights, filled with sun and the aurora borealis.

As they flew, the mountains fell away behind them. To the southeast, Mount McKinley and Mount Foraker rose to dominate the widening sky. Passing into the Farewell Burn, the troopers could see the awesome devastation wrought by the fire.

Some recovery was evident. Brush and small trees were about the height of scorched trunks left by the blaze. Though there were areas of rolling hills and some deep creeks, from the air it looked flat.

Watching the seared face of the burn stream under them, Jensen noticed what looked like a fog hugging the ground.

"Blowing snow," Caswell informed him. "The wind's picking up. It'll probably get worse through the afternoon."

Though there was a fair amount of snow, it was dry, and the relentless wind was uncovering large areas of grass and muskeg.

Roughly following the trail, it seemed a long way across open space before they spotted the small community of Nikolai and its Russian Orthodox church with three crosses along the roof. Later still, the low buildings of McGrath came into view. They counted a total of five mushers between Farewell Station and the airstrip where they landed against a steady blow.

16

Date: Wednesday, March 6
Race Day: Five
Place: McGrath checkpoint
Weather: Severe clear, moderate wind
Temperature: High 2°F, low −8°F
Time: Early afternoon

AS THE THREE TROOPERS CLIMBED FROM THEIR plane, Matt Holman pulled up in a van.

"If we wait ten minutes, a support plane'll be in from Anchorage," he told them. "There's something on it for you, Jensen."

Glad to be out of the small plane, Alex fired a pipe and brought Holman up to date on the Rohn stop. By the time he finished, the support plane was on the strip and rolling toward them.

"You Sergeant Jensen?" the pilot asked.

At the affirmative answer, he handed over a large sealed manila envelope. Alex climbed into the van to examine its contents. A note gave him negative findings on both the humane society and gambling theories. Several other pages included the autopsy reports on the three dead mushers and the dogs. There was nothing new in these but the results of the substance tests.

While Holman helped unload the supplies from the plane, Becker and Caswell climbed into the van to get out of the wind.

"Phencyclidine," Alex told them. "PCP. Angel dust. In the dogs, their food—and the container we collected from Schuller."

"Jesus," said Becker. "I didn't know PCP would do dogs that way."

"Neither did I. But here's a note from Dave in the lab. 'Phencyclidine was originally developed as a veterinary tranquilizer and is still infrequently used for that purpose. Even a small amount is extremely toxic, capable of causing disorientation, hallucinations, hypertension, agitation, combativeness, seizures, respiratory depression, and coma. It has a very narrow therapeutic window, meaning that a dose must be precisely measured in relation to body weight in order not to exceed its toxic limits. Most vets refuse to use it for that reason. Administration of ammonium chloride to acidify both blood and urine causes a shift of PCP out of the brain and enhances its renal excretion.' "

"Jesus, what a list of effects," Becker said. "That accounts for the dog that died. Difference in body weight."

"Yeah. More would have died if we hadn't shot them first. Of course we don't know exactly how much of the stuff was in that bottle to begin with, or how much dumped into the food. But the lab report indicates an extremely high dosage."

"What the hell is ammonium chloride?"

Caswell answered that question. "It's soldering flux, isn't it?"

"Yeah, but I wouldn't want to have to get it that way. It absorbs moisture, Phil. Would help the system eliminate the drug."

"But how the hell did the bottle get down to where Schuller says he found it?" Caswell shook his head, contemplating another round with the checkpoint reports.

"Those scratches on the sides have something to do with it," Alex told him.

He upended the envelope to dump out the container, now clean of any trace of PCP, in its clear plastic evidence bag. They looked at it again, passing it around.

Something spun through Jensen's mind as he examined the marks, a flash too fast to catch. He stared, concentrating. Finally, he shook his head.

"What?" asked Caswell.

"I don't know . . . something."

He held it up against the light. "Look, the marks on one side go up and down the length. The ones on the other side go more horizontal, against the curve, slightly slanted. Whatever held it ran two directions. Right?"

"Uh-huh."

"And put pressure on it, enough to mark it."

"Right again."

"What would cause that?"

"Umm . . . could have already been on the container, caused somewhere else."

"I don't think so. I think it relates. Anything else?"

Caswell shook his head. So did Becker.

"Okay," said Holman, climbing into the van. "You ready to go?"

* * *

McGrath is the communication, transportation, and supply center for a large area of interior Alaska. Two hundred and twenty miles northwest of Anchorage and 270 southwest of Fairbanks, the town lies in a looping bend of the Kuskokwim River, directly south of its confluence with the Takotna. In the width of the loop, two airstrips make a predominant north-south T, which fills the area so completely it leaves little space for the buildings of the town of over five hundred persons to nestle in under the eastern angle of the crossbar.

Incoming passengers walk directly from their aircraft into downtown. From the air terminal it is only a step to McGuire's Tavern. A door or two up the street (or landing strip, depending on how you use it) is a building that holds more airline offices, Beaver Sporting Goods, and the Iditarod Trail Café and checkpoint. At the eastern end of the crossbar the road bends right, around the Alaska Commercial Company store, and approximately two blocks past this bend the offices of the State Department of Fish and Game, the local law enforcement, are situated.

Before modern memory, the Upper Kuskokwim Athabaskan Indians established the area as a meeting place for trade and social interaction. They were still there when gold discoveries in the Innoko district to the northwest made McGrath a permanent settlement in 1906. During the next fifteen years of the gold stampede, it was the northern-most accessible point for the sternwheelers and riverboats that brought supplies and miners into the region. At that time the town was on the north side of the river, but erosion and flooding later forced a move to the opposite bank, rendering the town useless as a center for river traffic.

In 1908 a survey was commissioned to provide a

route for winter transportation and mail as far as Nome, and the Iditarod Trail was born. From 1911 to 1920, hundreds of people walked and mushed over it from Seward on their way to the gold strikes. In 1924 the first air-mail delivery in Alaska was made to McGrath.

During the race the Iditarod Trail Café found itself busier than usual as spectators, race officials, and mushers came and went, looking for food, information, and assistance. It was the first stop for Matt Holman and the three troopers.

Settling at a table by the window, they started on coffee and waited for hamburgers and fries.

"How's it going here, Matt?" Jensen asked the race marshall.

"Pretty good. Nothing unusual or suspicious. It's like we left all that in the pass."

"Hope so, but I doubt it." Alex frowned.

"Yeah, I know. It's beginning to make me damn nervous."

The hamburgers arrived, enormous and steaming, along with a second pot of coffee. For a time there was nothing but the sounds of appreciation around the table. Phil Becker was first to finish and sit back with a satisfied sigh.

"Either I've been out here too long or that was one of the best burgers I ever ate. Jesus, I was hungry."

Holman grinned. "Lil has run this place forever and her food is famous. Martin James says he starts the race just to get to McGrath and finishes it because of Lil . . . and McGuire's."

"Who?"

"Town watering hole that's the fan club and rooting section. During Iditarod it never closes. Packed with fans, locals, and a few party animals who don't care about the race but love the blowout. More than one musher has left town late, awash with goodwill from McGuire's. You'll see. Take you down later."

Jensen listened to Holman, slightly amused at his enthusiasm, but aware of the smudges of fatigue under his eyes. Responsibility for this race obviously wasn't an honorary position. He looked weary and sounded stressed.

We all are, Alex thought. And yet, whoever's responsible is still out there. He wondered how Jessie and her running mates were doing.

"Matt," he asked, "can you give us half an hour? I want to lay out what we know so far and see if, between us, we've got anything."

"Sure, but not much more than that. Got a hop to Ophir with a vet coming up."

"No problem. Now, you know Koptak's coffee was doped with secobarbital, but the head injury sustained when he hit the tree was the actual cause of death. Kline's gang line broke where it had been cut. A broken neck was the cause of death, but she would have bled to death from the internal battering otherwise. Just between us, PCP in the dog food got Smith's dogs."

"PCP?" Holman shook his head in disgust as he poured sugar into a fresh cup of coffee.

"Was there enough dope in Koptak's coffee to kill him without hitting the tree?" Caswell asked.

"No. The report says it was only enough to knock him out."

"So whoever dumped it in didn't mean to kill him," Matt said. "They couldn't have known he'd tangle with a tree."

"I think that's a fair assumption."

"You find out anything more about the bottle?"

"Not much. No fingerprints but Schuller's. I'm still convinced those marks mean something."

Caswell was frowning in frustration. "It's that damn bottle getting ahead of its contents that gets me. An empty bottle doesn't just float down the trail by itself."

Alex stopped dead and stared at him. "That's right. Empty. Someone emptied it. But not necessarily into the dog food." He turned to look at the other two. "Think about it."

They stared at him blankly until Caswell straightened and nodded.

"Of course," he said. "A red herring. Well I'll be damned."

Holman cleared his throat. "Hey, will someone let me in on this?"

Alex began. "Schuller found an empty bottle ahead of the Rainy Pass bunch. So far ahead that it couldn't possibly have been there when Smith died, right? But there were traces of PCP in the bottle, so at some point the murderer must have transferred the stuff into another container and then sent the bottle up the trail to get rid of it and throw us off."

"But how'd it get up the trail?" Holman asked.

"By sled, maybe?" Becker ventured.

"Exactly," Alex said. He dug into the pocket of his parka, pulled out the plastic container, and dumped it out of the evidence bag onto the table in front of Holman.

"You're a musher, Matt. Take a look at the marks on this. See? These run up and down, the others run back and forth. If you wanted to wedge it onto a sled without packing it into the bags, where could you put it to make those marks?"

Holman took the container and looked at it carefully. Then he looked up at Jensen and the half-smile of a new idea spread across his face. He nodded at the trooper and spoke slowly as he worked out the conclusion coming together in his mind.

"The up and down ones are sharper than the others. More scratches than rubs on that side."

"Yes?" Alex pushed.

"Probably between two different kinds of material, one harder than the other."

"Not harness." Holman spoke slowly. "Not cords for tying down the sled bag. My guess? It was maybe stuck between a stanchion and a toggle on the bag, maybe a bungee cord. Working against each other as the sled moved, they'd make opposite marks. Pretty soon, when the bag shifted, it would come loose and fall off."

"So whoever had this could have emptied it into something more disposable and put the bottle on any sled going out of Rainy Pass ahead of Schuller."

"Yeah," Matt agreed. "Or Schuller's. Might not have seen it fall off his own sled and thought someone else dropped it."

"So this clears anyone who left Rainy before Smith's dogs got him?" Holman asked, brightening.

"Well, not unless we can prove that's the way it was done. Even then, it's just possible that someone ahead planted the bottle or left it on the trail. We need proof before we rule out anyone."

"Listen," Caswell said. "Maybe the stuff was added to the frozen food earlier. It could be a two-person effort and the bottle was given to the partner to get rid of on the trail. We can't completely rule out Schuller, or any of the mushers who ran ahead of him, for that matter."

"Then why'd he turn it in, if he's involved?" Holman questioned.

"Make you think he picked it up, like he said," Caswell answered.

"Possible," Alex said.

"Can you prove it?" Holman challenged.

Jensen thought for a minute. "To dope the frozen food would mean elaborate planning. That doesn't fit the pattern of the other two incidents. Both were accomplished as circumstances and opportunity allowed, not planned more than a short time before they were committed. And the two-person scheme just doesn't feel right. I can't see the motive for it. Only one person can win this race. Split winnings can't be enough of a motive."

He turned to Caswell. "How many sleds were on the trail into Rohn ahead of him?" he asked.

"Six. Five men, one woman. Seven, counting Schuller, could have brought the thing down the trail. That includes the two who are here now."

"If it rubbed marks on the bottle, it may have left marks on the sled. Maybe not a toggle, but there may be a wear mark on a stanchion, if that's what it was."

"Going to be hard to distinguish from other normal wear marks," Holman commented gruffly. "Lots of those on all the rigs."

"Look at it again, Matt." Jensen handed him the bottle. "See where part of the serrated edge of the lid's worn opposite the sharp scratches? That should make a pretty distinctive mark on a wooden stanchion. We'll take a look at those sleds."

"Let's go." Becker started to stand up.

"No. Let's finish here first. Most of them are still on their way from Rohn. The ones in town aren't going anywhere for a while, are they, Matt?"

"Nope. Have to finish their layover. Those checkpoint lists help at all?"

"Helped us narrow it down some."

"Ones who were there?"

"Yeah. Cas?"

Caswell pulled out his notes. Quickly he reviewed the names of mushers and others associated with the race who had been in Skwentna, Finger Lake, and Rainy Pass. Reaching across the table, he laid the final sixteen names in front of Holman, who scanned them with dismay.

"My God. You really suspect all these people? I *know* some of these couldn't possibly—"

"Hold on," Jensen interrupted. "These are just the ones who were at all three checkpoints at the right times. We've got a lot of other stuff to consider.

"I think Cranshaw has a smart mouth, for instance, a chip on his shoulder. Schuller left Rohn without getting back to me. Martinson gave Phil a lot of flak, but it may have been all bluff. Hard to tell. Although I can't prove it, I don't think Bill Pete was involved. It was all he could do to shoot the last of Smith's dogs."

"You're a hundred percent right there," Holman affirmed. "Besides taking it pretty personal that anyone would try to hurt his race, some of those dogs he raised from pups. Smith bought them off him two years ago.

"Arnold and Ryan, you can cross them off this list. There isn't that kind of violence in either one of them, or Susan Pilch, either. Can't imagine it."

Alex was glad Holman had brought up Jessie's name. He wasn't sure how he could have defended his confidence in her.

"Tell me about Susan Pilch. In fact, we need personal information on all these people. Who are they? What motivates them? There's a lot more we need to know if we're going to solve this thing."

Holman gave him a look of resentful misery. "You want me to set somebody up," he said finally. "How the hell do you think I'm gonna do that?"

"No, goddamn it," Alex exploded. "That's not how it is. Think about it, Matt. You gotta choose here. Either we find out enough to catch this guy, or the stuff goes on. Anything you tell us is just a piece of information, like the rest. I'll tell you something. In Skwentna . . ." He stopped, catching his temper and realizing how close he had come to disclosing what he and Jessie knew about Koptak's thermos. "Never mind," he finished lamely. "But you get the picture. Now . . . what can you tell us?"

Holman handed the list back to Caswell and sat up, straightening his back and shoulders. "You're right. Be pretty stupid if somebody else died because I got pigheaded."

He leaned forward, his elbows on the table. "Tell you what. Let me get that vet and his stuff to Ophir. It'll only take an hour. Then we'll find a better place than this, somewhere the whole damn town can't listen in."

"Good enough."

Before they could get up from the table, a tall man with a checker's badge put a hand on Holman's shoulder. "Matt," he said breathlessly, "you better come. Someone's shooting off flares in the burn, the other side of Nikolai."

"Shit," said Holman. "Someone else'll have to get Chuck to Ophir."

17

Date: Wednesday, March 6
Race Day: Five
Place: McGrath checkpoint
Weather: Severe clear, moderate winds
Temperature: High 2°F, low −8°F
Time: Late afternoon

ON THE FAREWELL BURN, THE WIND WAS SCOOPING up the snow cover and hurling it defiantly in the faces of those laboring their way to Nikolai. Some sections of the trail were swept bare down to rocks and gravel. In others, snow had drifted in so heavily that it was impossible to see the stumps and broken pieces of dead trees before crashing a sled into them, crippling dogs, laming drivers.

Alex wondered how they could possibly spot a team on the ground from Caswell's Maule M-4. Then he saw the arch of a flare, rising out of the ground blizzard. At least they had the location. As they passed directly overhead, Jensen caught a brief glimpse of a waving figure beside the shadow of a sled and team.

"Whoever it is, he's not so hurt he can't wave," he

said with relief. But a second sled-shaped shadow was visible beside the first. This one had no waving figure.

"Damn," swore Holman from the seat behind Alex. "Solomon and Pollitt. They're the only ones who could be this far along. The three who left before them are somewhere between Nikolai and McGrath."

"Well, there's nothing we can do from up here." Caswell banked the plane and headed north. "The Air Force is on the way to McGrath with a helicopter. Hope the wind calms down so they can land. But at least those two know help's on the way. We better get back to meet the rescue team."

"Wonder which one's in trouble?" Alex said. "And what kind of trouble."

"Have we got another incident here?" asked Holman.

"No way to know. Have to wait for the fly boys."

By the time they returned, Tim Martinson had arrived at the checkpoint. Gail Murray came in half an hour later, forty minutes before Dale Schuller. None of them seemed aware of the problem behind them on the trail.

"I was last for most of the day," Murray told Alex. "I passed Dale about halfway from Nikolai when he stopped to rest his dogs, but I never even saw Mike or Rod."

"Why'd you come in by yourselves?" Jensen asked Martinson. "You agreed to keep together."

The big man took offense.

"I never agreed to that. Is this a race or a goddamn nursery school? Those guys in Rainy set that stuff up. I had nothing to say about it and I'm gonna run my own race. You got a problem with that, fucking arrest me. Now I got dogs to feed."

He stomped off toward his team.

Alex let him go, commanding his fists to unclench. Tempted to force compliance, he made himself take a deep breath and forgo personal satisfaction. He saw Martinson yank his lead dog to its feet, then look back over his shoulder. Alex watched until the musher drove his team out of sight down the street to wherever he would spend a few hours before going on to Ophir.

In the café, Jensen found Becker and coffee for them both. He sat down and warmed his hands on the heavy mug for a few minutes before pulling out his pipe and tobacco. Right about now, he thought, Jessie Arnold, having completed her twenty-four, would be leaving Rohn. With bad weather in the burn, he wondered how long it would take her to cross it. She'd arrive sometime early tomorrow, he guessed.

Looking up from his coffee, he found Phil Becker watching him. Becker had stayed behind in McGrath to examine the sleds of Rick Ellis and T. J. Harvey. Now the younger trooper shifted a little in his chair, shrugged his shoulders, and grinned.

"I saw it out the window. What do you think of him?"

"Who? Oh, Martinson. I can't make him out, but I think it's a front. I just wonder what's behind it. He sure doesn't want either of us to get inside the smoke he blows."

"Got a problem with cops?"

"Maybe."

A roar rattled the windows, and a large military helicopter with double rotors came down on the airstrip. Grabbing his parka, Alex gulped the rest of his coffee. "Check the rest of those sleds," he told

Becker. "See you when I get back." He reached the door as Holman, opened it, on his way in to get him.

Two hours later, after dark, he was back in McGrath without Holman. Hardly setting down, the helicopter paused just long enough to let him leap out before lifting off, Anchorage bound.

Ben Caswell came toward him from the company store swinging a plastic gallon of milk in one mittened hand. Alex waited, pipe clenched in his teeth, burning like a small furnace. Wind whipped the smoke away into the dark.

Caswell grinned. "We got a dinner invite. Holman's wife sent word, she's got a moose roast in the oven. I already corralled Becker, who has things to tell you. Where's Matt?"

"He stayed with Mike Solomon to drive Pollitt's team into Nikolai. He'll get a hop back in an hour or two."

"Pollitt okay?"

"No. He's pretty bad. Hit a piece of half-burned tree that trashed part of his sled and broke his leg. Compound fracture involving the knee. Solomon found him down beside the trail. Good thing one of them had flares. He couldn't have traveled anywhere but up and out."

"Any way it's related to the rest of this?"

Jensen pulled thoughtfully on his pipe before answering.

"I don't think so, Cas. Don't see how it could have been rigged. Still, it makes me sit up like an old hound when someone says 'hunting.' "

"Well, let's get on the outside of Mrs. Holman's dinner. Then we'll talk it around a little." They headed off toward a snug log house, two blocks from the airstrip. "With Holman running the trail, I feel like we ought to hang out the widow's lamp tonight."

Alex gave him a questioning look.

"Old custom. During the gold-rush days, the freight and mail drivers went out in all kinds of weather and the roadhouses hung out lanterns to let folks know that a team was on the trail somewhere in the great white. They kept those lanterns burning until the musher came in okay.

"Now they do it for the racers. Up in Nome they put up a lantern when the race starts in Anchorage and they keep it burning as long as even one musher's between the two points.

"McGrath doesn't usually have one, but maybe tonight we should."

Coming in from the cold, Alex found the warmth of the Holman house almost overwhelming. They had stripped off their parkas and boots and hung them with the rest of their outdoor gear on hooks in the Arctic entrance, a small, porchlike space between two doors designed to keep the cold from the main part of the house.

Relieved to take off the heavy insulated boots, Alex padded around, like everyone else, in his stocking feet. By the time they had finished Emma Holman's good dinner and were well into coffee, he was so tired he could scarcely see to set a match to his briar. However, he was soon yanked awake by Becker's news.

Wickedly, Cas had insisted that they take a break from the investigation while they ate, which, Jensen noticed, had been nearly impossible for Becker. Now he all but stumbled over his words in his haste to give Alex his news.

"It's there," he said. "Just like you thought. A worn spot on one stanchion. It fits the size of the bottle exactly, including the serrations from the lid, and rests right next to a toggle on the sled bag."

"Which sled?"

"Oh, yeah. You're going to *love* this one. Not Schuller. I went over every possible inch of his sled. Then I did the same with Martinson, who wasn't too happy, by the way. Nothing. It was Gail Murray's."

"Murray's?"

He nodded, smug.

Caswell grinned. "That's right, Alex. I impounded the sled. We got lucky. Murray said she had no idea what was up. She got a little rattled but was changing sleds here anyway and let us have it easily enough."

Becker shook his head. "She was completely confused. Schuller'd probably figure it out if he knew. We told her to keep it to herself, but . . ." He shrugged. "What do you want to do?"

Jensen hesitated, fumbling to get his thoughts in order. If I'm this tired, with good meals and time to sit down every so often, he thought, what can Jessie be feeling after standing up all day on the back of a sled, especially with that storm in the burn?

As he thought, a thumping in the entrance announced Holman's arrival. Emma emerged from the kitchen to greet him with a hug and the assurance that his dinner hadn't been eaten by someone else. As soon as he was seated in front of a full plate, Alex asked, "Matt, how long will Murray, Schuller, and Martinson be here?"

"Not long. They twenty-four'd in Rohn. Hardly anyone'll take more'n four or five unless the weather turns really mean."

Caswell drew circles on the tablecloth with the handle of his coffee spoon.

"It doesn't prove a thing, you know," he said,

slowly. "She wasn't in Rainy Pass when Smith's dogs were poisoned, even if she was at Skwentna and Finger Lake. All we know is that the container was on her sled long enough to make marks."

"Suggestions?" Alex asked, looking around the table.

Holman spoke after a minute of thought and a swallow of coffee. "We could apply a little pressure. Let's go down to McGuire's. It's the information pipeline. When they get ready to leave we'll hear it and can go watch. Just stand around and watch. It won't hurt to let them wonder why."

"That's fishing, Matt."

"Sure. But maybe we'll get a nibble. Nothing to lose."

Alex eyed a comfortable-looking overstuffed chair near the wood stove across the room and sighed. As much as he didn't appreciate the idea of the dark, cold night, he agreed they should go.

"Okay. But first tell us about everyone on the list, Matt. We still need your perspective."

Holman frowned and stuffed a last forkful of roast and gravy into his mouth. When he could, he growled through his chewing, "Don't like it much, you know."

"I know. We'll try to help you out. Start with Martinson, who's not a model of cooperation. He's given both Phil and me a hard time. He named Turner, Banks, and Bill Pete as having camped with Koptak in Skwentna, and he thought there might have been one more but said he couldn't remember who. Who is he? Where's he from?"

Stiffly, looking down at his plate, Holman answered.

"Wasilla. Moved from Delta Junction three years ago."

"What's his problem? Is he always this tough?"

"He's not real sociable, but he's a good musher. Honest. Great with his dogs. Had a hard time a few years back. Almost lost his kennel in Delta when some kind of virus went through his lot. It didn't leave him much. He's just getting back up there."

"Hey," Becker said, breaking in. "I forgot. When I talked to Mike Solomon in Rohn, he sort of apologized for Martinson. Said he was under a lot of pressure to make some money in this race or he would have to sell a bunch of his dogs to keep his kennel."

"Maybe . . ." Holman responded. "Know he went in debt pretty bad last year."

"What else?" Jensen asked.

"Not much. He's single. Got into mushing in sprint races. Then, before he went on his own, he worked with Redington, the guy who started this race."

"Okay. Schuller. He brought in Koptak, didn't stick around to answer questions, found the bottle, and again took off without checking with me. What about him?"

"From Fox, outside of Fairbanks. Probably just forgot to see you. He's got a good chance this year. Runs a really organized race. Gets it all down on paper ahead of time—when to rest, how much and what to feed. Like that. He keeps to himself, but he's always ready to lend a hand if it's needed. Won the rookie of the year first year he ran."

"Is he okay financially?"

"Yeah, I think so. Doing good this year."

"Murray?"

Before Holman could answer, Becker shook his head. "I just don't see that, Alex," he said. "Except for being in the wrong places at the right time, she doesn't seem the type. Besides, she gave us her sled and answered all our questions very openly."

"He's right," Matt agreed. "Gail's got the weight of her father's kennel behind her, too. John Murray has a real reputation as a breeder. They're good folks."

He reached across, took the list from Alex's hand, and went on hurriedly, as if anxious to get it over with.

"T. J. Harvey lives in Skwentna. My guess is you could clear him just by talking to folks there. He's their hometown musher, and everyone there helped get his fees together. Those kids think he walks on water.

"Ellis and Johnson are both from out of state. Montana. Minnesota. Ellis came in a month before the race and has been running his dogs out of Unalakleet to get them used to the coast. Doubt he knows local mushers well enough to get a mad on. He bought dogs off a couple of people though. Koptak, for one. Johnson drove up the highway just before the race.

"Ellis borrowed two or three dogs from Rod Pollitt—"

Jensen cut off his monologue to ask a question. "Pollitt seems familiar. Does he live in Wasilla too?"

"Close. Big Lake. You've probably seen him in Palmer. His girlfriend's a waitress at Jay's."

"If it's him, the accident in the burn sort of turns it around, doesn't it?" Becker asked.

"If it *was* an accident," Caswell commented.

"Oh, it was," Holman stated flatly. "No way that one could have been set up. Just damn bad luck."

He went back to the list. "John Grasle is a middle-of-the-packer. He's already dropping back. Trains outside of Fairbanks with his wife, and she's back with the bunch that didn't get into Finger Lake and Rainy in time to make the list.

"Still say Bill Pete's got no business on here, and neither do Arnold, Ryan, or Pilch. I know Jess. She's determined and stubborn, but there's nobody more fair. Does more than her share, too. Worked with another musher a while back but didn't like how he treated the dogs. Handles her own now. Better."

Jensen started to say something, then hesitated. Holman waited and Caswell turned his head to look at Alex.

"Nothing big," he said finally. "I was just remembering she said she wouldn't be able to race again next year without the money to get her team in shape." As soon as the words were out, he felt that he had betrayed her confidence, but he'd had to say it.

Holman tossed it off. "Sounds like half the mushers in the race," he said. "Only big names, with big kennels or a supporting business, don't have to worry about money. Big names mean big sponsors, too." He went on.

"Ryan's another one from near Fairbanks. North Pole. One of the most dependable guys I know. Before he tried the Iditarod, he helped out for a few years as a vet. Was in Rainy for three years in a row and Kaltag once. He's—"

"A vet?" Alex interrupted. Caswell and Becker both leaned forward. "PCP was originally a veterinary tranquilizer. Did you know that, Matt?"

Holman stared at him with a frown. "Can't say I did. But I think you're howling up the wrong tree. He's been working with the sports-medicine people on helping mushers keep their dogs healthier and . . ." His voice trailed off as he thought about it.

"Na-a-aw. Not Ryan! He babies his mutts. Can't be the only one who knows what the stuff would do to dogs."

"But he could get hold of it easier," Caswell noted.

"Yeah . . . Maybe."

"How about Bomber Cranshaw?" Jensen asked. "He was helpful in Happy Valley, but I think he's got a mean streak, sarcastic anyway. He's all mouth and gets defensive."

"Oh, that's just Bomber. Got a few hot spots. Giving you his bad side, I'd say. He's a pretty good musher, just talks a lot. I think under all that he mostly cares what the others think. You know, wants respect."

"Have money trouble?"

"He lost a couple of sponsors this year because he didn't do so hot last year. Don't know he's any worse off than anyone else."

"Doesn't like women in the race?"

"Mmmm . . . says so now and then. But he runs with Jess, doesn't he? Split up with his wife a couple of years back. She didn't like mushing, left and moved to Anchorage. Could be part of the problem, but he seems okay now."

"Still beat on his dogs?"

"Shit. Picked that up, did you? Not that I know." Holman shook his head in disgust as he looked back at the list and ran his finger down it.

"Who's left here? Susan Pilch, who's a real sweetheart. You can forget her. If she's got a problem it's taking too good care of her dogs. Her husband's a contractor and there's no short bucks there. And Mike Solomon, from Kaltag. A good friend of Smith's. He wouldn't know how to hurt another musher. Besides, I think he'd have a hard time in the village getting hold of PCP.

"There. That's it. Any questions?"

"Anyone on there who you think might want to win bad enough, Matt?"

He waited until he had looked again at each name, then stared straight at Alex before he answered.

"I won't finger anyone, Jensen," he said. "That's your job, not mine. I don't want any more killed, but I don't want any more of this either. Sorry."

"That's okay, Matt. You've given us a lot of help."

Holman got up, took his plate to the kitchen, where Emma could be heard rattling pans, and returned.

"Listen," he suggested, his grin back in place. "Why don't you guys park here for the night? Two of you can sleep in the other bedroom and one out here on the couch. Emma says she's got a new pancake recipe and would appreciate guinea pigs at breakfast."

Grateful to sleep indoors, they agreed, pushed back from the table, and headed toward their coats and boots.

"Going down to McGuire's, Em. You want to come?"

She came to the kitchen door. "No thanks. I know what that place is like during the race. You'll be lucky to get in the door."

She gave Alex a sympathetic smile. "Don't let that gang of tavern rowdies crowd you," she said. "Or this gang either. You look tired enough to fall over with a good shove."

"The cold air will wake me up," he told her. "Thanks for the dinner, Emma. It was great."

The air did help. Bundled once again in parkas and boots, the four men walked up the street and around the corner to the tavern. The door of McGuire's opened into a roomful of smoke and noise. The ceiling was so low that Alex, the tallest, felt its threat. A long bar stood along one wall, and the rest of the space was filled with mismatched tables, chairs, and tightly packed people.

As they moved farther into the bar, he could hear a guitar being poorly played and several voices shouting the words to a song about the Iditarod Trail. A pool game was in progress in the back, though the players could barely maneuver space for shots.

Toward the end of the bar they found enough room to squeeze in, and Holman ordered four of whatever was on tap. The room was stuffy and warm, but as the door seemed to be forever swinging to let people in and out, smoke and heat escaped frequently. Alex unzipped his parka and put hat and gloves in its ample pockets as he looked around the crowd. Some had been there most of the day, from the look of them. One man slept with his head on his arms at a table of seven or eight other celebrants. The din of conversation bothered him not in the least.

In a frame on the wall behind the bar was a hand-scrawled statement, signed by a previous race winner: "When I die I'm going to heaven because I've already been to the Farewell Burn."

"Solomon should be in before midnight," he heard someone say behind him.

"What's the word on Pollitt?"

"He's in the operating room at the hospital in Anchorage. Don't know yet."

Holman nodded an I told you so at Alex and turned to the only one of the three busy bartenders within earshot. "Schuller, Martinson, or Murray gone out yet?"

"Not yet," the man shouted back without missing

a glass as he poured mixer into half a dozen drinks. "Schuller slept for an hour and is down at the café getting fed. Murray's still at Sherman's. Martinson's over there." With a toss of his head he indicated a table across the room.

Alex turned his head in that direction and found himself meeting the direct, unsmiling stare of the big musher, who sat with three other men around a tiny table filled with beer mugs. After a minute he nodded, but received no recognition from Martinson. The man looked down at the glass in his hand, raised and drained it, thumped it back on the table, and stood up to pull on his parka. Ignoring the trooper, he turned and headed for the door.

"There he goes," observed the man who had remarked on Pollitt. "Schuller better hustle."

"Better let Gail know," said a woman near him, heading for the door. "Don't eighty-six my beer. I'll be back."

Holman turned to Jensen. "Martinson may beat both Harvey and Ellis out of town, and they're already packing up.

"Time to apply that pressure you mentioned, Cas," Jensen said. "There's no reason to watch Harvey and Ellis. You get Schuller. Phil, you know where to find Murray. Matt and I'll double the watch on Martinson. Let's do it."

Within an hour all four of the male racers had checked out of McGrath: Harvey, Ellis, Schuller, and Martinson, in that order. Across the airstrip, near the river, Jensen, Holman, and Caswell found Becker watching Gail Murray complete her packing, having put booties on all fourteen of her dogs. Having the three troopers join the group gathered around her didn't seem to bother her. When she was ready to start, she smiled and waved in their direction, pulled the snow hook, and went down the bank and onto the ice of the Kuskokwim.

Not one of the three they watched had supplied any clue to the puzzle. Martinson had glowered in Jensen's direction, but had said nothing. Schuller had gone about his business as if Caswell were not there.

Alex turned to Holman and yawned a yawn that popped his ears.

"Now," he started, when he could speak.

Becker interrupted. "Hey," he said, with a wicked grin, "let's go back to McGuire's. It can't be more than eight hours or so till the sun comes up."

Jensen stuck out a foot and tripped him neatly into the nearest snowbank.

18

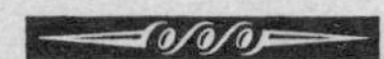

Date: Thursday, March 7
Race Day: Six
Place: McGrath checkpoint
Weather: Severe clear, light to no wind
Temperature: High −2°F, low −14°F
Time: Early morning

"ANYTHING ON POLLITT?"

Breakfast was over and Caswell had gone to service the plane. Becker left, stuffing a last strip of bacon in his mouth, to check out the arrivals at the café. Alex and Emma were finishing their coffee when Matt, out well before daylight, showed up to join them.

"Out of surgery, doing okay. Won't be running dogs for a while, but the doc said it wasn't as bad as he thought it would be."

"Solomon got out last night?"

"Nope. Stayed over. Came in to see the vet just as I left to come up here. Arnold, Cranshaw, and Ryan're in," Holman told him. "Saw Jess at the checkpoint an hour ago. She asked where you were."

"They okay?"

"She looked pretty whipped and worried, but

everybody does when they get here. She and Ryan went to bed down the dogs."

"Damn." Alex set down his coffee. "I think I'll go find out."

As he stood up, he heard someone knock on the door.

Jessie Arnold stood there, her face pale under windburn.

"Hi," she said to them in an exhausted voice. To Alex, "I have to talk to you."

"Coffee?" said Emma as she went to get it.

Alex helped Jessie with her parka and boots before he brought her across the room to the table.

"Sit," he said. "Thanks, Emma. Get some of that hot stuff into you, Jess. Whatever it is, it'll wait five minutes."

He could see how tired she was by the way she dropped into the chair. Something was wrong. He exchanged looks with Holman, who said nothing. They waited while she sipped the steaming coffee.

Emma came out of the bathroom with a towel, a facecloth freshly wrung out in hot water, and some medicated cream. She held them out. "Here, Jess. Wash your face and hands. You'll feel better."

Alex saw Jessie's eyes fill with tears at the kindness, but her voice was level when she spoke her thanks. She held the cloth to her face and sighed, then wrapped both her hands in its heat.

"Oh God, that feels good," she said.

As she rubbed cream onto her face and hands, she turned to look at Alex and took a deep breath.

"My gun is gone," she said. "There was a moose in the trail just outside of town. It was easy to go around, but when I reached into the bag to check my gun, it wasn't there. Bomber fired a couple of shots with his to scare her off. After we got here, I went through my sled while the pups ate. It's not anywhere in my gear."

Jensen was suddenly all trooper.

"What kind of a gun?"

"A Smith and Wesson .44."

"Koptak had one."

"Yeah. He told me what to get when I bought mine."

"When did you see it last?"

"During my twenty-four in Rohn. I checked and cleaned it. Made sure I could get at it in a hurry." She held her mug for Emma to refill.

"Exactly when did you clean it?"

"Soon as I got in, while I waited for the dog food to cook. I wanted to get done before it got too dark."

"So it could have disappeared during your twenty-four in Rohn or anywhere from there to where you saw the moose. Was anyone besides Cranshaw and Ryan in your camp while you were cleaning it who could have seen you put it away?"

"I've been thinking ever since I realized it was missing. Schuller stopped to see Ryan. Martinson brought back a piece of Bomber's harness that got mixed with his in Finger Lake. Gail Murray came to talk to me. They didn't stay long because they were about to go out. Next day, practically everybody taking twenty-fours was there sometime. Almost all of us who don't wear our guns carry them in the bag below the handlebar. It's the first place to look."

"Have you said anything to Ryan or Cranshaw?"

"No. Jim asked me if something was wrong, but I told him I was just tired. Alex, I'm scared. I didn't lose it."

"You have a right to be scared. On the burn, was anyone in your gear?"

"Both Jim and Bomber, with my permission. But I was there and I think I would have seen. There were several stops, twice with other people. I can't watch everything every minute. In Nikolai we all went inside for a while, but our teams were out where everyone could see them."

"And get at them. Including Ryan and Cranshaw, who, I'll bet, both went in and out."

"Yes."

Jensen walked across the room thinking hard. From the front window he could see a plane taxi across the end of the street.

He turned back and looked at Holman who was watching him, listening silently. "Matt?"

"Yeah?"

"You have a gun Jessie can borrow? If she buys one in town, whoever's got hers will know it."

Holman got up and vanished into the back of the house. He returned with a shotgun and a handgun in a holster. "Take your pick, Jess. You can have both if you want."

She shook her head at the shotgun. "If I shoot that from the sled I risk hitting my dogs. If I step off, they could take off on me when I fire. I'll take this one. Thanks, Matt. I'll get it back to you."

"In Nome. You going on with those two?"

"Yes, I'm going on. With them?" She shrugged. "I don't know. I guess it depends."

"Well, if you are, I guess we'd better have a look at their gear first. Right, Jensen?"

"Afraid so."

Jessie sat up straight in her chair. "But should they know my gun's missing? Should anyone know?"

"If we do it at the checkpoint as they leave, and check 'em all, it'll seem less suspicious," Holman suggested. "Don't have to say what we're looking for. That way we catch everyone who was with you in Rohn and the burn."

"Good idea," Alex agreed. "How long till you go, Jessie?"

She looked at the clock on Holman's wall. "A little over three hours."

"You better get some rest. Emma, do you mind if she stays here?"

"Of course not. Come on, Jess. You want a shower?"

"Oh, yeah, but I'd better sleep first and use it to wake up. All my clean clothes are on the sled."

"I'll get them," Alex told her. "Where is it and what do you want?"

She described the sled's location. "There's a small red duffel in the back of my sled bag. My friend, Jan Thompson, is watching my sled, and I told her to scream her head off if anyone touched anything. You better show her your badge or something."

"How long do you want to sleep?"

"Hour and a half. No more."

"I'll have it here by then, Jess."

"Thanks, Alex." She gave him a look like the hug she had given him in Rohn and followed Emma to the bedroom.

As he turned to the door, Holman stood up too. "I'll go along."

They booted up and threw on parkas. Hurrying down the street, Holman said, "Jess, huh? You could do a lot worse than that, Jensen." Then, before Alex could answer, "I'll go talk to the checker."

* * *

Alex returned in two hours to find Jessie sitting by the stove in one of Emma's bathrobes, running her fingers through her hair to dry it. She looked scrubbed, tired, . . . and wonderful.

"I shouldn't have done the shower," she said. "It'll be harder to go back out, but it feels so good to get clean."

He set her duffel on the floor beside her chair and looked down at the back of her neck, exposed as she leaned toward the heat. It was all he could do to keep from reaching out to lay his hand on the damp curls of her hair.

"Where's Emma?"

"To the store for a box of shells. Didn't want me to go."

He stood looking down at her, saying nothing, wanting to hold her, wanting to tell her . . . he wanted her? That he didn't want her out there with some maniac? That it scared the hell out of him? What?

Suddenly he was angry with himself for not knowing what to say or do with his feelings. She had given him encouragement with her hug. What was wrong with him?

Aware of his silence, she stopped drying her hair and looked up. "Alex?"

He started to turn away, but then let her see his confusion.

For a long minute she looked at him. Then, with one easy motion, she stood up into his arms. She lifted her face, he reached for her mouth with his, and his fear, anger, and want got all mixed up with the taste of toothpaste. She was warm, smelled of soap and shampoo, and she kissed him back, thoroughly.

Then she buried her face in his shoulder and laughed. "Well, now I know," she said.

"Know what?"

"About your mustache. It's nice, but it tickles."

"I'll shave it off." Smiling.

"Don't. I like it."

"Really?"

She kissed him again.

When it was over, he looked down at her and frowned.

"I've been thinking. We've got to talk."

"Oh, Alex, I can't. I've got to get dressed and back down to the team. There's a lot to do before we leave."

"But that's the point. I don't want you back in it."

"Alex!" She stepped back from him, shaking her head, astonished. "You don't . . . Now, wait a minute."

"Stop and think, Jess. This isn't spur-of-the-moment stuff. It's calculated and deadly, and whoever did it is still out there. We're getting closer. He's made a mistake or two. But we don't have him yet.

"Stealing your gun says he may be aimed at you now. If you're out of the race you won't be a target. Please, Jess."

She glared at him. "In a minute you're going to say 'Trust me.' Damn it, Alex. A couple of kisses and you're in charge of me? Wrong! Nobody's going to dictate my race for me. That's it."

"That's *not* it. Something could go wrong out there, and I'm scared to death I can't protect you. Goddamn it yourself. I *care* about you. Isn't that obvious? It's *only* a race."

Her voice was terribly quiet. "Give . . . me . . . a break."

She had looked straight at him while he talked, her

face pale, lips stiff. Now she didn't say anything, just stared at the floor.

"Jessie?"

When she still did not respond, he walked over and stood at the window, staring out at an empty lot next to the house, frustrated, helpless, and angry. What was wrong with this woman that she wouldn't be reasonable? What made her feel she had to finish a race when her life was on the line? All of this was happening too close around her. The odds were terrible.

He remembered the limp feel of Ginny's body in Happy Valley, the carnage of Steve's death in Rainy Pass, and George's face. All the blood and death in the snow could have been hers.

So far he had cleaned his hands of the blood of three people and some dogs he didn't bother to count. He turned them up and looked down at them as if he could still see it there. A thing he hadn't recalled in a long while crossed his mind, an image of Sally in the hospital in Idaho, not long before she died.

They had been trying to put a needle into her arm, but there was hardly a place left that hadn't been used repeatedly. Dazed with pain, she had still been aware and fought against it. She had hated needles. It had been all he could stand to watch the nurse try until her hands were shaking and she had to let another make the attempt.

When they finally got the needle into a vein, it spurted a few drops of Sally's blood on his shirt sleeve as he held her hand. With relief, he had blinked back his tears of frustration and love as she relaxed her grip. His fingers had been numb, and when he looked down, he saw that she had held on so tightly that three of her nails had broken the skin, each cutting a near half-moon in the back of his hand.

He turned his hands over. Only one of the small scars was still visible, fading. She hadn't been able to hold on tight enough.

The memory carried a tired surge of sadness. He didn't want anyone to hold on, to depend on him like that again and then die. The thought of it made his stomach turn over, and for a moment he wished intensely he'd never met Jessie. But it was stupid to pretend that he had a choice in that now, wasn't it?

"Alex?"

Her voice jerked him back. When he turned, her expression had altered. She was back in the chair, looking up in appeal.

"Sit down. Please. I need to try to explain something to you."

He came back then, slowly, and sat.

After a minute, she took a deep breath.

"I know how it looks, but really, Alex, I'm not trying to be stubborn. It scares me—bad. But I can't just drop out because I'm scared. I'm not the only one in the race or any more at risk than the others, am I?"

"I don't know Jess. I wouldn't think so except for your gun. We don't know why it was stolen."

"But I think the odds can't be all bad or it would have been me instead of Ginny. Anyway, that's not what I'm trying to say.

"I told you this is my fifth Iditarod. I don't think you understand what that means. It means I've been breeding dogs, raising them, working with them all these years to prepare for this race. Every race is *this* race. As soon as I got home from my first race I started putting together the best team I could train. Every year I do that.

"I've bought dogs, traded them, tried them out,

found out what kind of pups turn into good racers, sold and gotten rid of as many as I kept. With a lot of hard work, I've built a racing machine. I know which dogs will go in any kind of cold, which run best in the wind, and which can take the weather without dehydrating. We understand each other. Tank knows, almost before I do, what I want and what to do about it. He's a great leader. And the rest know me, trust me and what I ask them to do. They love it, the running, as much as I do. I *love* it, Alex, or I wouldn't do it.

"Every year, as soon as the race is over, we rest and get back in shape. Through the spring and summer I train all the dogs. In the fall we start training runs with the ones I may want for the race, hundreds of miles of runs. By February we're in top form and ready to go again.

"I had a good team last year, but the team I'm driving now is the best I've ever had. I can't stand to waste that, Alex. The focus of my life for the last five years has been this year's race. I can't throw that away. I just can't."

She paused, stood up, and paced for a minute back and forth across the room, thinking. He could see she wasn't finished and waited. Finally she came back and, sitting down, reached out for his hands.

"You want to catch whoever is responsible for George and Ginny and Steve, don't you?"

"Of course."

"What would you do if someone asked you to give it up because you might get hurt?"

"They wouldn't. It's my job."

"But if they did?" She pushed. "If I did?"

"I'd have to ignore it and go ahead," he said

slowly. "The risk goes with the job. I knew that when I took it."

"Do you like what you do?"

"Yes. Usually I like it a lot. There are things about it I don't enjoy. People getting killed out here, for instance, and the sort of person who killed them. But I value the process of solving the cases, the skills I have and using them."

"So do I," she told him. "I mean I love what I do, and I do it well. It takes skills, too. I don't like getting so tired I can hardly function, or freezing half to death once in a while. But all the rest makes it worth it, just as your job does.

"That's why, though I understand your wanting me to quit, I have to ignore it and go on with what I need to do. Can you understand that? This race is a thing I need to do for myself. It's important. Do you see?"

The anger had left him completely. The frustration remained, but he did see. He was still looking at the race as if it were a game, an event, rather than the culmination, the motive for the dedication she was describing. Although he didn't feel the way she felt about it, he knew she was right. He wished she wasn't, because it meant he had to back off and watch her make her own choices.

He stood and pulled her up to hold her close. This is going to be important, he thought. He put his face against her damp hair and closed his eyes.

"Yes," he said, "I do see. I don't like it, but I see. I know exactly what you're saying and part of me agrees, but another part's scared to death and still wants you out of it. This is all happening so fast we'll just have to trust each other and sort it out later. Just promise me you won't take any chances, okay?"

She nodded against his ear.

The door opened and Emma Holman came in, smiled, and said quickly, "The others are right behind me, if it matters."

Although they stepped away from each other as the two troopers followed her in, Alex didn't feel it really mattered at all.

19

Date: Thursday, March 7
Race Day: Six
Place: McGrath checkpoint
Weather: Severe clear, light to no wind
Temperature: High −2°F, low −14°F
Time: Late morning

ALEX TOSSED HIS GEAR INTO THE PLANE, PAUSED TO light his pipe and look across the runway toward the store, where Becker had gone for last-minute supplies. Caswell climbed down from the pilot's seat, where he had been cleaning the inside of the windshield.

"You're looking thoughtful again," he remarked.

"What did you think of Holman's information on the mushers last night?"

"Well, I can understand his feelings, but he might have told us more. I think we could narrow the list a little."

Jensen nodded. "Let's put them in priority order and see what we get. Motive is the thing now. They all had opportunity."

Caswell flipped his notepad to a clean sheet. "Go."

"Martinson first, then Cranshaw and Ryan. After that, Schuller, but he's marginal."

"Why?"

"Why Schuller?"

"No. All of them."

"Martinson's attitude. I think he's desperate. The fact that he might lose his kennel gives him a damn good motive, and he'll only make *big* money if he comes in first, or close. I think he's got an obsession with winning. He's also a loner, self-contained. Didn't show any concern for the victims at all. Something about him bothers me, a lot."

"Could be afraid and covering up, trying to look tough."

"True. He's hiding something. It's a game of nerves, but I think he's capable and has had every chance. I still put him first, but not far ahead of Cranshaw."

"What's the motive there?"

"That's harder to pin down. Holman said he lost sponsors. If he doesn't do well he may lose more and knows it. You know how you pick up when somebody's thinking something different than what he's saying? That's Cranshaw. An egotistical son of a bitch. He's got a mean temper and holds a grudge, I bet. Doesn't like women in the race, but has learned to cover.

"Jessie says he's sorry about Koptak's death, but here's the thing, Cas. That doped thermos had the initials G.K. painted on it. George Koptak, right? But the killer may have thought it was Ginny Kline's. She filled it for George when she did her own in Skwentna. If he killed the wrong person, it should shake him a little."

A low whistle was Caswell's only comment.

"I want to go on keeping it quiet. And that the stuff

in Smith's dog food was PCP. I told Holman to keep it close."

"Which brings us to Ryan and his vet experience?"

"Right. There isn't much in terms of a motive, and Holman thinks he's okay, but I can't overlook the coincidence. His work with sports medicine would make a perfect cover. We don't know much about him either. What makes him tick?"

Caswell pulled a notebook from his pocket. "This is the press book they put out every year." He thumbed through it. " 'James Ryan, veterinarian from North Pole, Alaska. Raised in Minnesota, where he learned to raise, train, and race his own teams. Moved to Alaska in nineteen eighty-one and first ran the Iditarod in nineteen eighty-seven. Was a volunteer veterinarian from nineteen eighty-three to nineteen eighty-six at various checkpoints. Now working in sports medicine, this quiet, thirty-eight-year-old musher enjoys country-western music, traveling, and spending time with his partner, Patty Jakes.' Sounds pretty ordinary, Alex."

"Yeah, so ordinary you might forget he was there. Is he covering? But Jessie's confident of him. She's glad to run with him and seems pretty good at people."

"Alex . . ."

"Yeah?"

Caswell looked at him, waiting.

"Yeah, I know. I can't forget him just because she likes him. But I don't want to suspect him because he's running with her either."

"Make up your own mind,"

"Indulge my intuition. Leave him third, then, and let's see what we can find out about him."

"Who else?"

"Schuller and Murray we *have* to keep because of that damn bottle. Murray's okay, I think, no motive. But Schuller found it, and he slipped out of Rohn without seeing me.

"We can put the out-of-state people off the list for now—Ellis, Johnson, and Talburgen. Pete, Pilch, Grasle, and Harvey just don't show any motive. And Arnold," he said deliberately. "It may be intuition again, but that's as objective as I can be, Cas."

"I agree. Don't get defensive. That leaves Banks and Solomon. I put them with your last bunch. Pollitt's out of it."

He drew heavy lines under the first three names, then, hesitantly, under the fourth on the list. "Martinson, Cranshaw, Ryan, and Schuller. Right?"

"For now. From here on I want to know where they are, who they're with, when they eat and sleep. If they spit, I want to know it, but I'm not sure how. We can't be out there with them. I want all the information we can get from Anchorage. Call headquarters and have them get Fairbanks going on Schuller and Ryan. Palmer can check out Martinson, and we'll have to take care of Cranshaw. Here comes Becker. Let's get going."

The younger trooper came up in a hurry and dumped a sack of groceries into the open door of the plane.

"We may have a problem, Alex. Holman says Bomber Cranshaw pulled out a while ago in an awful hurry."

"Alone?"

"Yeah. Matt went through his equipment, down to the last toggle, but he didn't have Jessie's gun. Just his own, not a forty-four. It had been fired twice, he said, to scare a moose, just before he got here."

"That's right. Ryan with Jessie?"

"Yeah. I think you better talk to them. Something went down."

Crossing the strip, they found the two packing the last of their equipment.

"What happened? Becker says Cranshaw took off without you guys."

Ryan nodded and went on packing. Jessie stepped away from the teams to answer him.

"He took off, all right. Becker said we'd better tell you before we left. Bomber went by himself because he's mad at me."

"Tell me."

She nodded. "When he brought his dogs back down to where Ryan and I were camped, he was already mad. The checker had told him to get ready for a sled search and he didn't like it."

"What do you mean, when he brought his dogs back down? Wasn't he camped with you guys?"

"No. He lives here, so when we checked in, he went home to his cabin, on the edge of town someplace."

"Why didn't you and Ryan go with him?"

"Well, he did ask if we wanted to come, but it didn't seem like he was too hot on the idea. I figured he wanted some time to himself and we didn't really want to go anyway. Bomber has been a pain since Rohn, so we weren't sorry to split up for a while. Besides, I wanted to talk to you about the gun."

"And when he came back?"

"Like I said, he was mad. He stomped around, complaining that we weren't ready to go, even though it was earlier than we had planned. He bitched about the sled check, troopers, and unnecessary delays, until I finally got fed up and told him why.

"He really exploded and accused me of telling you it was him or Jim. I told him I hadn't, but he said . . . Well, he got nasty. Jim told him he was out of line, but that just made him madder. He said I lost my damn gun, that a spacey bitch wouldn't remember. Then he said he wasn't going to run with a couple of idiots and took off."

"I bet his sled check was a disaster."

Becker agreed, with a disgusted expression. "I understand he was not a happy camper."

"And they found nothing?"

"Nope. His gun had been fired, but we know the reason."

"How did Ryan take it when he heard you had talked to me?" Alex asked her, lowering his voice and walking her away from the rest.

"Okay. I told him I didn't think it was him. He asked a few questions after Bomber left, but he thought the search was a good idea and seemed worried my gun was gone."

"What do you want to do, Jess?"

The frown left her face. "I want to go, of course."

"With Ryan? Is there someone else?"

"Not if we want to go now. Why? Alex, you don't think . . . ?"

"I don't trust anyone, Jessie. I don't know. Let's just say I'd feel better if there were more than two of you."

She thought about it, then shook her head. "This is one of the necessary chances, Alex. It's time to go."

"Then go give it your best shot."

The smile lit up her face. "Come on, Ryan," she called, heading for the sled. "We're out of here."

As the two sleds disappeared over the riverbank, Jensen turned to Becker. "Where's Holman?" he asked. "I want a look at Cranshaw's place. It's time to take this apart."

Back on the runners, following Ryan on toward Takotna and Ophir, Jessie felt better about going on. Alex had thoroughly shaken her, as he had meant to, with his concern that she might be in danger. But his trust of her judgment and her own determination was substantial enough to override her nerves and get her out of McGrath. Once on the trail, feeling the exhilaration of motion, her anxiety fell away.

Thinking of Alex, she could almost feel the warmth of him against her. Maybe he could trim his mustache just a little. How unexpected, in the middle of the race, with dogs, other mushers, and the trail demanding most of her attention to find herself thinking of him so often.

The quiet shush of runners on the snow, and the live movement of the sled as it flexed over irregularities in the trail, were soothing. Jim looked back and waved as he went down the bank of a small creek and round a turn. The dogs were running enthusiastically after their long rest, and it was good to be moving.

A couple of miles from McGrath, they were winding their way from marker to marker, in the maze of tracks and trails, through creek beds and stands of willow that filled the river basin. Half the residents of McGrath supplemented their incomes with subsistence hunting and trapping, and they made new trails all winter as they came and went on sleds and slow machines.

Around another turn, she found Ryan pulled over. "Got to switch a dog," he yelled as she approached. "Go ahead. I'll catch up."

She drove by without stopping and went up the bank of a creek. The willows thickened near creek banks, and the trail twisted to accommodate them. In half a mile, over the subtle sounds of the team and sled runners and between her own sparse commands to the dogs, she was vaguely aware of the whine of a snow machine in the distance, growing louder. Glancing back, she saw no sign of Ryan behind her.

Attentive to the team once more, she saw the ears of her leader suddenly come up as he slowed, then stopped. Damn snow machine, she thought. Should know better than to run the marked trail against dog teams. Tank began to bark and lunge; before she could react, a moose scrambled out of the willows to the right of the trail in front of her dogs.

It was huge, a full-grown bull, over eighteen hundred pounds of unpredictable stubbornness. It halted on the packed snow of the trail, perhaps twenty feet directly ahead of Tank, who, with the rest of the team, was now hysterically lunging and barking.

Quickly, Jessie threw the snow hook and stomped it down. "Tank! Shut up. Hey, stop that! Quiet," she called, but they ignored her. Snorting, the moose assessed the threat before it with angry eyes, pawed the snow with one large, sharp hoof, and lowered its head. Then, with no more warning, it charged the dogs.

Jessie heard snarls and yelps as the animal flailed through her team, kicking and stomping. Instinctively she thrust a hand into the sled bag for her gun. Frantically realizing her mistake, she threw herself and the sled over to the right, away from the threat of the slashing hooves. The moose passed over her, one long, bony leg thrusting its hoof into the snow beside her shoulder, as she lay curled in the partial shelter of the sled.

Instantly she rolled to her knees and, reaching under her parka, snatched Holman's handgun from its holster. Raising herself to peer over the sled, she braced the gun on a stanchion with both hands, ready, but the moose was gone. For whatever reason, it hadn't turned to renew the attack, disappearing instead down the trail toward McGrath. The sound of the snow machine seemed to have passed her somewhere to the southwest and could now be faintly heard, dying away.

Heart pounding, light-headed with adrenaline, Jessie sank back, gulping great lungfuls of air. Keeping the pistol in her hand, she stumbled to her feet and went, full of apprehension, to see the havoc that had been wreaked on her team.

The barking had stopped, but she could hear whining and panting as she came up to the tangle of harness and dogs. Most were on their feet, and Tank stood in the middle of the pack, where he had chased the moose halfway back to the sled. Having dragged his teammates along, he had thoroughly snarled the lines. Two dogs were down, one licking a grazed flank, the other a cut foreleg.

Replacing the gun, Jessie knelt and carefully examined the injuries, relieved to find that neither was serious. Years of experience allowed her knowledgeable fingers to determine that there were no broken bones or hidden hurts as she untangled the lines and examined each dog in turn. With a little first aid, all could continue the race. Had the moose turned to fight, the story would have been different for the dogs, who could not escape or defend themselves in harness.

When deep snow makes it difficult for the long-legged giants to reach their willow browse, they are hungry and aggressive. A starving moose is mean and dangerous. Lacking sufficient food, its body burns fat and, after that, protein, which increases irritability and causes hallucinations. This also happens in humans, as many mushers, deprived of sleep and not careful to include enough fat in their racing diets, will attest.

Jessie, hardly believing her luck, wondered why the moose had run on without stopping. Opening her sled bag to get salve for the two injured dogs, she was again conscious of the distant whine of a snow-machine engine. Good God, they were everywhere. Dying away to the north, it suddenly stopped, as if it had been turned off.

She hoped the moose had not run headlong into Ryan's team behind her. Where was Ryan? He should have caught up with her by now. Carefully she spread the salve over the abrasions on her hurt dogs, petted and loved them all a little, and rechecked the harness, straightening out a couple of last-minute kinks. Still no Ryan. Should she go back to see? What if the moose had taken out its anger on his team? Yes, she would head back. Too narrow to turn there, she would first have to go on to a wider spot. "Come on. Let's move, guys."

Around two corners, a wide spot appeared at a split in the trail. As she approached she noticed there were no pink tape markers to indicate which fork to take. Strange, but she turned around anyway. "Come haw, Tank. Come haw. Let's go back now." Obediently he came around, leading the rest of the team back past the sled, and soon they were headed back over their own tracks.

A quarter of a mile later, Jessie realized the markers had once again disappeared. Not one waved at her from twigs or laths at intersections with other trails. What the hell was going on? She stopped and walked to the front of the team, where she could see farther. Except for her own runner marks in the trail, there was nothing to guide her at all. All she could do was go slowly, watch carefully, and trust Tank's nose to get them out of this tangle.

And where the hell was Ryan?

20

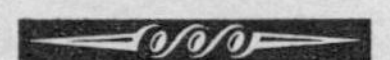

Date: Thursday, March 7
Race Day: Six
Place: McGrath checkpoint
Weather: Severe clear, light to no wind
Temperature: High −2°F, low −14°F
Time: Late morning

CRANSHAW'S CABIN LAY HALF A MILE NORTH OF McGrath in a slightly wooded area, out of sight and sound of any other residence. A sign on the unlocked door read "Make yourself at home, but leave it the way you found it." Jensen elected to take Bomber at his word. He'd make sure they put it back together after they took it apart.

Nothing in the one big room was left unexamined, but nothing they found told them much. A note on the table instructed "Jim—Make sure they get plenty of water. Thanks, B." This was clearly meant for the person feeding the twenty dogs who lived in individual houses behind the cabin. Their frantic barking had greeted the four men on arrival. The stove was still barely warm, and a skillet, bowl, and spoon, wiped rather than washed, sat on the table beside the note.

Two shelves of a rough bookcase were filled with a well-thumbed collection of *Playboy* magazines. Caswell, going through a chest of drawers, came up with a few joints in a plastic bag and some loose marijuana; less than was legally allowed. A dusty, unloaded shotgun hung on the wall by the door. To Holman's amusement, Cranshaw seemed to have cornered the market on baked beans and Jack Daniels; three cases of each were stacked in one corner. "You suppose he won't have one without the other, so they come out even?"

While the other three replaced Cranshaw's possessions, Alex went through the storage shed outside. There were several gas and oil cans, full and empty, a can of kerosene, and some tools on a shelf. Woodworking and engine-maintenance tools, they looked well cared for and oiled against rust.

A neat stack of wood, split for the cabin stove, was piled against an outside wall. In front of the shed were tracks of a snow machine in the new snow.

"Might have loaned it to anybody, Alex, or left it in town," Holman responded to his inquiry. "Jim Miller may be using it, instead of his own, to go back and forth to feed the mutts."

"Find out, will you, Matt."

The search confirmed nothing, positive or negative. They found neither Jessie's gun nor any suspicious drugs.

They closed up and walked back to town, Jensen sunk in silent thought all the way to the checkpoint, which was busy with mushers coming in from the burn.

"I've got to get hopping here," Holman told them. "You going out?"

"Soon as I make a call," Alex answered. "See you up the line?"

"Yeah. I'll be jumping close to the front as I can get. Checkers'll know where I am. I'll ask about Miller and the machine."

"Thanks, Matt. See you later."

They watched him hustle off to organize the rest of the race.

"Amazing," said Caswell.

"Get the bird warm," Alex told him. "I've got one call to make."

He returned quickly and started speaking before he was fully inside the plane. "Anchorage says Martinson was arrested for assault last year, a month after the race. Broke a guy's jaw in a Wasilla bar fight. Dismissed when the other guy admitted he started it and refused to press charges.

"Now get this," he continued in a growl. Tension drew lines in his forehead as he stared out the plane window at the section of riverbank where Jessie had vanished with her dogs two hours earlier. "It's been kept quiet, but Ryan was named in a case in Fairbanks, along with some other guy who was selling steroids to high school and college jocks. This guy claims he got the stuff from Ryan, who says he prescribed it for the guy's dogs with no idea it was being resold. They'd have a hard time convicting Ryan of anything, but the state board license review called Minnesota to check. At one time, before moving here, Ryan was licensed in both states. But he lost his Minnesota license in nineteen eighty-one for abuse of prescription pharmaceuticals. And the last nail—Steve Smith was the witness who turned in the pusher in Fairbanks. His kid is a bodybuilder."

There was silence in the cockpit when he finished, then a long, low whistle from Caswell.

"Well," he said, "doesn't look good for Ryan, does it, Alex?"

"Yeah, let's go have a chat with him. Now."

Flying toward Takotna, they looked down on loops of the river as it wound its way north through the rolling hills toward Ophir. Compared to the misery of the Farewell Burn, these hills were good mushing country. Dogsled travelers would be able to see for miles back across the way they had come. After running mostly northwest since Nikolai, from Ophir the trail would turn almost southwest, into the gold country, where mining still went on to a limited degree.

During the early part of the century, hundreds of miners made their way into the area. Creeks around these all-but-empty districts bear names that recall the search for gold: Fourth of July, Maybe, Goldbottom, Yankee, and Tango.

Caswell flew his small plane low enough to watch for mushers on the trail, giving the troopers the opportunity to get a feeling for the country. More than halfway between McGrath and Takotna, Jensen sited a lone racer, knowing it could not be Jessie, since she would be with Ryan.

As he lost sight of the team, Caswell spoke into the radio. "Put on the headset, Alex," he instructed. "It's Holman."

"Jensen. We got an emergency. Jessie just brought Ryan into Takotna on her sled. Moose ran through both their teams and kicked the hell out of his. Three dogs dead, four injured. He caught it pretty good, too. Got a kick in the head that'll need stitches, and it stomped him enough to break a few ribs. He's unconscious at the checkpoint. We're getting a plane up with the McGrath EMT to take him to Anchorage, but it'll be half an hour. Can you get in and take over there?" He paused for breath.

"Affirmative. Is Jessie all right?"

"Yes. Repeat. Yes. She's fine. But, Alex . . . she thinks someone drove the moose into them with a snow machine."

"We're almost there now." He glanced at Caswell, who nodded vigorously. "Did you find out about the times here and in Ophir?"

"Yeah. Harvey, Ellis, Schuller, and Martinson all went through Takotna between three and five this morning. Ellis, Schuller, and Harvey checked into Ophir between seven and ten. They're still there, but Martinson hasn't showed up yet. Cranshaw went through Takotna ten minutes before Jessie got there with Ryan."

"But he left an hour ahead."

"Right."

"And Martinson's overdue to go . . . how far?"

"Thirty-eight miles."

Alex considered it, with a little mental finger counting.

"Anything on Cranshaw's snow machine?"

"Miller says it's missing. He was using it to feed the dogs and took it to his place last night. Gone when he got up this morning."

"Would it be possible to . . . ?" Alex started to ask.

"Borrow a snow machine, come back to run that moose through Jessie's team, return, avoid Takotna, and go on into Ophir?" Holman finished. "Just barely, but a big risk of being seen somewhere."

"And Cranshaw's machine hasn't been seen?"

"Right. But they're everywhere in this country.

People borrow them all the time, especially during Iditarod. Kids joyriding. We've had five reported in the last four days, including two today from north of town."

"Coming in," Caswell interjected, as the plane lost altitude.

"I'll get back to you through the ham as soon as I know what's going on. Thanks, Matt. Wait—one more thing."

"Yeah?"

"How long will the leaders stay in Ophir?" Jensen asked.

"Not long. By the time you could fly up there, the first three'll be gone."

"We could catch Martinson."

"Probably, unless . . . He could be in some trouble out there."

"One of the reasons I want to find him. If he's not, I want to know where he's been. Over and out, Matt."

21

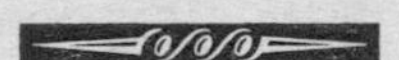

Date: Thursday, March 7
Race Day: Six
Place: Takotna checkpoint
Weather: Severe clear, light to no wind
Temperature: High −2°F, low −14°F
Time: Midafternoon

RYAN WAS OUT OF THE RACE. IN THE CHECKPOINT cabin, Jensen examined him. Though he was not comatose, he was fading in and out of consciousness with no real awareness of what was going on around him. The moose's hoof had caught him behind the ear, a glancing blow that opened about four inches of scalp. There was no depression of bone, but Alex was sure he was concussed. His breathing was normal, so the broken ribs had evidently not punctured a lung. They put a gauze and snow pack on his head, monitored his pulse and breathing, and waited for the EMT, who arrived within the thirty minutes Holman had estimated.

The man examined Ryan quickly and thoroughly and started an IV before they carried him to the plane. In less than ten minutes it was back in the air, heading south.

The checkpoint vet and Becker had gone on a snow machine, with an empty freight sled bouncing behind, to collect Ryan's sled and bring back the dead, injured and still healthy dogs. Becker would search the area, though the tangle of trails and overlapping tracks offered small chance of revealing clues that would identify any particular snow machine.

In the empty checkpoint, Alex turned to Jessie, who stood beside him, watching the plane disappear. Her parka and hands were caked with Ryan's dried blood. A smear of it lined one cheek. He laid his arm around her shoulders.

"Come on. Let's clean up and talk about it."

"Because of the way the sound traveled," she said a fcw minutes later, as they sat with Caswell to discuss the incident. "I heard the engine before the moose went through my team. I expected to see a snow machine coming at us when the moose burst out of the brush. Then the sound went farther to the southwest. But when I was taking care of my hurt pups, I heard it again going north, till it stopped, like it was shut down."

"But you thought it was more than one machine," Caswell commented.

"I know," she answered carefully. "But I don't think so now. I think I was only listening some of the time, hearing just parts of it in between what was happening. It could have been just one."

She told them about the missing marker tapes, Tank's leading them back to the trail, how she had found Ryan with his injured team, and struggled to get him on her sled and into Takotna.

"I was really scared when he kept passing out. He was bleeding so bad and all I had was gauze from the first aid kit that wasn't half enough. I got him in his sleeping bag before we left. Looks like it went through a war. I thought we'd never make it back." She looked down at her hands. They were shaking.

"Jim's not as bad as he looks, Jess," Alex told her. "You know how head wounds bleed. He'll be okay."

"You know what I think?" she said slowly. "I think someone moved those markers so I'd get off the trail, then ran that moose right into us."

Alex met Caswell's half-frown.

They both spoke at once.

"If there was only one machine . . ."

"Did you see anyone else . . . ," Alex continued at the other man's nod, "anywhere after you left McGrath?"

"Not till we got here."

"From the plane, I saw someone a long way behind you."

"Probably Mike Solomon. He was going to leave next, I think."

Outside, Jessie's team began to bark. As if he had been conjured, they heard Solomon pull up.

"Good," said Jessie, getting up. "I can go on with Mike."

The troopers stared at her.

She spoke to Caswell. "I'm pretty stubborn. Ask Alex."

She went out the door. "Hey, Mike," they heard her say. "Got a minute?"

The ghost town of Ophir is a series of old, abandoned houses and buildings of logs and weathered gray boards. At least two of these were once roadhouses, but many have been pulled apart for their building materials, so hard to come by in a country where trees grow slowly and are limited in height by permafrost. Fire had claimed most of the other structures through the years. An old dredge lies silent and motionless near the trail.

They dropped onto the river ice rather than land at the airstrip, which was over two miles out of town.

The checkpoint cabin was not large, but it had been so solidly built from squared logs back in the thirties that it still served as a retreat for a couple from McGrath, who came in every year to man it during the race. Outside, they found the sled and team of only one musher, Martinson. As they ascertained its ownership, the checker stepped through the door.

"Where is he?" Jensen asked, with a nod toward the sled.

"Asleep inside."

"When did he get in?"

"Two hours ago. When he pulled in, Ellis was just leaving."

"Did he say what took him so long?"

"Said he got lost."

"That's right. I got lost," said a belligerent voice from the door behind them. "What's going on out here?"

Martinson, pulling on his parka, stepped out to confront Jensen and Becker.

"What the hell are you harassing me for this time?"

"Mr. Martinson—" Becker started.

"Come on," Martinson interrupted. "You've been at me every time we crossed paths since Rohn, and you've made damn sure we crossed them. What the hell do you want?"

"We want," said Jensen, stepping forward, "to know where you've been and what took you so long to get here. We aren't harassing you. We have the right to ask anything of anyone to figure out who is attacking mushers in this race. You aware that Jim Ryan was stomped by a moose outside of Takotna?"

"Yeah, Bob told me." He gestured toward the checker. "What's it got to do with me?"

"It's possible someone drove that moose into him."

"If they did it wasn't me. I wasn't anywhere close. They'll tell you what time I went through Takotna, and I took a bad turn between here and there. Lost over two fucking hours while I went the wrong way and back. Damn snow-machine tracks. Rested and fed my dogs before I came on through to Ophir."

"According to our calculations you had just enough time to go back to the place Ryan was attacked, then return here, avoiding Takotna for the second time."

"But I didn't. Do these dogs look like they had been run that many extra miles?"

The team didn't look exhausted. Though all the dogs lay on the snow, resting, many of them had their heads up, watching what was going on at the sled. One wheel dog stood up and whined.

Jensen didn't mention the snow machine.

"Did you see anyone while you were off the main trail, or on the rest of the way here, for that matter?"

"Not a soul."

"But you can't prove where you were."

"No, but I didn't spend my time going backward."

"I'd like to have another look at your sled."

"What the hell for? Can you do that without my permission?"

"No," said Jensen shortly, having had about all he could take of the man's countentiousness. "We could have the checker do it, though. Matt Holman has made it mandatory in McGrath, will here if I ask him. Let's just say it may be to your benefit to let us and

I'll make it damned hard on you if you won't."

With his grudging permission, they went through the contents of his sled and found nothing. He carried a rifle, rather than a handgun, but it was cleanly packed in a soft case in the side of his sled bag and had not been fired recently.

Alex shook his head at Caswell, who had tied down the plane, come up from the river, and was watching the procedure with interest.

"Well?" demanded Martinson, who had not assisted, but had glowered and insisted that they precisely repack the gear they had searched.

"Nothing to indicate you are involved," Jensen told him. Then, resenting the musher's attitude and still suspicious enough to be stubborn, "But nothing to say you're not, either. I haven't scratched your name off my list, Martinson. A little cooperation would go a long way with me. You might think about that."

The musher said nothing to the troopers in response, but spoke instead to the checker. "I'm going on out, Bob. There's no rest to be had here. I'll pull the dogs over down the trail a few miles."

The checker waited for Alex's sharp nod before he agreed, having seen everything essential while the sled bag was open.

In ten minutes all that was left of Martinson were the tracks of his sled and team heading out of Ophir. Becker stood looking at them, concern on his face.

"What do you think?" he asked.

"I'd like to think he'll get lost and we won't have to put up with him again."

"I'd better check the plane," Caswell commented. "Did a pretty slipshod tie-down."

Jensen turned to look back down the trail toward Takotna.

"Might as well tie her down good. We're not leaving here until Cranshaw shows up."

Two hours later, a little sooner than they expected, Cranshaw pulled into Ophir. The minute he stopped the sled, the dogs lay down, ready to rest. Bomber was not a man to baby his team.

As the checker went through the familiar accounting routine, Jensen watched Cranshaw's sidelong glances at the waiting troopers and listened to the noisy, unnecessary chatter he exchanged with the official. The business over, he seemed to gather himself, turned, and walked straight up to Alex.

"Bill says there was some kind of accident with Ryan and a moose."

"Yeah. He's on a plane to the hospital in Anchorage with a head injury and broken ribs."

"Aw shit." He looked away toward the trail he had just quit, framing his next question. "Is Jessie okay? Did she go on?" His tone was flat, but Jensen sensed a tension.

"She's fine. She's on the trail with Mike Solomon."

"Good. Good. Hate to see her drop out now. Well, got to feed the mutts," he said, half-turning to his team.

"Just a minute, Mr. Cranshaw. We have a few questions."

"Not now, okay? The dogs are hungry and I got to get 'em settled for a couple hours' snooze. Then we'll see about it."

"We'll see about it *now*, Mr. Cranshaw. If you don't mind. We'll only take a few minutes. If we don't get back in the air, we won't make it to Iditarod before dark. Do us a favor here." The crack of authority in his voice contrasted with the polite words, and Cranshaw swung back sharply, a hint of challenge on his face.

"You *do* like to throw around that trooper shit, don't you, Jensen? God, you assholes are all alike."

Caswell stepped up to stand beside Alex, a study in poised relaxation, silently confronting the musher, hands thrust into his parka pockets. Becker walked a wide circle to put himself between Cranshaw and his team.

"Shit," Cranshaw said. "All right. What the fuck do you want?"

"You lost almost an hour getting to Takotna, then went right through."

"So?"

"Where were you in that hour?"

"Hell, I made 'em take it easy getting back into it. They're greedy to go when they're rested. Let 'em go too fast and they'll dump too much energy and go flat on you. I stopped to snack 'em twice.

"You know your snow machine is missing in McGrath?"

Impatiently he shook his head, but he grinned, as if pleased to catch Jensen in an error. "Shit. I loaned the machine to a guy who's feeding my other dogs while I'm gone. He's got it."

"Jim Miller says it was gone when he got up this morning. He's using his own."

Cranshaw's head came up in seeming surprise. "Goddamn it. Fuckin' kids. They'll find it somewhere out of gas and probably bashed up."

Good save, thought Alex.

"We think a snow machine drove the moose into Jessie and Ryan."

He watched the other man think about that one.

"And *you* think it was me, in the extra time *you*

say I took. Aw shit, man. Why the hell would I do that? They're friends of mine."

"But you got pissed and took off this morning by yourself."

"Listen." Cranshaw's jaw tightened and his hands clenched into fists as he stiffened. "I didn't need her accusing me of stealing the gun *she* lost. Making you guys think I'm responsible for this shit. If she wants to suck up, it's her mistake, but she can fuckin' leave me out of it. Okay?"

"You have a problem with Jessie and *me?*"

"Shit, no. She's smart. It won't take her long to figure out what troopers are full of and that will be it, so I've got no reason to care."

Alex felt himself boil. Cranshaw seemed to be letting his anger overcome caution. Something in his eyes said he was coldly aware of every word and calculating the effect.

"You're not doing yourself any good with that kind of jealousy, Cranshaw."

"What jealousy? I like Jessie. I just think this should be a man's race. They fuckin' confuse the issue. They're a distraction. They have a place, just like men, but, goddamn, it's not the Iditarod, or any other trail."

"We'll have a look at your sled, Cranshaw."

"I oughta make you get a warrant."

"You got something to hide?"

"Not a damn thing. Be my guest." He made a sweeping mock bow toward the sled and its contents. "Mind if I get down to the important things now?"

Half an hour later, the troopers were again airborne. There was little to say about Cranshaw, and Alex was silent, letting his temper cool. Flying west they passed over Martinson and his team, running over fairly flat ground on a trail that wound gently through spruce and birch stands, gradually climbing into the hills of the Beavers, which rise like a terrace in the Kuskokwim Mountains.

Ninety miles separate Ophir from Iditarod, the town from which the race and the mining district both take their name. The last great stampede for gold had taken place in this area, which the Ingalik Athabaskan Indians had called Haiditarod, "the faraway place," long before white men found it to be true. During the years of extracting gold, sleds hauling heavy loads of freight, pulled by dogs or men on snowshoes, marked the trail over these hills so deeply in places that it is still easy to follow, even in new snow, by the depression alone.

Midway through the flight, Holman called. Over the crackling static of the transmission, he informed them that a McGrath kid had been caught with Cranshaw's missing snow machine.

"Took us back to where he says he found it. The tracks in the snow are damn close to the trail, about a half-mile from where Ryan got stomped. Seems Jessie might be right, huh?"

In brooding silence, Alex stared out the window at the hills.

The sun ahead of them went down into a band of cloud along the horizon, and darkness began to fall slowly, deep shadows defining the spaces between the hills. Looking closely they identified all four of the racers headed for the silver prize at the halfway point. Harvey and Ellis, running within a mile of each other, led Schuller and Murray by only a little. It would be a race into Iditarod sometime during the night.

"Looks like we'll get some weather," Caswell commented. "The report says there's a front moving in slowly along the coast. It could come in late tomorrow, or hold off for two or three days."

"Three days would suit me fine," Jensen told him. "I don't like the idea of bouncing around up here in bad weather."

"Bouncing around, hell. You've obviously never seen weather like they get around Norton Sound. We'll be sitting it out wherever we are when it comes in. Nobody flies in that."

"Could we handle being grounded?" Becker asked. "Do we have enough food and stuff?"

Caswell laughed. "You've got your priorities straight, Phil. We could make do for a while."

After the emptiness of Ophir, it was a surprise to see several planes at the edge of the river ice when they reached Iditarod, the last of the light fading fast. Pulling in near them, Alex was glad to drop onto the ground. Caswell's plane flew well enough, but it made him feel like a grasshopper, with his long legs folded into the narrow space below the instrument panel.

As they went up the bank toward the lights of the checkpoint, he hoped the opportunity for sleep would come early. It had been a long day. The temperature had dropped steadily throughout, and he intended to sleep in his clothes, if necessary, to stay warm, but he wanted to do it soon.

A wall tent, glowing in the twilight, welcomed them to the checkpoint. A fire in front of it heated a kettle of water and an enormous coffeepot. As he stopped close to warm his hands, Alex wondered whether Jessie would sleep or run through the dark. He hoped she'd be okay wherever she was.

Goodnight, Jess, he thought. Go well.

22

Date: Friday, March 8
Race Day: Seven
Place: Iditarod checkpoint
Weather. Clear and sunny, moderate wind
Temperature: High −4°F, low −11°F
Time: Early morning

IT HAD BEEN LIGHT FOR TWO HOURS WHEN JESSIE and Mike Solomon dropped down through the surrounding hills into the wide valley of the Iditarod River. A navigable waterway, the river had been the reason the town of Iditarod became the center of the mining district in 1910. When the water was high in those early summers, this was as far as the paddle wheelers could come with their loads of freight and supplies for the gold-rush community.

As they came out of the hills, Jessie began to look for buildings in the distance. From past years, she knew the tallest, the old, abandoned Northern Commercial Company, would be visible before they reached town. Tired and past ready for a rest and hot food, she finally spotted its peaked roof on the far side of the river and followed Solomon's team down onto the ice for the run across.

Passing three small planes, including the one she recognized as Caswell's, they located their supplies in a neatly organized line of bags and loaded them onto their sleds. Up the bank, the checker waited, clipboard in hand.

Rather than pitch their tent, the troopers hauled their gear into the old Northern Commercial Company building. Although it tilted to one side, it was sound enough to provide shelter and allow access to all of its ancient two and a half stories.

After a dinner from cans, Alex went straight to bed, where he slept instantly.

A little after midnight, Caswell shook him awake, much to his groggy displeasure.

"Come on, Alex. First musher's on his way. You gotta get up."

"The hell I do. Let him come."

"No. You said to wake you up, no matter what. You've gotta see this. I promise it's worth it."

"What's worth it? Won't he still be here in the morning?"

"The silver. The halfway trophy. It's a big deal. There must be a dozen reporters out there."

Oh yeah, the silver, Jensen thought resentfully. What made me get into the law-enforcement business anyway? But he stumbled out of the warm bag, glad he had followed the instinct to sleep in his clothes, and took the cup of steaming coffee Caswell offered him.

Outside the old building, they walked toward the riverbank. He could see the bobbing light from a headlamp and, illuminated in its glow, a team of dogs just beginning to cross the ice.

"Hey," someone said, loudly, "there's another one."

Coming down the opposite bank was a second headlamp.

"Who is it?"

"Can't tell yet, but it should be Harvey and Ellis, unless Schuller got the drop on them."

As they watched a race develop between the two mushers, he saw that Cas was right about the news media. Video cameras with blinding lights were everywhere, competing for vantage points. Three thousand in silver made good press.

Swinging out to the side as if to pass, the second team was gaining perceptibly on the first. Shouts of encouragement broke out among the spectators. Neck and ncck, the two teams dashed for Iditarod. As they came within range, the bright lights caught the colors on their sled bags and clothes, enough to identify them.

"Damn! It's Harvey and *Murray*," a KTUU reporter yelled. "COME ON GAIL!"

"Back up! Give them room," the checker shouted, as the sleds reached the bank, and flew up it.

The spectators divided, forming a corridor just as one team gained the advantage and whipped through them, forcing the other into second place.

"It's Murray by a nose," a fan called out. "By a bunch of noses."

The camera jockeys ran toward the checkpoint cabin, where the teams had been whoa'd to a stop. The rival mushers now grinned at each other and shook hands.

"Good run, Gail," Harvey congratulated her. "Worth about three thousand. But I'd've had you if I hadn't had to carry Hot Shot." He patted the head of a dog that protruded from the bag of his sled.

"Maybe not," Murray laughed. "Luck of the draw, T.J. I gave you a run."

"And picked up the halfway jinx. Now I know you won't beat me to Nome, anyway."

"Yeah, Gail," a reporter said. "How about that old jinx?"

"What's he talking about?" Alex asked Caswell.

"It's a superstition this award has picked up. Since the race started, back in nineteen seventy-three, only one person has ever won the halfway silver and gone on to win the race. Dean Osmar did it in nineteen eighty-four on the northern route. No one has ever been the winner after taking it here in Iditarod."

"We'll see about the jinx," Murray was telling the reporter. "Just have to wait and see." She opened her sled bag and waited while the checker affirmed the presence of her mandatory gear. Then the media claimed her.

Two Alascom officials set a large two-tiered silver trophy down in the snow by her sled. On her knees beside it, Gail Murray watched with everyone else as one of the officials opened the drawstring on a canvas bag and poured three thousand dollars' worth of silver ingots into the upper bowl. Shiny new, specially minted, they tumbled musically, filling it and overflowing into the lower basin.

Reaching out, she took two from the bowl, held them up, and smiled for the photographers. When they finished their questions and turned off the lights, she got to her feet and walked over to where the checker was still going through Harvey's sled.

"Hey, T.J. It was close enough so you ought to have this to remember." She handed him one of the ingots, which he accepted with a grin as she pocketed the other.

"She's not going to carry all that silver to Nome?" Jensen said.

"Not a chance. Alascom will take it up for the banquet. She'll pick it up there. Glad you got up?"

"That's debatable."

"Oh, go on back to bed," Caswell told him. "You'll be better company tomorrow."

Alex didn't argue, and was glad in the morning. He slept later than usual and woke to find himself alone in the ruins of the Northern Commercial Company building, sun shining in one broken window. He was hungry, but what he really wanted was a shower and shave. He settled for half a bucket of hot water, begged at the checkpoint, which he used to scrape off his whiskers and wash what he could of his upper body. Feeling almost human again in a clean shirt, he went to look for Becker, Caswell, and some breakfast.

Schuller and Ellis had come in shortly after Murray's win. Martinson had followed them by two and a half hours. Just after daylight, Bomber Cranshaw had pulled into the checkpoint, and he now slept in his sled at a point on the riverbank away from the checker's tent. The first four were gone, on their way to Shageluk and Anvik. Martinson was repacking his sled when Jensen walked by, but he ignored the trooper.

After eating Alex once again tackled Cranshaw, with even less result. The musher sulked and said little.

"Would I be stupid enough to steal my own machine, then leave it that close to the trail?" he demanded sourly.

"Maybe," Jensen commented to Becker. "If he

thought it would throw suspicion away from him. On the other hand, Martinson could have figured we'd suspect Cranshaw of just that kind of duplicity."

The day was sunny, defying Caswell's weather forecast. The abandoned buildings of Iditarod cast dark shadows from their weathered sides. Curious, Jensen wandered over to take a look at the remains of what had once been the center of their third largest gold-producing district in Alaska.

In October of 1910, advertisements in the *Iditarod Pioneer* indicated the existence of eight saloons, six cafés, six general mercantiles, six attorneys, five clothing stores, three hotels, two banks, two doctors, two dentists, two tobacco shops, a barber, a drugstore, an undertaker, a bathhouse, a music store, and a candy store. Construction of these businesses, and houses for the residents, required that all the usable timber be stripped from the hills for miles around. To the present day, there have been almost no trees of any size near Iditarod. The few buildings still standing define the old streets.

A concrete vault stands by itself. The building around it, once a bank, has long since disappeared, demolished, probably a board at a time, for firewood. In the vault lie the remains of old records of deposits, withdrawals, and loans, each telling its own silent tale. In its heyday, the Iditarod District yielded up over fourteen million dollars in gold.

Alex fingered a few of the crumbling paper records of those long-ago transactions. Then he walked past the rest of the tumbledown buildings, back to the Northern Commercial Company store.

Inside, counters and shelves that were once filled with merchandise now held only dust. Old account books were still on shelves in the office, filled with lists of debits and credits for the inhabitants of the town and its surrounding mining camps. Amused, Alex wondered if ghosts of those who died owing the company might still haunt the building. He could almost imagine the sound of voices and footsteps in the empty rooms. Upstairs he found rooms for boarders, one with a number of old bunk beds.

What had once been a bustling boom town was now empty enough to echo. He decided he'd like to come back and see it in the summer.

Going out the gaping front door, he met Caswell on his way in.

"Is there anything else we can do here now? If not, I have a suggestion."

"What's that?"

"Let's go on to Kaltag. They've flown gas in for us from Nome. We can fill up the plane and take on the additional cans of fuel. Then, if this storm hits, we'll be ready for it."

"How far is it?"

"About a hundred and thirty miles if we fly from here, cutting off two sides of a triangle. Following the trail west to Anvik, then north to Kaltag, would be almost two hundred and fifty."

"Sounds like a good idea. We can wait for them there, or come back down if we need to."

"Right."

"Let's get our gear."

Heading for the plane, they found Solomon and Jessie checking in.

"Everything all right?" he asked Solomon, who was nearest.

The musher smiled shyly. "Yeah. Pretty calm, except for a wild ride after some caribou in the dark last night. The mutts should know better by now.

They never catch anything, but they never give up."

Jessie looked up and smiled as he approached.

"Hi, trooper. Caught any bad guys?"

"Not yet. You okay?"

"Tired, always tired, but fine. It was a good run."

She turned to open her sled for the checker, then back to Jensen.

"Have you heard anything about Ryan?"

"The hospital says he's okay. No permanent damage. Check with the ham, he sent a message for you this morning."

"Oh good. I miss him."

"How's Solomon?"

"Mike's really fine. He's sort of quiet and sweet, but, boy do these Yukon mushers know their dogs. Emmett Peters, the Ruby Fox, helped him train. Now there's a sharp one for you. Wish he was racing this year."

He grinned at her enthusiasm.

"Listen, Alex, I want you to hear something Solomon told me last night. Hey, Mike."

The musher stopped what he was doing and walked over.

"Will you tell Sergeant Jensen what you told me about Tim Martinson?"

Solomon shuffled his feet and looked uncomfortably at the ground.

"What is it?" Alex coaxed him.

"Well . . . Heard him swearing at Ginny Kline at Skwentna. One of her dogs got loose and got into it with one of his over a bitch in heat. He yelled at her: 'If you can't control your damn dogs, you shouldn't be out here.' "

"Hmm . . . You think it was personal? Or would he have yelled at anybody?"

"Anybody, I think. I don't know. Could have been anybody's dog."

"Thanks, Mike."

Solomon nodded and went back to his team.

Jessie waited for his comment.

"One more piece for the puzzle, Jess."

"Just thought you ought to hear it."

"How long will it take you to get to Kaltag?" he asked.

"Two more days. Why? Are you going up there now?"

"Yeah. Cas wants to make sure the plane is set to ride out the bad weather they're expecting. We used up a lot of the fuel we were carrying. He doesn't just fly that plane, he wears it. So what he says goes. Still, I'm not entirely comfortable being two days up the road, so to speak."

She looked up at him, caught more by the tone of his voice than his words. "What? Is there something else? Last night was completely quiet. No problems."

He frowned. "Maybe that's what's bothering me. Too quiet. I slept like a log last night and found myself wandering around in these old buildings like a tourist a little while ago, like I hadn't a care in the world. Something feels wrong. I don't want to let down the guard, Jess, or for you to either."

"Yeah, I know," she said. "But from here on this is serious business. We're getting into it and shutting out everything else, I'm afraid. That's the way it's run. You need your concentration."

She frowned and shivered.

"You really okay?"

"Yeah . . . That moose and Ryan getting hurt shook me more than I thought. It could have been me. I thought about it, off and on, all night and was jumpy as hell at every shadow in the trail. But . . . yeah. I'm fine."

"Want out?"

"No. But I'm glad to be running with Mike."

"Just keep in mind that we can be back anywhere between here and Kaltag in a matter of hours. I wish you weren't out there."

Her eyes widened.

Damn, he thought. I didn't mean . . .

Her mouth tightened, but she said nothing.

Easy, Jensen, he told himself. Easy. She's tired. She's scared, like everyone else. So are you. Don't push it.

Carefully, respectfully, he tried, "I'm sorry, Jessie. I didn't mean I don't appreciate what you're doing. Just keep in mind that we're here. That's all. Okay?"

Her mouth relaxed, but she didn't smile.

"Okay," she said, as Solomon pulled his team around hers, heading for a resting place. "I've got to go, Alex."

"I know. Jessie? Are we fighting?"

Then she smiled. "Hell, no," she said. "We don't know each other well enough yet to do a good job of it, and I've got a race to win."

She stepped onto the sled and bent to the snow hook.

"Hey," he said suddenly.

She straightened and turned back.

"Buy you dinner in Nome?"

"Well . . ." She hesitated a moment. "After I get a shower and a lot of sleep, that sounds good. And, if this race goes as well as I want it to, I'll buy the champagne."

She pulled the hook and moved away before he could respond.

She had meant what she said about winning and he felt it. She wasn't running just to finish well anymore. Scared or not, she was racing to win if she could. It frightened him deeply to think that, for whoever was responsible for Smith, Kline, Koptak, and Ryan, it might be a reason to focus on her.

23

Date: Friday through Sunday, March 8–10
Race Day: Seven, eight, and nine
Place: Kaltag checkpoint
Weather: Wind and blowing snow, clearing on Saturday
Temperature: High −8°F, low −27°F
Time: Friday morning to Sunday afternoon

WHEN ALEX LOOKED BACK AT IT LATER, THE SECOND half of the race seemed to have gone faster than the first. Perhaps it was partly because the country was flatter, with less contrast than the pass and canyons. The trail ran along a series of low monotonous hills, then along the long, gentle bends of the Yukon River. After a portage, the route followed the coast in a sweeping curve for over two hundred miles around Norton Sound until it reached Nome, crossing the sea ice in two places.

From the map, he knew that the mushers continued west through Shageluk to Anvik, where they took to the river highway for almost a hundred and fifty miles, passing Grayling and Eagle Island, before coming to Kaltag. Flying straight to Kaltag from Iditarod, he saw only hill after rolling hill, although Caswell drifted a little west to give them a look at the mighty, mile-wide Yukon.

The inactivity of waiting in Kaltag for the two days it took for the first sled-dog racers to arrive left Jensen frustrated and tense.

The storm swept in, stranding the race leaders for almost half a day at Eagle Island. It broke in the early morning hours, only to hover ominously, threatening to close in again.

From radio information, they followed the race, now well over halfway to the finish line. When the weather allowed, Holman's Iditarod air force kept track of the teams' locations. Two-thirds of the route would be complete in Kaltag: only three hundred and sixty miles left.

Two groups of leaders developed, running within hours of each other. Harvey, Schuller, Murray, and Martinson formed the first group, leapfrogging each other up the trail. Ellis had dropped back to the second group, several of his dogs suffering from diarrhea and dehydration. He joined Cranshaw, Solomon, Arnold, and Banks, who had caught up in Anvik. The next closest mushers were at least six hours behind. Not immediately threatening.

Everyone was pushing hard and watching closely for advantages. No one stayed long in any checkpoint, pausing only to care for their dogs and get just enough sleep to keep them going. Sleep could be had when the race was over. The mushers were averaging a couple of hours' rest a day.

A few racers still drove teams of at least fifteen dogs. Some were down as low as nine or ten. To start the race a musher must have at least seven and no more than twenty dogs. He must have at least five on the tow line at all times, including at the legal finish. Dogs may not be added to a team after the start.

There comes a point in the race toward the finish when a carefully considered decision must be made on the number of dogs to keep in a team. More dogs mean a stronger and, usually, a faster team. But the more animals a musher has to maintain, feed, and care for, the more time is required at each stop. Fifteen dogs have sixty feet that may need booties replaced and wounds tended.

This late in the race, everything must be decided and performed in a foggy-minded state of physical and mental fatigue. It is understandable that no one has ever won the race in the first year of running it. Strategy is everything, but unpredictable luck can be taken advantage of, if a musher is in top form and ready for it.

The Yukon River's very size precludes the sharp snakelike loops of smaller rivers, the volume of its water bending it into wider, more gradual curves. High on one of the bluffs framing one of these curves stands the village of Kaltag, facing east, swept by the winds that follow the river down from the Arctic mountain ranges to the northeast. Weathered log buildings stand near the bluff, with more modern frame houses farther away. Usually one of these, home to a bush pilot and his family, serves as the race checkpoint.

In a state of anticipation, the 250 villagers wait for the Iditarod racers to come through each year. Reporters and photographers begin to arrive soon after the checkpoint officials and equipment are flown in. There is always someone looking down the river hopefully, even though updates from the radio indicate it will be hours before the race reaches them.

Like a winter festival, the Iditarod is a reason for celebration in each community through which it passes, particularly those isolated in the great alone of Alaska's interior. Cut off by the cold and darkness of winter, cabin fever sets in among the residents in late February and early March, as the days begin to grow longer and the wait for spring seems endless. "Freezing in the dark builds character," says one Alaskan proverb. But often it encourages depression, claustrophobia, and boredom, which are alleviated by the excitement of the race.

Children spend most of the twelve hours of daylight sliding down steep riverbanks on everything from sleds to plastic garbage bags, always watching for a musher to appear. When the first sled is sighted the shout of "Dog team! Dog team!" rings out, bringing everyone to the bank to watch and cheer it into Kaltag. For the next week the celebration goes on, reviving the spirits of winter-weary villagers. When the last musher has come and gone, they know spring cannot be far behind.

Though Alex was restless he passed the time talking to the locals about the race and dog mushing. The villagers were proud that, until he died in 1981, Edgar Kalland, one of the last survivors of the 1925 serum relay to Nome, lived in Kaltag, managing the store and post office.

The original race to Nome was no sporting event, but a deadly serious race with death. Diphtheria was diagnosed in town late in January of that year, and the Nome doctor, knowing that the local Eskimo inhabitants had no immunity to the disease, never having been exposed, feared an epidemic. Sufficient serum was located in Anchorage, but airplanes were a new concept to Alaska, and the weather was too cold to fly without risking the only such medicine in the state. It was decided to transport it overland by dogsled.

The serum was taken by train to Nenana, and twenty freight teams and drivers were organized to run it over the trail to Nome. The temperature fell to fifty below, and the serum was wrapped and insulated carefully to protect it against freezing and breakage on the rough trail. In a remarkable 127½ hours, the serum run was made. Although the serum arrived frozen, it was still viable enough to stop the epidemic.

Alex asked the checker, Mick Lord, a former racer, about the changes in sleds since the serum run.

"Most mushers used to use the traditional basket sleds built of hardwood and tied together with strips of rawhide, or *babiche.* Not a bit of metal on them. Now they have plastic runners and rubber tread where the driver stands, to keep him from slipping. The brakes and snow hooks are a little different now too, but the biggest change is the toboggan body. A piece of heavy plastic runs under the whole sled, attached to the runners and protecting the basket. It slides easier, especially in deep snow, but it makes the sled a little stiffer than the old, flexible ones. Lots use them, but a few still race with the old kind. Depends on the musher. One Eskimo guy still uses carved ivory toggles on his sled bag."

Saturday night, Alex slept poorly. Bad dreams woke him twice. Finally, unable to get back to steep, he dressed and left the tent to pace the riverbank.

Puffing morosely on his pipe, he walked about half a mile before turning back. A sense that something was about to happen pervaded his thoughts. He felt helpless and stranded. Snow fell, drifting on a light wind, making it impossible to see the frozen river. The curtain of isolation was broken only by a faint light or two that seemed farther away than they were.

There had been no incident since the moose attack, but that didn't quiet his suspicion that they were far from finished with whoever was threatening mushers. Bits of information turned over and over in the roiling stew of facts in his head. He couldn't shake the feeling that he should be able to figure out who was responsible for it all, but a solution to the puzzle wouldn't rise to the surface where he could skim it off, see it singular and whole. It was a feeling that came at a certain point in almost every challenging case, familiar but annoying.

In the partial shelter of a storage shed, he stopped and sat down on a pile of snow-covered lumber. He was cold and considering going back to his bed, but he repacked his pipe and thought about Jessie instead, thoughts he knew he had been avoiding.

Elbows on knees, he puffed smoke into the dark, thinking over his attraction and confusion.

Wanting her physically was easy. It was the emotional part that gave him the shakes. He no longer found comfort in the false intimacy of casual one-night stands. They left him feeling hollow. You could talk yourself into just about anything, but emotionally you were never fooled. Mornings after were haunted by an emotional hangover for which there was no quick hair-of-the-dog chaser. Avoidance was better than the embarrassment of forgetting a name.

Jessie made him aware of an emptiness inside himself. Under the obvious competence and good humor was the confidence of a woman who knew herself attractive, but didn't trade on it. Who was openly warm and sharing, but not indiscriminate. She clearly knew the value of commitment to what she chose to do.

He wanted to know what mattered to her, what she thought funny, sad, trivial . . . and yet didn't want it. He felt pressured by his own pleasure in her.

Am I feeling guilty because of Sally? he wondered, but it didn't ring true. It had been over eight years, after all.

He thought about those years and how he had lived them, not allowing anyone to get too close. His life was quiet. Now, suddenly, because of Jessie Arnold, it felt crowded and noisy. I don't want anyone else's problems, he thought. I want it quiet and calm, controlled and . . . lonely?

If you don't feel, you don't hurt, but you don't laugh much either, or give, or get. He felt as if he had been living in the center of a great silence. Even with all the people he met, places he went, and things he did, he had isolated himself. At times, he felt if he went very carefully, quietly, without speaking or making a sound, no one would know he was there.

He put his head in his hands. He felt raw and disturbed. I haven't given much to anyone in years, he thought. I don't think I know how anymore.

Caswell came around the end of the shed to find him, having followed his footprints from the tent. He took in the dejected shape of elbows and knees on the angular pile of lumber.

Alex didn't realize he was there until Cas laid a companionable hand on his friend's shoulder.

"Middle of the night bejeebers got you?" he asked, sitting down and hunching his parka hood closer to his ears.

"Yeah, I guess," Jensen replied, relighting his pipe. "Couldn't sleep."

"The case?"

"Can't come up with any real answers. I feel like we're wallowing around."

"Maybe we just don't have enough information yet."

"I don't want to get it from another dead musher," Alex said bitterly.

"Nope. That all?"

Alex exhaled a long stream of smoke, staring into the falling snow. "No, Cas. That's not all."

"Jessie Arnold?"

"Yeah, I guess."

"Yeah, you *know*. I been watching. She scares the hell out of you, Alex. Why?"

More smoke, no answer.

"She's pretty. She's bright and tough and talented. She likes you. That gets you, doesn't it?"

A deep breath. "Maybe. That and all that goes with it."

Caswell was quiet for a long time, thinking. He pulled a knee up and clasped his mittened hands around it. Then he talked to himself, looking toward the invisible river.

"You know, I've never been sorry I found Linda. She's my best friend, and I don't have to prove anything to her. She makes sure what happens outside gets put in perspective at home. She's funny and wise and I never know what she'll say next. Things without her would be black and white. She puts the color in my life."

He paused and turned to meet Jensen's watchful eyes.

"Color's not a bad thing in your life, Alex. Might not hurt to try it."

Standing up, he brushed the snow from the seat of his pants.

"Now, let's find some coffee, or go back to bed. We're gonna freeze our *cojones* out here."

The next day Jensen found himself, with the rest, looking down the empty river more often. Caswell played cribbage with the radio operator, and Becker used the time to catch up on his sleep. Alex walked up and down the bank, puffing on his pipe.

About two o'clock in the afternoon, a plane landed on the ice below the bluff and Matt Holman crawled out. Moving like an old man, he climbed up and stopped beside Alex, red-eyed and grizzled with a three-day beard.

"Hi," he said. "Got a place where a guy could catch some z's?"

"What happened to you?" Jensen asked.

"Not sure I wanna think about it," Holman responded with a tired grin. "Kind of silly now.

"After the leaders took off for Eagle Island, I got a feeling something was gonna happen to somebody out there. So I flew to Grayling and got on a snow machine. Thought I'd buzz up and catch a hop from Eagle Island. Halfway up it socked in and I spent five hours going the last twenty-five miles.

"Blew so bad I couldn't see where the ice stopped and the banks started, so I bumped into them a few times, which kept me on the river. Scared to death I'd miss the turnoff and go till I ran out of gas and froze, but I made it. Dragged myself into the checkpoint and collapsed. Just got to sleep when the weather cleared and support flew in to pick me up. So, here I am."

"And nothing happened?" Jensen asked.

"Nothing, except I frostbit my nose. Everyone's okay so far and really pouring it on. Won't be in until late tonight. All I want now is some more sleep and food. Anything going on here?"

"Not so you could tell. Hot cribbage game between Caswell and the ham operator. Which mushers were in Eagle Island?"

Holman grinned as he turned away from Jensen and started for the checkpoint. "She's okay," he tossed back over his shoulder. "Said to tell you so." Without looking back, he continued, "Sort of glad you have a vested interest in this, Jensen. Means you're doing your best work. Kick me out if I'm still asleep when they come in."

24

Date: Saturday, March 9
Race Day: Eight
Place: Between Eagle Island and Kaltag
checkpoints (seventy miles)
Weather: Overcast, clearing, wind
Temperature: High −10°F, low −22°F
Time: Early morning

OUT ON THE ICE OF THE YUKON, THE LEADERS OF the race struggled into the wind, battling their way toward Kaltag. Trailbreakers had marked the route up the east side of the river, knowing the worst of the wind would hit the west bank. Heading almost directly into the wind for hours at a time demoralizes dogs as well as drivers. Blowing at a steady twenty to thirty knots, the gusts sometimes reached fifty or even sixty, battering sleds and teams the length of the run, from Anvik to Kaltag.

Past Grayling, on the sixty miles to Eagle Island, the weather deteriorated, catching the race leaders on the ice, with no option but to continue until they reached the checkpoint. Along with increased wind came fine, granular snow and temperatures that dipped to twenty below.

Even at zero, a person or dog standing still in a fifty-knot wind experiences a chill factor of minus sixty degrees. A team doing even five miles an hour adds another ten- or fifteen-degree drop. Any portion of a musher's body exposed to the wind risks almost instant frostbite, and many mushers come into checkpoints with patches of white on their faces, the first indications of danger. Ski masks and goggles are worn by most, but they must be closely checked for small openings that would allow windblown snow to filter in next to the skin.

Under these conditions, a good lead dog is vital. Racers breed for strength, determination, and grit in their best leaders, knowing that somewhere along the Iditarod Trail, the time will come when that good leader may be all that keeps them in the competition. Dogs that will go anywhere, anytime, are priceless. Some mushers have won the race more than once, only to lose their best leader and never win it again.

To keep their teams moving forward, many drivers get off the runners of the sled and walk, helping the dogs, periodically changing the order of the team to relieve those in front, giving them extra food and rest, but always pushing, always moving toward Kaltag and, ultimately, Nome. For a musher already sleep deprived, the additional physical and mental strain frequently produces a trancelike condition of hallucinations. Far from any trees, on the broad, flat, snow-drifted surface of the ice, a musher may duck to avoid a sweeper, or drive wide around a moose that isn't really there. It's not unusual for them to see buildings or people in the trail that disappear before they're reached.

Always present is pressure of the competition. As little as an hour can mean the difference in winning or losing at this point. All the racers watch one another constantly, afraid someone will sneak out and drive to get ahead and stay there. No one sleeps well, for fear they will sleep too well and waste time, or another racer will make better time. Mushers are obsessed, paranoid, and irrational in the last half of the race.

Jessie and Solomon left Eagle Island before five on Sunday morning, the ninth day of the race, with seventy miles between them and Kaltag. After being crammed into the small cabin for almost eight hours, waiting for the storm to blow itself out, Jessie, like the other eight leading mushers, was frustrated and tired of anyone's company but her own.

Although the worst of the storm was over, wind still blasted down the river and the temperature still held at twenty below. She had carefully booted all her dogs before leaving, knowing that the fine snow crystals on the ice would be as abrasive to their feet as they were to her skin, wearing away at any exposed pads and toes.

"Come on Tank. Let's take them out now. Hike, Sadie. Go on, Chops."

Well rested, they dropped onto the ice and into the wind with more enthusiasm than she felt. She could hear Mike talking up his own team ahead of her as they crossed back to the east bank and headed upriver.

It was still dark, but a thin band of open sky brightened below the clouds to the east, throwing the stunted spruce trees into black silhouette against it. She wished she were alone and couldn't hear even the sounds of another driver, the way it was on early morning training runs on the Knik Flats at home. This time of day was one of her favorites; the other was the half-lit end of it, when blue and gray shadows softened the landscape. Whistling up the dogs, she hurried them until she caught up enough to call to Solomon.

"Why don't you go on ahead, Mike," she said. "I'm going to drop behind you a little. Need some time to myself for a change, after the crowd last night."

He frowned. "Sure that's a good idea? You think maybe we should stay in sight of each other?"

"Oh, just for a little while. I really need some space, and I like to watch it get light with just the mutts for company."

Hesitating, he finally agreed. "But you run in front. I'll give you ten minutes' start. When you're ready for company, drop back and I'll catch up. Then I won't have to wonder if you've had to stop."

A few minutes later she had her wish and was gliding smoothly along the ice on the back of the sled, with only the sound of the wind in her ears.

Glorious, she thought. Freedom. She loved the solitude of mushing.

Three or four miles later, as the light grew stronger, the wind died until she could hear the panting of the dogs and the swish and scrape of her sled runners. The glow before sunrise was reflected off the endless snow and ice. It was like traveling through the inside of a pearl. She removed her goggles and rolled back the ski mask to appreciate the sudden calm, knowing it wouldn't last long. On the Yukon it seldom did.

Movement on the riverbank caught her attention, and a lump of apprehension filled her throat. Not again. Not now. What was that shadow that slipped swiftly between two trees above her? "Haw," sharp and urgent, brought quick response from Tank and the rest of the team, swinging them left, farther onto the ice. Then a second movement from above showed her what she was seeing.

Wolves. A pair of them, silent as the trees they threaded. Curious, one stopped, then the other. As Jessie and her team passed directly below, they stood like statues, watching their domestic cousins pull that strange thing that carried a human on its back.

The hair rose on the back of Jessie's neck. She turned her head to keep the pair in sight as long as possible.

She had never seen a wolf in the light. Many drivers had reported their glowing eyes suspended in the reflection of a headlamp, but they were almost never observed during the day. In the flat half-light these were only canine-shaped shadows, but a thrill all the same. She felt no threat; her team, having caught no scent, was oblivious.

What a gift, she thought. And only because I was alone. Two teams and they would never have appeared. She looked around carefully at the shape of the banks and the curve of the river in the soft light and thought of Jon Van Zyle's stunning impression, painted for the official 1989 Iditarod print. He had portrayed a pair of wolves on this same stretch of the Yukon.

Spirits raised, she put a tape in her Walkman and began to sing along as they moved north, gathering energy with her enthusiasm. Tank, in the lead, looked back at the sound of her voice and seemed to grin as he trotted out a little faster.

25

Date: Sunday, March 10
Race Day: Nine
Place: Kaltag checkpoint
Weather: Clearing, light to no wind
Temperature: High −11°F, low −24°F
Time: Late evening

AT SIX O'CLOCK, SCHULLER, MARTINSON, AND MURray came into Kaltag, looking as if they had left most of their consciousness on the trail somewhere. They walked around half-asleep and responded slowly to questions.

As Mick checked mandatory gear, Schuller leaned over his dogs, stripping off booties and inspecting feet. The long run over solid ice had been hard on their pads. The murmur of his voice was comfort and encouragement for the tired dogs.

"All present and accounted for, Dale. Pretty bad out there?"

"Could have been worse." Schuller groaned as he got to his feet and stretched against the ache in his back. "We may get more of it, if the reports are right."

"That's what I hear. Go on. Get 'em out of here for some rest."

Mick walked back to Martinson's team. The dogs were all spread out, exposing their bellies to the cool snow.

The big musher opened the bag and stepped clear of the sled, without looking in.

Mick went through the gear and looked up questioningly.

"Okay. Sleeping bag, ax, food, booties. Where's your trail mail, Tim?"

"Right here, in the back, in that plastic thing."

"I don't see it."

"Oh, hell. Let me." Irritated, Martinson shoved the checker aside and dug through the rear of the bag. "It was right here."

He tossed gear from the sled. When half the sled was empty and the mail had not yet appeared, he stared into the bag, as if willing this vital cargo to materialize.

"Goddamn! It's got to be here somewhere."

He frantically hurled the rest of his equipment from the sled. Cooker, clothing, a jumble of assorted items, but no mail.

"Could you have left it at the last checkpoint?" the checker ventured.

"No! Damn it. I don't take it off the sled. Ever."

It was obvious that, exhausted and frustrated, he was approaching explosion. Rapidly, he went through the whole pile once more.

"Son of a bitch!" he shouted, throwing a boot ten feet into a snowbank. "Some bastard son of a bitch stole my mail."

"Tim." Mick tried to get the musher's attention as a bag of jerky followed the boot. "Tim, hold on. Take it easy. Go through it again. Or, better yet, let someone else. We'll call Eagle Island and check." He looked across the crowd that had gathered to watch and meet Alex's eyes beseechingly.

Knowing it would only make the situation worse to intervene, Jensen shook his head.

"Shit," said the checker. "Somebody go wake up Holman."

It was a bleary race marshall who staggered from the checkpoint house five minutes later.

"Found it yet, Tim?" he asked.

"No, goddamn it. Hell, no. Somebody fuckin' stole it."

"Aw, you don't know that."

"Well, it's not here and I sure as hell didn't take it out."

Okay. Let's take it from the top. Without all your mandatory stuff, I can't let you go on. The ham's trying to raise Eagle Island. If it's there, maybe we can get it flown up, but you'll have to wait. If it's not . . . we'll have to disqualify you."

All the starch and bluster seemed to go out of the big musher. Without a word, he sat down on his sled, his head in his hands.

Holman stood looking down at him, silent. In the minute or two before Mick came out of the checkpoint shaking his head, nobody moved. It was so quiet that the sound of Martinson's ragged breathing was the only thing Alex could hear, except for the whine of a faraway snow machine.

Matt stepped forward to lay one hand on the musher's shoulder. "Tim," he said, almost tenderly. "Tim, I'm sorry. It's not here."

At this point, half an hour after the first three, T. J. Harvey pulled up the bluff to park his sled beside Gail Murray, who was still waiting to be checked in.

He looked at Martinson, sitting dejectedly on his sled, and asked Murray, "What's going on?"

"What a bummer," he said when she explained. "And he doesn't have any idea what happened to it? Could he have lost it somewhere?"

"Not likely, the way he takes care of his stuff. You know how picky he is."

"Yeah."

Mick was now going through Gail's sled, and she breathed a sigh of relief as he checked off her trail mail and other required items. Leaving her team, she went into the checkpoint to see how much space there was for drying gear.

The checker started on Harvey's sled bag. Like Schuller, the musher worked with his dogs while he waited. Martinson, finally on his feet, carelessly shoved gear back onto his sled.

After a minute of rummaging through Harvey's bag, Mick stepped back, a puzzled expression on his face.

"T.J.," he said. "Ah . . . come here a second, will you?"

"What?" They both looked into the bag.

"Is this yours?" The checker held up a plastic container of Iditarod mail.

"Yeah, sure."

"Then, is this, too?" He held up a second container, exactly like the first.

"Huh?" Harvey's mouth dropped open. "Where'd you get that?"

"Here, in your bag."

Martinson, hearing the astonishment in Harvey's voice, looked up to see Mick holding both containers. He lunged toward Harvey, grabbing the front of his parka.

"You bastard!" he yelled.

With one powerful swing, he punched the other musher in the face, dropping him into the snow beside his sled.

Then Jensen did step in, as did Caswell, who had come out of the checkpoint. They grabbed Martinson before he could swing again. With the help of the checker, they held him as he struggled to reach the fallen man.

T.J.'s nose bled profusely down the front of his parka as he sat up and wiped at it with the back of one hand. "Hey," he said, groggily. "Hey. I didn't . . ."

"You stole my mail!" Martinson roared, trying to throw off the troopers. "Should have fuckin' got rid of it, you son of a bitch."

Holman came rapidly around the sled to help Harvey to his feet.

"Tim!" he shouted, standing between the two mushers. "Martinson. *Shut up*. Calm down. Give us a chance, we'll sort it out. Just shut up and get inside."

Martinson finally gave up and allowed himself to be pushed into the checkpoint, still swearing. Holman followed with Harvey who wiped at his nose with a grubby bandana.

By separating the two, it was possible to question Harvey without interruptions from Martinson, but no clear answer came from the session. T.J. swore he hadn't known there were two containers in his sled, had never seen the second one. In fact, no one could tell which had originally been his. They both looked exactly alike.

"All I know," he told Alex, "is that when I checked into Eagle Island yesterday, I had all my required gear, including the mail. If the other one was in my sled, no one noticed it."

"Was anyone near your sled at that checkpoint?" Jensen asked.

"Could have been. We didn't sit around outside to watch them, with the wind howling all night long. Everybody went in and out to check on the teams."

Later, Gail Murray put in a word for T.J.

"I really don't think he knew it was there," she said. "You don't know him like we do. Besides, why didn't he get rid of it, like Tim said? Pretty dumb to leave it in his bag for the checker."

"What about Martinson?" Alex asked her. "Would he put it in Harvey's bag to blow it for him?"

"And risk being disqualified? I don't think so."

"Got any other ideas?"

She had to admit she hadn't.

Holman allowed both men to continue the race, conditionally. They were to avoid each other and, he told Martinson, if there was any attempt at all toward Harvey, he would instantly be disqualified. The threat seemed a sufficiently effective restraint.

"If there's one thing Tim's worried about it's not being allowed to finish the race," Matt said to Alex later. "He wants to win it more than anything. Don't think he'll take chances."

By the time Jessie and Mike arrived an hour later, an uneasy truce had been achieved. Exhausted, cold, and windburned, they ran their dogs into town as the still angry musher stumped off to care for his team. Jessie looked more worn than Jensen had yet seen her, but so did they all. There was a smile of greeting on her face when she saw him. He wanted to hug her, but, because of the crowd around the checker, contented himself with returning the smile.

"How long here?" he asked, walking with her to a spot near Solomon where she could rest her dogs. She was buoyed up by the performance of her team.

"Three hours," she answered. "Fifth. We're fifth, Alex, and only an hour behind Schuller. Three hours of dog rest is enough."

"And you?"

"Well, no. But if it's a choice between sleep and winning, I can sleep when it's over. It's only three days to Nome. Besides, even fifth would give me enough money to run again next year. Fifteen thousand."

Where does she get it? he wondered again. Where do any of them?

"I saw wolves this morning," she told him. "Oh, Alex, they were incredible. Dark shadows on the bank above us. They didn't seem to be afraid at all, just stood there watching us go by. It was like a dream."

"How many?"

"A pair, like Van Zyle's print. I wish you could have seen them."

Watching to see his reaction, she stumbled over a rut in the packed snow. He reached quickly to keep her from falling.

"Thanks," she said, regaining her balance. "It's like being on a boat. You get off and everything goes on moving for a while."

He stood looking down at her, his hands still on her shoulders.

"God," she said. "I'm so gone I can't even walk, but I'm glad you're here."

As he pulled her close, he caught a glimpse of Solomon's shy grin over her shoulder.

"I know I can't help you. But is there anything I can do?" he asked when he let her go.

"You dear man. I've got to feed the gang first, but then I would trade half of them for a hot cup of tea with lots of sugar."

"You got it."

26

Date: Sunday, March 10
Race Day: Nine
Place: Between Kaltag and Unalakleet checkpoints (ninety miles)
Weather: Clear, increasing wind
Temperature: High −11°F, low −24°F
Time: Late evening

UNEXPECTEDLY, THE WEATHER HELD AS THE RACE leaders pushed on to Unalakleet, over the Kaltag Portage from the Yukon River to the coast of the Bering Sea. The crest of the Nulato Hills and a rolling series of ridges called the Whalebacks were the only obstructions, easy to cross. The trail ran up the Kaltag River, through a low east-west pass, and down the Unalakleet River, past Old Woman Mountain.

The route, centuries old, is used by the people of the interior to reach the sea. It marks the dividing line between two groups of native residents: the coastal Inupiat Eskimos and the Athabaskan Indians of the interior.

Schuller and Martinson left Kaltag together at nine o'clock in the evening. This time, however, they were closely followed, not only by Murray and Harvey, but by Cranshaw, Solomon, and Arnold as well, all driving hard, increasing the pressure. Ellis and Banks were close behind them.

During the three-hour rest at Kaltag, Bomber approached Mike and Jessie to offer a stiff half-apology for his temper tantrum in McGrath and ask to join them. Alex watched uneasily as the three of them left together. He studied each leader intently as they left, knowing one of them had to be responsible for the murders. When they had all gone the three troopers loaded the plane and prepared to make the hop from Kaltag to the coast, hoping the wind would not be too strong for them to land in Unalakleet, where the wind had been known to blow planes off the runway before they could taxi to a stop.

Less than half an hour after the last sled disappeared to the west, the wind dropped and seemed to be holding its breath. The storm still threatened. Trailbreakers reported from Unalakleet that the trail was in excellent condition, although the snow was a little deeper than usual. Unless the weather changed, it would take the mushers approximately fourteen hours to make the ninety-mile trip to the largest village community anywhere along the Iditarod Trail.

As the three troopers flew in the dark, they could see none of the mushers on the trail. Other than twice spotting the bobbing light of a headlamp, Alex saw nothing until the lights of Unalakleet appeared on the western horizon.

They had no trouble landing and tied the plane down securely before finding their way to the checkpoint. Although the lodge that doubled as a hotel was crowded with race followers, the troopers managed to get a room that had a single bed. Two of them would sleep on the floor. Jensen insisted Caswell take the bed, reminding him that he wanted a fully alert pilot.

"If the weather takes the turn they keep warning us about, I don't want to take any more chances. I want you rested."

"If it does, we'll be drinking lots of coffee and waiting for it to clear," Caswell reminded him. "There's absolutely nothing to stop that wind all the way from Russia, cold as Stalin's heart."

Late as it was, the lodge was full of noisy people eager for the race to reach them in the morning. The café was crowded, but, as Unalakleet was a dry community, it served no alcohol. This didn't put a damper on the high spirits of those who awaited the first mushers, and Jensen suspected an outside supply. As the race drew closer to the finish line, tension increased, not only among the racers and their teams, but also for those following their progress. For the next few days rules would relax somewhat and authority would look the other way, as long as a semblance of order was maintained.

The troopers crowded themselves into chairs around a small table, which they shared with the ham operator on a break and Holman, who had flown in earlier in the evening, seemingly recovered from his Yukon River trials. Conversation slowed as they turned their attention to enormous bowls of firehouse chili. Starved for greens, Alex stared in disappointment at the small bowl of shredded lettuce and carrots, topped with one limp slice of tomato, that the waitress set in front of him.

"Lucky to get that," Holman told him with a grin, "Each tomato and lettuce leaf comes in by plane from Anchorage. Might as well ask for gold."

Stuffed and blinking with fatigue, Caswell agreed with Alex that sleep was next on the agenda, and they left Becker talking with Holman. Alex heard the young trooper come in sometime later to crawl into his sleeping bag. It roused him slightly, and he lay for a few minutes listening to the small sounds from downstairs. Some of the fans were still enthusiastically anticipating tomorrow's racers.

Lying on his back, staring at the dark ceiling, he tried to let his mind drift and not think of the case. He remembered that in the morning he would have been on the trail a week. *Who is it?* It seemed much longer and yet not as much as a week. *Had to be Cranshaw or Martinson.* The whole race, with its competition and the celebration it inspired in the villages through which it passed, seemed isolated from anything else that could be happening in the rest of the world. *Although there was nothing specific on either of them.* He realized he had not seen a paper or a televised news broadcast since he'd left Palmer and hadn't missed them. *Maybe they should be looking at Schuller again? Harvey? Murray?* Caught up in the case and the race itself, he felt suspended in time, as if, when he returned, things would simply pick up where he had left them and go on without a break. *Damn it.* His eyes flew open once more as he huffed with irritation and turned on his left side. If he couldn't sleep, he might as well try to find some answers.

Three people had died and one had come close. This was no dream. Carefully he reviewed the mushers he still felt any reason to suspect. Could he find anything in what he knew of their characters to help solve the problem?

Martinson and Cranshaw still headed his list, but how about the others?

Dale Schuller, who was so quietly focused on the race that he seemed to have almost no personality away from his dogs and sled, was competently going about the business of reaching Nome first, if possible, keeping strictly to himself. Or was he? But he couldn't have run the moose into Jessie and Ryan.

Gail Murray seemed too long a shot for the same reason, but there was nothing else she could not have been responsible for. She certainly kept a low profile, but she defended Harvey actively enough, which seemed out of character for a murder candidate. Unless she was very smart. Still . . .

T. J. Harvey. He too was out of position for the moose, and would he really have forgotten to remove the mail container from his sled if he had taken it at Eagle Island? There must have been all kinds of opportunity to discard it between there and Kaltag, where it had been found. Or had Martinson set him up? Harvey and Ellis were both hard to suspect of stashing the plastic PCP container on Murray's sled, considering that they had been running hard for McGrath before taking their twenty-fours. Harvey seemed likeable enough, cooperative and good-humored. How could you tell, seeing him only on his way in and out of checkpoints?

Oh, hell. Again he sighed and rolled over. He would think about Jessie and leave the case alone till morning. Wonder where she is? *I'm trying to put up a fence without posts, like I warned Becker.* Her hair is like silk. *These other mushers just don't fit in right.* Wish she was here, right here, warm against me. Hmmm.

Intuition screamed that it was either Cranshaw or

Martinson, but which? There appeared to be a remarkable sense of inferiority lurking somewhere in both men. Neither exhibited the generosity that comes from self-respect and confidence.

Whichever, the whole motivation rose from trying to win the race without earning it; to run the hypothetically shortest distance possible, a direct line, between the start and finish without traveling the long curve of reality, which meant competing against better racers. If you can't beat them, eliminate them.

From his experience with other criminals, he had learned to expect and watch for inordinate selfishness. They wanted what they wanted immediately, easily, without waiting or paying the price. Seemed to assume they deserved it, that they were special, above paying their dues.

Uninspired, he shifted again from one side to the other in his bag.

Phil Becker's disembodied whisper floated through the dark, snatching him out of his contemplation.

"If you don't stop thrashing and go to sleep, I'm going to throw the nearest boot."

The pounding of a boot on the door dragged him from the bright dream of a swift-flowing Idaho stream and three trout on the bank as he fought to land a fourth. Becker opened the door for Holman, who stomped in with three cups of coffee, his voice like an alarm clock.

"Hey. Rise and shine. Got something for you, Jensen. McGrath called when we cranked up the radio. Got a Takotna trapper says he saw a guy on a snow machine just about the time that moose stomped hell out of Ryan. Passed him on the trail headed southwest. Description fits Martinson, right down to the parka color. Whadda you think?"

"Jesus, said Becker.

Alex pulled on his jeans and reached for coffee. "Did he see the face? Could he identify him again?"

"Seems to think so. Says it was a big guy, dark, with heavy eyebrows."

Calculating rapidly, Alex drank half the cup and began to pack his pipe. "You got a supply plane coming in anytime soon that could bring him up here before Martinson leaves?"

"One here that could hop back and get him, but it'd be faster to find one out of McGrath and skip the return."

"Right. How long?"

"Early afternoon, easy. Martinson'll get in here about noon and have six hours' layover."

"Let's do it. We'll pay the freight, whatever it is. This could be the break. Nail him cold before he has a clue."

27

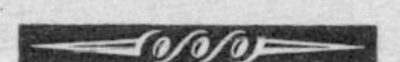

Date: Monday, March 11
Race Day: Ten
Place: Unalakleet checkpoint
Weather: Overcast, increasing wind
Temperature: High −10°F, low −21°F
Time: Noon

THE FIRST SEVEN CAME INTO TOWN WITHIN AN HOUR and twenty minutes of one another, at noon. Martinson had jumped over Schuller for a ten minute lead, but he dropped two of his dogs as soon as he arrived. He was now down to twelve, while Schuller still had fourteen.

Half an hour later, Jessie arrived in third place, having passed Bomber, Harvey, and Murray. Harvey was next, with Bomber right behind him. Murray and Solomon completed the group at twelve forty-five. All Jessie's dogs looked strong. Murray dropped one. So did Harvey and Solomon.

Race regulations required a six-hour stop before the last, long run up the coast, Everyone wanted to get it over with, catch some much-needed rest, and head out. They were all leaving room for strategy in the last 270 miles.

The mushers began to sort their gear, taking only what was required and necessary for the next two days, leaving anything they could spare, to lighten their sleds. Every ounce counted. Three of them—Murray, Martinson, and Arnold—changed to the lighter sleds they had had shipped in.

With so many mushers in town at once and the outcome still in question, village excitement soared. School let out for the day and children ran everywhere. As each musher came into town the siren sounded and church bells rang to announce them. In front of the lodge, it seemed that all five hundred residents, plus out-of-towners, stood around assessing the relative merits of the teams as they checked in. Between arrivals they wandered back and forth, watching the ice of the Unalakleet River for more arrivals.

The sun came out shortly after noon, but the wind picked up, whipping snow from the ground. Clouds soon replaced sunshine, and the chill factor drove many indoors. They knew it would be several hours before more racers made their way over the portage.

Before going into the checkpoint, Becker asked Holman about the dogs that had been dropped. Only one, Martinson's, looked really tired. The other four seemed capable of continuing, even eager.

"None of 'em'll finish with all the mutts still in harness," Matt told him. "It's time to leave the slow ones. Team can only go as fast as the slowest. Some of these dogs're running their first Iditarod, training, sort of. Or they're older and slowing down some. Next two or three villages, they'll all leave mutts. The winner'll probably make Nome with just the eight or ten fastest.

"They'll drive the teams hard, really push. It'll be

a sprint soon. There'll be almost no rest for dogs or mushers till the finish. They need their strongest and best. Dogs can take it. They're tough. Drivers have to hope they are, too."

At two o'clock, the plane carrying the Takotna trapper set down neatly on the strip, despite the crosswind. Half Athabaskan, short and spare, Joe Garcia greeted them with a nod. Jensen thought it a strange name for the interior of Alaska, but all kinds of men got gold fever in the old days. They snow machined him to the hotel and went up the back stairs, to avoid meeting Martinson. Garcia sat on the bed, drinking coffee and nodding as Alex explained the setup.

At two-thirty Holman called a mushers' meeting in the room next door, ignoring complaints from the racers. The room was crowded with seven mushers, Holman, and the checker when Alex accompanied Garcia through the connecting door.

In the silence of suspended conversation, the trapper looked carefully at each face, narrowing his eyes.

"See anyone you recognize?" Jensen asked quietly.

Once more the sharp eyes assessed the gathering, then turned back to Cranshaw. Raising his hand, he leveled one bony finger in Bomber's direction.

"Him. Lives in McGrath. The rest? No. No one I know."

"Nobody you've seen?" Jensen pressed.

"No. The man I saw on the trail is not here."

As quickly as it had materialized, their lead disappeared. In the room now empty of mushers, Jensen fumed in frustration, kicked a chair, and dropped dejectedly onto the bed.

"Goddamn it, Cas. I thought we had him."

"Yeah."

"Who the hell did he see on that snow machine? There's not one other musher in this group who fits the description. Could it be an outsider? Have we focused on the wrong people?"

"You really think so?"

"No, damn it. Just a hunch, not fact."

"Well, we could stop the race. Impound the sleds, body search everyone, question them all till something shakes out."

"And still come up empty, maybe. No. I don't like that either, but we've confronted them as a group here. Whoever it is may go cautious on us now."

"Or desperate."

"Yeah."

Impatiently finishing the six-hour stop, Jessie watched Martinson leave, then Schuller. She finished packing her sled and talked to Solomon as she waited.

"Sorry, Jessie," he told her. "You'll have to go ahead from here. Just isn't my year. My mutts aren't as fast as yours."

"I'm sorry too, Mike. Third—I really didn't think it would happen, and my guys still look good."

They did. All eleven dogs were healthy and ready to run. Already hitched to the sled, they waited at the checkpoint for the last thirty minutes to tick by. Although some of them lay down in their harness, all were watching closely for Jessie to step onto the runners. Tank got to his feet each time she passed the back of the sled but finally sat down, half-ready, his tail sweeping snow.

"Listen, Jess. They still haven't got whoever's trying to wreck the race, and I think it's still dangerous out there." His back toward the checkpoint, Solomon opened his parka to reveal a handgun in his belt. "You need this? You have one?"

"Thanks, Mike." She leaned close to avoid being overheard. "I have one. But you're a good friend. Thanks."

The checker came up. With her hidden gun, Jessie suddenly felt like a thug.

"Ready?" he asked. "Five minutes to blast-off."

She hugged Solomon and went forward to talk up her dogs, now all on their feet, sensing imminent departure. Tank woofed and strained at his harness as she ruffled his fur. "Good boy. Want to go, huh? Okay." She gave a pat and a word of encouragement to each dog, then stepped onto the runners and pulled the snow hook.

"All right. Let's go guys. Take 'em out, Tank." The team leaped forward, heading swiftly north.

As they pulled away, she saw Alex standing on the steps of the lodge. As he waved, she grinned. Taking off a mitten, she held up one index finger, indicating her intention to make it to Nome first, and was rewarded with his smile.

Watching her go, Jensen didn't feel much of the smile. There was a coldness in the pit of his stomach.

He, too, was thinking about guns. Jessie's had never reappeared. Now he wished he were going with her, knowing Solomon was not. She was going to be very much alone, with Cranshaw and Harvey directly behind her.

Alex felt strongly that if anything else was going to happen, it would be soon, possibly in the approaching darkness on the forty miles between Unalakleet and Shaktoolik, or the following fifty-eight-mile run to Koyuk.

"What's the weather prediction, Ben?" he asked Caswell, who stood beside him.

"Not looking good. The wind is supposed to pick up, and another storm is headed for the coast, due to hit soon."

"Have we got time to make another hop up the coast?"

"If we leave right away, we could make Koyuk, maybe Elim. We'll have to watch it, though."

As soon as they could load the plane and warm it up, they took off. Holman, also heading for Koyuk, waved them off and went to help a reporter load video equipment into a Cessna 185 Skywagon for the short trip.

The view from the air was spectacular. Still well below the Arctic Circle, the sea freezes out from the shore each winter. As it freezes, the force of the tide, combined with driving wind, cracks and moves the ice, shoving up giant blocks and breaking it apart to expose open water, which then refreezes. Until it gains solidity deep into the winter, the frozen sea is frightening, creaturelike, as it groans and barks in its own violent voice. Later, during the most intense cold, it creaks with the tide in a deep vibration, talking in its restless sleep, waiting for spring to wake and break it again.

From Unalakleet to Shaktoolik the trail runs mostly over land, following the slight curve of the shore. To reach Koyuk, however, mushers must venture onto the sleeping ice giant of Norton Sound.

Although the line between land and sea ice is not obvious, somehow the mushers know when they have crossed onto the sound. For those running their first race, the knowledge that far below their sled runners lies ocean, with its impermanently subdued salt water, makes them feel small and vulnerable. A feeling of danger and the transience of nature inspires an almost giddy sense of relief when the crossing is over. Experienced mushers respect the ice bridges between Shaktoolik and Nome, never quite losing their awareness of the power of the sea over which they travel.

Jensen, Becker, and Caswell watched in silent awe as they passed over, barely able to pick out the line of stakes and tripod markers carefully laid by the trailblazers to guide the racers across. They looked like toothpicks in the snow, flagged with the familiar pink surveyors' tape, only visible when they were flying low.

"Jesus," whispered Becker. "You couldn't pay me enough."

Jensen remembered the race won by Libby Riddles. She made this crossing alone in a severe storm, bravely walking into the face of the wind, creating enough of a lead to break away from the rest of the field. He had wondered at the guys who elected to stay safe in Shaktoolik. Now he suddenly realized what an incredible thing Riddles had done, brave or foolish, when she crossed, foot by foot, from one marker to the next, giving herself the edge. He no longer questioned the wisdom of those who waited it out.

They were approaching Koyuk when he realized he could not see the ground. A white fog had blown in from the west. Glancing toward Caswell, he discovered a frown on the pilot's face. At that moment the plane took a slight drop and began to dance, vibrating slightly.

He felt his stomach lurch.

"We got problems, Cas?"

"Not yet, but I want to see that gravel strip soon.

The storm is about to hit. Check your belts, guys. I don't want one of you in my lap. This may get worse before I can set it down."

Alex looked back to see Becker, wide-eyed. He grinned.

"Don't sweat it. If Cas can't get us down, no one can. Right?"

"Right. Why doesn't that make me feel better?"

The motion of the plane now subsided into irregular jerks and bounces as they flew north, searching for the lights of the village.

Caswell could be heard speaking into his microphone, but to Jensen's untrained ears it was mostly uninterpretable pilotese, interrupted by jounces.

"Can't you reach anyone?" Becker asked.

"All the villages from here to Nome are uncontrolled landing sites," Caswell told him. "That means you're on your own. No radios, except for other pilots. I got through to Unalakleet, thinking we'd better turn around and head back. They've closed the strip. The storm has blown in there already. It seems to be coming in from the south, following us up the coast. We'll have to make a run for it, find a place to land as soon as we can. Koyuk's out. Wind's too strong and I don't want to waste the time. We'll aim for Elim, but I think we're going to wind up in Nome. They have radio and can talk us down if they have to."

With that, he turned his attention to the plane. For what seemed like an interminable amount of time they slid around the sky, heading mostly west. The wind picked up, tossing them in unexpected directions.

Cinching his safety harness as tight as possible, Alex tried to keep his knees and elbows out of Caswell's way and to ignore his stomach. That became almost impossible when Becker lost his lunch into an evidence bag, but he managed to control himself until the ventilation system could remove most of the unsettling odor.

Caswell paid attention to nothing but keeping them airborne. Always impressed with his fellow trooper's flying skills, Alex now realized the true extent of his ability. He responded so quickly to movements of the wind-driven machine that he seemed to anticipate them. Perhaps he did.

If I don't live through this, I'll never blame Cas, he thought. He knew by the absurdity of the thought just how scared he really was.

It grew darker, and it seemed as if they had been thrown around the cockpit for hours. Jensen's right arm began to ache from hitting the door. Becker was moaning quietly from the rear seat when Caswell began to speak tensely into the microphone. Another ten minutes and the jouncing gentled slightly. Straightening in his seat, Alex looked down to see lights under him.

"Nome," Caswell said, and he continued his tense communications on the radio. As the ground came up beneath them, Alex could see how much they were still being blown around. The strip moved up and down as Cas fought to bring the plane into contact with its surface. They bounced three times and slid sideways as they taxied in, Cas fighting every inch. Two figures in parkas ran to throw their weight against the plane, and another directed Cas into the shelter of a small hangar. They stopped moving, and Caswell was out the door in an instant to make sure the halt was permanent.

Alex opened his own door, stumbled out onto the ground, and threw up.

"Who the hell taught you to fly like that?" he asked Caswell as they unloaded the secured Maule M-4.

"A guy in Anchorage named Bunker, who knows more than I'll ever learn. Why? You want a lesson?"

"Not in a million years. But I'd sure like to shake his hand."

28

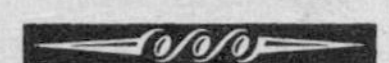

Date: Monday, March 11
Race Day: Ten
Place: Nome checkpoint and between Shaktoolik and Koyuk checkpoints (fifty-eight miles)
Weather: Blizzard conditions, blowing snow and heavy winds
Temperature: High −19°F, low −27°F
Time: Early evening

"BUT I DON'T WANT TO BE IN NOME, DAMN IT," JENsen told Sergeant Ken Carpenter of Detachment D, Nome Post. "If anything happens, it will be back down the trail. There's got to be some way to get to Koyuk or Elim, even White Mountain."

The tall, half-Eskimo trooper in charge shook his head and tried again to explain, but he wasn't saying what Jensen wanted to hear.

"Alex," Caswell interjected. "There's just no way. As long as this storm has us socked in, you can't get anywhere. You know that, you just don't like it. I don't either, but there is nothing, I repeat, nothing, we can do about it."

Jensen stopped, leaned on the desk, and took a deep

breath. Then he apologized to Carpenter, and to Caswell, for good measure.

After taking care of the plane and collecting their gear, they had taken a cab directly to Carpenter's office, where he was working late, in case of trouble. Iditarod week in Nome is the biggest event of the year, and half the population, plus more than a thousand nonresident race fans, was crowded into the local bars in celebration of the approaching finish. With several hundred folks thoroughly awash with alcohol, there was always some trouble—seldom anything serious, but something.

The ground blizzard was now howling through town. The few people on the street scurried from one shelter to the next, clutching one another to avoid being blown off their feet. The south side of Front Street turns its back on the sea, but the blizzard thrust its frigid fingers between buildings. Out on the ice, a person turning his back on such a storm would actually feel his breath being sucked from his lungs by the strange vacuum created by the wind.

Inside the drinking establishments of Nome, from the Polaris to the Breakers and on down to the Board of Trade, bands imported from Anchorage pulsed loud enough to drown the sound of the wind, as well as any serious attempt at conversation. Dance floors, little larger than a barn door, were packed with gyrating patrons. Hobo Jim, a regular in the Nome Iditarod celebration, sang repeatedly, "I did, I did, I did the Iditarod Trail," as the crowd clapped and loudly followed along.

Alex would notice all this later. Now he turned and dropped into a chair.

"Okay," he said. "I give up. We wait. But let's

figure out what's available to us. Can we get through on the radio?"

Caswell and Carpenter gave each other a look to decide who told him the rest of the bad news. Carpenter lost.

"Very iffy," he stalled. "Depends on the conditions between here and there. We can try. We can also keep in touch with Iditarod headquarters here, to see what they get."

Cas tackled the issue head-on. "The best we can do right now is hope this blows itself out in less than a week. We might as well find something to eat and get some sleep."

"A week?"

"It has been known to happen. We are damned lucky to be here. And, believe me, no one is running on the trail in this. They will hole up in the closest checkpoint and wait it out. Just like us."

"Good God. I hope so."

He had no way of knowing how the night would be spent by mushers on the ice of Norton Sound, between Shaktoolik and Koyuk.

Arriving in Shaktoolik late in the evening, after a cold, windy, but reasonable run from Unalakleet, Jessie found Schuller and Martinson still at the checkpoint, debating a move on Koyuk. While she fed and cared for her dogs, they decided to wait and see if the wind would lessen early in the morning. All three of them went to get some sleep.

Two hours later, as if it had tired of toying with them, the wind abated. Staying with a friend, Jessie woke to, if not the sound of silence she hoped for, at least a comparative quiet. Going out to check, she found both men readying their teams for departure.

"If this holds we can get across most of the ice," Schuller told her.

"Naw," said Martinson, seemingly in a better mood. "We're just getting some practice packing sleds. Go back to bed."

"Right behind you," she replied instantly, knowing it was a make or break situation. If she allowed them to get ahead of her and was blocked by a returning storm, she would forfeit all possibility of winning. So tired she could hardly stand, she started preparations of her own.

"We're almost ready. Won't wait for you."

"I don't remember asking you to."

Schuller grinned and went back to booting his dogs.

In thirty minutes they were gone. She followed them ten minutes later, having booted her dogs and, hurriedly, packed her sled. On each trip into the house, she was almost overcome by its warmth. She ignored the temptation to linger. Protests from her friend had no effect on her determination, but she was grateful for several thick ham sandwiches and a thermos of well-sugared coffee, which, stashed inside her parka, disappeared with her into the dark and onto the ice.

For the next hour and a half, she followed the tracks of the two mushers, who ran before her. Several times she thought she saw a headlamp behind her, but she had no way of knowing who it could be. If the order had been maintained, it would be T.J., but now that it was really a race, it could be Bomber or Gail Murray, who were also pushing hard. She hoped it was the latter, but was soon distracted by the wind as it began to rise once again.

Soon it was blowing so hard that it wiped out the

tracks on the trail in front of her as effectively as if they had never been made. The only thing that made forward progress possible was the emergence, from the white nightmare the wind had become, of the trail markers, one after another, spaced more than a hundred feet apart. Most of these were simply slats stuck into the snow, but a few, regularly spaced, were tripod markers, a little easier to spot in the whirling storm.

Slowly, walking ahead of her team, Jessie found each marker. It grew worse until finally she couldn't see the next one. Stopping the team, she moved forward until she located it, then went back for the dogs. She remembered reading Riddles's account of her perilous crossing in the same kind of weather. It encouraged her, as did the fact that, somewhere to the north, Schuller and Martinson also struggled through the maelstrom.

She stopped periodically beside each dog to wipe away the snow that packed their fur and coated their faces. She could feel it on her own cheeks and tried to keep the tunnel of her parka hood turned away from the direct force of the wind. She was sure the wind chill had dropped to well below minus fifty in the gusts she estimated at seventy miles per hour. She pulled a ski mask from her sled pack, put it on, and pulled her hood back up. Her hands and feet were warm, but she paid close attention to them. Hypothermia could catch up in a matter of minutes in this kind of cold.

Slowly, they proceeded along the trail of sticks. The name of the game now was patience and care. Care not to freeze, not to get off the trail, not to panic. She wondered how far ahead Schuller and Martinson were, and how far she could go. It was over fifty miles from Shaktoolik to Koyuk. How far could she possibly have come? In the hour and a half before the storm hit, perhaps fifteen miles. The dogs were still moving well, but soon she would have to camp, wait until morning, and hope that this blew over, even a little.

Once again she left the team to go forward and find the marker. As she went back to call the dogs, a trick of the wind stratified the snow. For just an instant, she thought she saw the light again. Next to a tilted slat, she waited. Again she saw it, sure this time it was real. Who was back there? Harvey? Cranshaw? Or someone else? Suddenly she was frightened. If she was forced off the trail for any reason in this weather, she could be lost, buried in snow and never found. Breakup in the spring would send her body into the sea with the rest of the ice.

She now moved forward with more purpose, working carefully so as not to go too fast or miss any vital element in what was fast becoming flight. One mistake could cost her everything. Drive as far as possible, she thought, keeping the last marker in sight until she could see the next one. If I can't see it, stop the dogs, walk ahead to find it, return and drive forward once more. Keep moving. She didn't want to know who was on the trail behind her. Better to stay ahead.

This is crazy, she thought. It's got to be T.J. or Bomber. But what if it isn't? Worse—what if it is and one of them is the killer in the pack? Suddenly she felt completely isolated, alone in a way she didn't like.

She remembered Holman's borrowed gun. At the next marker, she put it in the pocket of her parka, along with the box of shells.

What seemed like hours had passed, and whoever

followed her hadn't caught up. Tired, hungry, and desperate, she was still moving one marker at a time. Everything seemed unreal. The last time she had cleaned his face, Tank had whined and licked her hand. Although she had switched him with her second-best leader to give him a break, she knew she couldn't keep the dogs going much longer.

Stumbling forward, she tried to shield her face with her mittened hand as she looked for the tripod that should be there. Instead, a large lump of snow came into view, the size of a packing crate.

"Cruiser. Tank. Come on guys," she shouted to the dogs.

Suddenly the lump moved, startling her back away from it. The head and shoulders of a man appeared above it. A hooded figure stepped around and moved toward her.

In panic, she turned to run away, tripped, and fell. The figure reached to help her up. She recognized Dale Schuller's green parka as he put his mouth close to her ear and yelled to be heard over the howl of the wind.

"Jessie? That you?"

Relief flooded through her, weakening her knees.

"Oh God, it's you, Dale. Thank God."

She didn't bother to share her fears of the last few hours.

Schuller and Martinson had turned their sleds on their sides and crawled in between for some protection. Now they pulled Jessie's around beside theirs, creating a three-sided shelter. Dumping almost everything from the sled bags, they piled the gear against the runners, heavy stuff on top so the rest wouldn't blow away. They put anything flat down between the sleds to keep their sleeping bags off the snow. With some effort they tied a piece of canvas onto the stanchions to form a makeshift roof.

Taking turns within the limited space in the dark, they struggled to remove as much of their cold outer clothing as possible, put on something dry, and climb into their heavy cold-weather sleeping bags. They managed somehow, knowing that if they didn't, their frozen clothes would thaw as they rested, drenching the bags and leaving them vulnerable to the cold.

Trying to pull up her bag's zipper, Jessie thought her cold fingers would fall off, but she grew a little warmer as she lay still, letting her body heat warm the bag and her mittens, which she had placed under her to dry out. Remembering the sandwiches and coffee, she shared them with the other two. Although by now the sandwiches were half-frozen, nothing could have tasted better. The coffee, still warm from the thermos, helped thaw them.

Huddled as close as possible, they all gradually grew warm enough to doze.

Before settling into restless sleep next to Schuller, Jessie shouted to him over the howl of the storm. "Someone has been behind me for a long time without catching up. I kept seeing the light."

He shouted back. "It's probably T.J. If he shows up we'll let him in. Don't worry. It won't do any good. He'll be okay."

The last thing she thought about as she drifted into exhausted sleep was the terror that had clutched her earlier and how glad she was that these two were in the middle of Norton Bay. It would have been easy to miss them. She hoped it was T.J. behind them, but she felt sorry for him if it was.

29

Date: Tuesday, March 12
Race Day: Eleven
Place: Between Shaktoolik and Elim checkpoints (106 miles)
Weather: Overcast, decreasing wind
Temperature: High −14°F, low −21°F
Time: Early morning

AFTER FOUR HOURS OF FITFUL SLEEP, THEY WOKE TO find the storm had died again. It was warmer, and so dark in the shelter of the sleds that Jessie thought she had only slept a few minutes. When Schuller pushed at the canvas roof, wind-packed snow cascaded from it, allowing light and cold wind into their retreat.

They struggled out of their warm sleeping bags and back into cold parkas, pants, and boots. When Jessie stood up to yank on an extra wool sweater, she looked out to find them alone in a world of endless white. Not a dog was in sight, but close to the jury-rigged shelter was a barely perceptible set of tracks. Someone had passed them as they slept.

Martinson whistled and shouted his leader's name. In a moment three teams of dogs were shaking themselves out of snow-covered resting places, where they had slept warmly buried, tails to noses. Their survival had been less at risk than that of their human companions.

"Should we get a fire going?" she asked Tim Martinson.

"With what?"

"I've got some charcoal somewhere, and a can of Blazo."

"Too much trouble. Let's cold-snack the dogs and run on into Koyuk while the wind's down."

Schuller agreed and Jessie was glad, not really wanting to fuss with the usual routine. The dogs would be fine. There would be hot coffee and food at the checkpoint.

All the gear from the sleds was buried under drifted snow. They dug it out, repacked, and went on, taking turns breaking trail. The going wasn't so bad in the dim, early light, especially with the tracks to follow.

"Wonder who it was?" Schuller said just before they took off.

"And why he didn't stop," Jessie added.

"Wanted to get a jump on us," Martinson determined, "and it worked."

"Doesn't look like Harvey. He's pushing that toboggan rig, and it doesn't drag like this. It might be Bomber's."

When they came off the ice at Koyuk, Schuller's speculation proved correct. Bomber Cranshaw's sled was parked at the checkpoint. Inside, he was cleaning up an enormous breakfast of sourdough pancakes, eggs, and sausage, which made Jessie almost break her rule of always feeding her dogs before herself. She warmed her hands and face quickly and went back out to care for them.

Martinson finished feeding his twelve and disappeared toward the food. Jessie, caring for eleven, wasn't far behind him, but everything seemed to take hours. She was working on the dogs' feet when Schuller stopped beside her.

"Hey, Jess. Can you spare any of that super goop you put on your mutts' paws? Old Betsy has a problem with a front foot. The boot tore last night, and she picked up some grainy snow between the second and third pads. Got a pretty deep split in the webbing. Your stuff really worked on Widget during the Kusko."

"Sure, Dale," she said and handed him the tube.

He squeezed out enough onto two fingers to do the job and gave it back.

A few minutes later, as she collected the empty dog bowls so they wouldn't blow away, he reappeared with a cup of coffee and a sausage patty folded inside a pancake. Thankfully, she drank the coffee, then ate the sandwich as she repacked the sled bag.

It was enough to make her stomach clamor for more. Inside, she ate enough pancakes and protein for three people. Though she was stuffed, she still felt the urge to eat, her system telling her how many calories she had burned to stay warm on the ice.

They stayed only three hours in Koyuk before heading for Elim. Neither Harvey nor Murray had come in while they rested.

Bomber was the first to pull out. Like Martinson, he still had twelve dogs in harness.

"If I don't see you guys again, it's been nice racing with you."

"Don't count on it," Martinson told him. "You'll see the back of me soon enough."

"I don't know. A couple of your dogs look pretty short-legged."

"You'll think you're running dachshunds if you try to keep up once I shift into high gear."

Nome was now only 150 miles away. The closer they got, the more Martinson's temper seemed to improve. He thinks he has a good chance of winning, Jessie thought. But so do I.

As she booted up her dogs, she wondered what had happened to Murray and Harvey.

Schuller was leaving two of his, including Betsy, which she knew must disappoint him. For the first time in his four years of Iditarod racing, this dog would not cross the finish line with him. He also took a young male named Pepper out of harness, which left him with a strong team of twelve. Jessie watched him rub Betsy's ears affectionately as he talked to the checker who would take care of her. The vet knelt beside the old dog, going over her injured paw with gentle fingers. She licked his hand but had eyes only for Schuller, knowing she was being left behind.

He looked back at her as he pulled out. As soon as he was out of sight, the dog laid her head down on her paws dejectedly. Jessie let Tank get her team going just behind him, a little sad herself.

The trail from Koyuk to Elim swung back to the sea ice, following the curve of the shoreline, which was surrounded by steep rock cliffs topped by projections like sentinels. Then the trail turned back abruptly onto land and into low rolling hills. Just before reaching the checkpoint, they were on the ice once again, with more cliffs to the right.

By midevening Jessie was in Elim, forty-eight miles beyond Koyuk. The wind had whipped across the sound all day. Though airborne granular snow blasted head-on at times, scouring her exposed skin, she was able to complete the trip in just under seven hours.

Martinson, good as his word, had passed Cranshaw halfway between the two checkpoints and disappeared into the distance. Schuller, then Jessie, both passed Bomber just before Elim, but he repassed, to arrive five minutes ahead. They pulled in to Elim to find him in serious conversation with the checker.

"You're sure you only saw him once before you went onto the ice?"

"Yeah, sure. He pulled over to let me by. I saw his light for a minute or two in the storm but went on into Koyuk without seeing anyone else. I even missed the ménage à trois camped out there. That snow was blowing pretty good."

His comment on their emergency shelter, obviously intended for their ears, infuriated Jessie. She could tell it angered Schuller, too.

He snapped. "If you didn't see us, how do you know we camped together?"

Bomber grinned maliciously. "I said I missed it, not didn't see it," he said. "Maybe I should have stopped, huh?"

Schuller took a step in his direction, but Jessie caught his arm.

"Don't, Dale. It's not worth it. He's just being stupid."

"You're right." Shaking his head, Schuller turned to the veterinarian, who stood ready to check the condition of his dogs.

Cranshaw stared at Jessie until the other two were out of hearing.

"You're doing pretty good this year, Jess," he said.

"I've got a good team and they've stayed healthy."

"No better than mine."

"Well, we'll see. Don't forget two years ago." She reminded him of the year she had passed him just a few miles from the finish line.

He didn't respond, but stood looking at her belligerently.

"See you lost your trailbreaker," he said finally, with a sneer.

"You mean Mike?"

"Yeah. Wore out his dogs."

His insinuation stung. She felt anger flare again, but caught herself before she spoke. *He's trying to get you. Don't let him.*

Silently, she looked at him, feeling her face grow hot. Her lips felt stiff.

"That's not fair, Bomber. I break my share of trail."

"So you say."

"What's wrong with you?" she burst out. "I don't deserve that and you know it."

"Aw, come on, Jess. You've had help all the way up the line. Just like Murray and all the other women. If not from Ryan and Solomon, then from that idiot trooper."

She was incapable of speech, so angry she wanted to hit him. Incredulous, she struggled to hold her temper.

Bomber scowled at her, assessing the effect of his accusations.

Jealous. He's jealous, she thought. But it seemed more than that. He was also tired and really angry. I think he actually believes it, she realized. He's afraid I'll beat him again, and he's setting up excuses in case I do.

Carefully calm, she said, "I'm sorry you feel that way. It isn't true and you know it, if you're fair."

He whirled and stomped off toward the checkpoint.

Jessie watched him go, feeling limp, as adrenaline drained from her system, leaving her more tired. She had thought he was over this prejudice.

"What are you smiling at?" Schuller asked. She hadn't seen him return, and she jumped at the sound of his voice.

Smiling? She realized she was and why. She was exhilarated. Bomber was afraid she would not only beat him, but the rest, too. For the first time in the race, she really knew that, given the right conditions, she could.

"Nothing important," she told Schuller. "Just the same old stuff." She wouldn't let Bomber reach the finish line ahead of her. He had just guaranteed it.

She studied Schuller for a moment.

"What's wrong, Dale?"

His frown of concern told her it wasn't good news.

"T.J.'s been hurt," he said. "Solomon and Murray found him unconscious by his sled last night, in the hills before they went down onto the ice. Looked like he parked his team to give them a snack, tripped over something, and fell, hitting his head on a block of frozen fish he was about to feed them."

"God. Is he okay?"

"Yeah, I guess. They turned around and took him back to Shaktoolik. He came to after they got him in. He's got a lump the size of a baseball on the side of his head and can't remember much about it."

They looked at each other, both thinking the same thing. Jessie expressed it.

"Are they sure he just fell?"

Schuller considered his answer, kicking at the runner of her sled.

"Hell, I don't know, Jessie. I guess if they weren't

wondering about it, they wouldn't be asking questions, would they?"

"He's out of the race, then?"

"Oh, yeah. No chance. They'll fly him out as soon as the weather clears."

"Are the troopers in Shaktoolik?"

"No. They're in Nome. The storm drove them up the coast yesterday and they haven't been able to get out. Holman finally got in there this afternoon from Koyuk."

"He had to want to get there pretty bad to fly in this stuff."

30

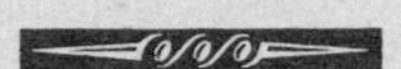

Date: Tuesday, March 12
Race Day: Eleven
Place: Nome checkpoint
Weather: Overcast, decreasing wind
Temperature: High −15°F, low −24°F
Time: Late afternoon

HOLMAN WASN'T ALONE IN WANTING BADLY TO BE somewhere else. Throughout the day the storm had progressed in waves up the coast to Nome, driving Alex to new heights of irritation.

"When it dies down here, it's still blowing like a son of a bitch down there, and vice versa," he complained to Caswell and Becker. They were having coffee at Iditarod headquarters on the south side of West Front Street, a block beyond the finish line.

On their way to check out the current race positions they had passed a well-guarded group of prisoners from the Nome correctional facility. The men were setting up slatted snow fence and shoveling snow to create the chute, a 175-foot-long raised area where, tomorrow, the winner would cross the line and officially complete the race. The fences would hold back the crowds, while the raised finish line would allow them to see what was going on.

Crowning the chute was a massive long arch with two enormous burls on either end. It was supported, fifteen feet in the air, by heavy wooden tripods. Into one side was carved "END OF IDITAROD DOG RACE, 1049 MILES, ANCHORAGE, NOME."

"There aren't any trees that big out here," Alex said to Caswell. "Where'd they get that thing?"

Caswell smiled, glad to find something to distract Jensen from his preoccupation with the weather.

"Fairbanks," he said. "A logger named Red Olson, who owned the log back in 1974, thought the race needed a finish-line monument, which he conned the Fairbanks Lions Club into building. When they had it done, they put the whole thing into a plane and had it flown to Nome. When it got here, the race committee found he had shipped it C.O.D., over five thousand pounds of it. There was over a thousand dollars of freight due.

"They took up a collection from everybody in town to pay the bill on something they hadn't even seen. Then Olson came to town, they put it together and set it up. It's beginning to need some repair after standing outside for years, but it sure makes a great finish-line marker, doesn't it?"

Fans and officials came and went from the race headquarters, which was located in a medium-sized auditorium. One small room held radio and computer equipment, operators keeping close track of the racers as they went through the checkpoints. Behind a counter near the door, Iditarod volunteers sold souvenirs: enameled pins, sweat shirts with the race logo, mugs, suspenders, posters. Another booth did a brisk trade in soft drinks, hot dogs, cinnamon rolls, and whatever else the cooks of the community brought in. All three troopers had sampled bowls of moose stew a short time earlier.

A large hand-drawn map of Alaska, the race route carefully marked, filled one wall. Officials moved colored flags with individual names along the line as they received word of the standing of the mushers on the trail. Those who scratched were pulled off to one side.

From the map, Alex knew that Murray and Solomon had made it in and out of Koyuk. The other four—Martinson, Schuller, Arnold, and Cranshaw—had completed more than half the forty-eight miles to Elim. The weather was slowing the race, not stopping it.

The news of T. J. Harvey's accident had come through on the headquarters radio. Alex spoke to Holman, who had talked to Harvey and the village health aide in Shaktoolik.

A community of less than two hundred people, Shaktoolik has no resident doctor, dentist, or pharmacist. Daily health and medical needs are met as well as possible by a resident health aide. Medical professionals visit once or twice a year. Anyone requiring emergency treatment is flown to the Norton Sound Regional Hospital in Nome.

"We'll bring him in as soon as this weather clears," Holman had assured Jensen over the radio. "He's not in any danger that we can tell. Has a massive headache but seems to be holding up okay."

"What do you think, Matt? Was it an accident?"

Holman's answer came slowly. "Don't know. Could have been. T.J. doesn't remember anything. Says if someone hit him, he didn't see them. I didn't see where it happened, but Solomon's no dummy.

Said he looked for footprints, but the damn blowing snow had covered everything, even Harvey. Lucky they found him. He could have frozen to death."

"What did he hit his head on?"

"Chunk of frozen fish he was about to cut up for his dogs. Solomon brought it in with him. Harvey's blood's on it, and it matches the mark on his head. Would have had to fall awful hard to make a lump that size."

"So it's possible either way."

"That's a roger. You got anything else?"

"No. You coming up?"

"Soon as I can. Holman, out."

"Is he going to fly in this stuff?" Becker questioned Jensen.

"Not if it's bad. I think he had about all the flying he could take getting into Shaktoolik."

"I can relate to that," said Becker, still unfavorably impressed by their trip from Unalakleet.

Although the storm had momentarily subsided, fierce wind swept the street, and the temperature hovered menacingly in the minus range. Jensen was glad to step through the door of the Nugget Inn, where Carpenter had found them a room by calling in a favor from the owner. It was tiny, dark, and once again short on beds. This time Caswell insisted on taking the floor. "We're not going anywhere soon," he said. "I'll be fine."

The lobby was crowded with out-of-town race fans seeking shelter from the wind. In the Gold Dust Saloon, ten feet and two steps down from the hotel's front desk, Alex could see that most of the tables were filled.

"Let's get a beer," Caswell suggested. "You've got to see this bar."

They crossed the room to climb up on tall bar stools. To one side a large picture window faced the ocean, though in the dark little could be seen but snow, whipped up off the sea ice and flung against the glass with some force. The bar was impressive, filling one whole wall with polished wood, mirrors, and shelves of glassware. The heavily carved bar, with its old-fashioned lamps, recalled the goldrush days of not so long ago.

"This is what an Alaskan bar should look like," Caswell enthused. Overhearing his comment, the bartender smiled.

"Thanks," she said. "We like it. You guys here for the race? Of course."

"Yeah, sort of."

"They'll be in tomorrow. Late. Martinson is running first just outside Elim, but Cranshaw, Schuller, and Arnold are right behind him. They're all moving fast, even with the snow." She nodded toward the window. "We'll get a report soon."

"What time is it?" Alex asked her.

"Almost eight. Where you from?" She smiled and set their beer in front of them. During a quick and casual check, which Caswell observed with a grin to Becker, she had assessed the wedding-ring status of both the other troopers. Turning to Alex, she set his brew down last and addressed the question to him.

Aware of her attention and Caswell's amusement, Alex felt his ears redden.

"Palmer," he told her and drowned his discomfort in a long swallow of Budweiser.

As she moved down the bar to mix drinks for the cocktail waitress, several people stood up at a table behind them.

"Let's move," Jensen suggested. "More comfortable there."

"Oh, I don't know." Becker gazed innocently at the ceiling. "I sort of like it here. How about you, Cas?"

"Yeah, Alex, I just got comfortable. It's pretty interesting here, you'll have to admit. Great detail and decoration."

"Come on you two. Move it." He sat down at the vacant table, facing away from the bar, pulled out his pipe, and began to pack it with tobacco.

"I'm back to Cranshaw and Martinson," Jensen said when the others joined him, grinning. "And I don't like it that Jessie's out there running with them."

"I know you want to get back down there, Alex," Caswell said.

"Being stuck here makes me crazy," he admitted.

"If we knew that Harvey's accident was another attempt, it would eliminate Schuller and Martinson, wouldn't it?" asked Becker.

"But we don't know that it wasn't an accident."

At that moment, the bartender turned up the radio. The hourly Iditarod report was coming on, and everyone in the bar grew quiet to hear it.

As anticipated, Tim Martinson had reached Elim first, at seven forty-three. At seven fifty-six, however, having passed Dale Schuller and Jessie Arnold, Bomber Cranshaw pulled in second. The other two were in sight of the checkpoint.

"Hey," a woman in a bright yellow jumpsuit said to her husband. "Frank, she's going to win. You just watch."

Noticing the grin on Alex's face, she turned to him. "You know her?"

He nodded. "Yes, we know her."

31

Date: Tuesday and Wednesday, March 12 and 13
Race Day: Eleven and twelve
Place: Between Elim and White Mountain
checkpoints and beyond (forty-six plus miles)
Weather: Clearing, light wind
Temperature: High −13°F, low −19°F
Time: Late evening to midafternoon

TWO HOURS IN ELIM, BARELY ENOUGH TIME TO FEED the dogs, then Jessie was off again, behind Martinson this time. Beating Bomber out of the checkpoint established a second-place position she was unwilling to give up. The team was doing great, and she encouraged them, knowing they would have a required four-hour rest in White Mountain, in preparation for the last sprint through Safety to Nome. What mattered now was holding on, not letting anyone get away from her.

The storm appeared to be dying at last. Turning off her headlamp long enough to regain her night vision, she could see clouds. In the clear dark sky between them, a few stars drifted overhead. After a minute or two she turned the headlamp back on.

She could not remember ever being so tired. But knowing the whole thing was almost over sustained her, as did being second. Far behind her on the ice she could see the bobbing headlamps of Bomber and Schuller; occasionally she could see Martinson's ahead.

Remembering the look Cranshaw had given her as she passed him leaving Elim, she shivered. If he could have arranged it, she was sure that look would have stopped her from ever running again.

According to the rules, a musher must give way to another who comes within fifty feet and asks to pass. Outside of Elim Bomber had pretended not to hear her request until she had made it three times. If Schuller hadn't been in sight, she wondered if he would have refused completely. She suspected he might and resolved to stay ahead of him if she could.

She considered turning off her headlamp and running in the dark, so he wouldn't know where she was, but the light helped keep her awake. As tired as she was, she was afraid an unexpected rough spot might tumble her off the sled. She couldn't risk it at this point, so the light stayed on.

For eleven of the twenty-eight miles to Golovin, the trail followed the shoreline, curving slowly to the southwest. To shorten the route around Cape Darby, the trailbreakers had taken the way inland through the Kwiktalik Mountains. Jessie followed Martinson across the portage, away from the sea. After running so far on ice and through gentle hills, mountains that rose over a thousand feet above her seemed enormous. The trail was rough and choppy, frozen and swept by the storm.

When they completed the passage and dropped

down onto the ice for the northwest run to Golovin, the wind hit hard again.

At three in the morning she arrived at the checkpoint to find Martinson stretched out on his sled bag, his team around him. A few villagers stood discussing the merits of his team and watching the dogs finish their dinner, standing far enough away to avoid disturbing their meal. Martinson sat up as she pulled in from Golovin Bay.

When she had settled her team and finished feeding them, he wandered over to where she was repacking the equipment in her sled.

"You're really pushing me, Jessie."

She grinned. "Good. I plan to keep it up."

He took a long, thoughtful look at her remaining ten dogs. "They look good."

"They are. I left one in Elim, but the rest are doing fine. How're yours?"

"Okay. I dropped two. Want some coffee?"

She stopped what she was doing to turn and look at him. Though they had been in races together in the past, she had never run near him. Given his hostile behavior throughout this one, his offer surprised her.

"Sure, Tim. I don't want to go to sleep, just rest a bit. Coffee would be great. Here. I'll be over in a minute."

He took the metal cup she handed him and clomped off in his heavy boots to the fire he had going near his team.

After checking her own, she followed him. She squatted as close to the fire as she could to warm her hands and took the cup he offered. He settled back on his sled with his own cup. In companionable silence, they watched the flames.

She had just raised the cup to take a sip of the

steaming coffee when a voice called her name and a figure appeared out of the darkness. "Jessie, you got here." It was Alice Yupanuk, an Eskimo friend.

Jessie stood up to greet her with a hug.

"Alice. Good to see you."

"Sorry I wasn't down here to meet you. They woke me up to tell me you came in. You look tired, Jessie."

"Don't remind me. I'm so tired I don't dare stop in one place too long or I'll fall over. Tim, this is my friend Alice Yupanuk."

He nodded and smiled from his place on the sled.

"Here, Jessie. Hot chocolate." She pushed a thermos into Jessie's hands. "You drink this now. I got reindeer stew on the stove. You both better come eat."

"Oh, Alice. I'd like to, but if I come in where it's warm I'll never leave. I've got to stay awake, at least till White Mountain."

"No problem. I'll bring some down for you two." And before Jessie could protest, she was gone up the hill to her small house where the lights shone through the windows.

Turning back to Tim and the fire, Jessie held up the thermos.

"Want some of this?"

"Ah . . . Well, sure."

She dumped the coffee out of both their cups and poured in the rich chocolate drink. It tasted heavenly.

In just a few minutes Alice was back, carrying a covered kettle and a large paper bag. From the bag she took bowls, spoons, and hot buttered bread. She ladled stew from the kettle and handed them each a full bowl and spoon. Alice ate a small bowl of the stew herself and contentedly watched them, providing refills until they groaned and turned the bowls over.

The large kettle was still half-full and stayed warm on the fire.

"What a treat. Thank you, Alice," Jessie said, handing her the thermos as they were drinking the last of the hot chocolate.

"No problem," she said again. She grinned at Martinson. "You going to win, Jessie? Beat this guy?"

"I hope so, Alice. I'll sure try."

During the meal, Bomber and Schuller pulled in. Schuller waved as he started to care for his dogs.

"They friends of yours?" Alice asked.

"Well, yes."

A smile spread over the small woman's face. "Bet they're hungry."

With a parting hug, she was off to feed Schuller and Cranshaw.

"Nice lady," Tim said, watching her go. "Everybody is so generous with what they have. It makes you feel . . ."

"Welcome," Jessie finished. "She must have made that stew yesterday and kept it hot all night for when we came in."

There was a long pause, then he looked up at her.

"Listen, Jessie. I don't want to worry you, but I think you should watch out for Cranshaw. There's something funny about that guy, and he's pretty angry at you right now."

"What do you mean, funny?" she asked, suddenly alert.

"That's just it. I don't know what I mean. He's acting real weird. I overheard him in Anvik, telling Paul Banks how you made him and Ryan break trail and never took your turn. How you had to have help all the time."

Anger rushed through her once more, so strongly

that her fingers clenched around the cup. She sat very still, thinking.

"You believe that, Tim?"

"No, Jessie. You're a good musher. I've never heard you ask for help from anyone. You've broken your share of trail in the worst of weather, from what I know. I just thought I'd better tell you what he's saying. You don't have to prove anything to me."

He paused and flashed his crooked grin.

"Besides, I'm not about to let you in front of me now, even if you did have something to prove."

She laughed and felt the anger recede.

"Thanks, Tim," she said. "I'll watch him, but I don't really think there's a problem if I don't let him get to me."

"You're probably right. He's just jealous. He thinks this should be a man's race."

Jealous, she thought. There it is again. Does everyone in this race know about Jensen? Wait a minute, she told herself. He could just as easily mean Bomber's jealous of my being in second place, afraid I'll come in ahead of him.

But she knew she and Alex hadn't bothered to try to hide their interest in each other. Why should they? And that was a part of Bomber's anger too, even if Tim didn't say it.

"Thanks for the warning," she said, getting up to go back to her team. "I'll stay away from him."

The rest of the night they ran to White Mountain, arriving just after eight the next morning. Schuller came in forty minutes behind Jessie, ahead of Cranshaw this time. Only seventy-seven miles remained of the long trail, and it was assured the race would end on this twelfth day. Even though times were slower than usual because of bad weather in a few places, it was still a respectable showing.

With four required rest hours before they could go on, the mushers fed their teams and left them alone to sleep.

While the dog food was cooking, Jessie emptied her sled bag of all it carried and began to sort out everything she could do without. From here on she would carry only essentials. Her mandatory gear went back in first, then the cooler full of a hot batch of dog food for the next leg of the trip, followed by a few clothes, snacks, and little else. She left out the cooker and charcoal. She also discarded all but one set of extra batteries for her headlamp, two tapes for her player. She put all she was leaving into heavy plastic bags she had sent in along with her supply drop.

As she carried the rejected gear to the checkpoint to arrange for it to be shipped back to Wasilla, she saw Schuller and Martinson, both surrounded by gear they had removed from their sleds.

Martinson stood, a sweater in each hand, calculating their relative merits. "Oh, hell," he muttered, tossing both on his heap of rejects. Jessie laughed.

Cranshaw's sled, parked away from the others, was surrounded by watching kids. His head snapped around at the sound of her voice, and he glared. Taking advantage of his inattention, one of the boys reached out to lay a finger on his gun, which lay, temptingly, in plain sight. "Hey," Bomber yelled, turning back quickly. "Get your hands off that."

As he turned, his parka opened and Jessie caught a glimpse of metal at his belt. He grabbed up the gun and stuffed it into the handlebar bag. The curious boy jumped as if he had been struck, ran a few steps, and stopped to make a face at Bomber's back.

Jessie empathized with his impudence.

"Lighten the load time," Dale called out as she passed him. "How you doing, Jessie?"

"Good. Hanging in there."

"Watch out. I'm going to turn up the burners now."

"Give it your best shot. I've got most of an hour on you."

"I can hope your mutts quit in Safety."

"Not my guys."

This was something they all worried about. Safety was the last checkpoint before Nome. Through the years, tired dogs, used to stopping for a rest at each checkpoint, refused to go on through it. Some quit and wouldn't be driven on until they had rested to their satisfaction. Frustrated mushers watched themselves slip several places in the standings as others came through and passed them. Races had been won and lost on the whim of a team in Safety.

As soon as she completed her chores, Jessie tried to feed herself, but couldn't find her appetite. She picked at her mom's macaroni and cheese, drank several glasses of orange juice, and stretched out for an hour's sleep on the sled.

When she got up at the end of the hour, she was so disoriented that for a minute she hardly knew where she was. It took her another five just to get in motion. Again she drank juice, then went to rouse the dogs.

She waited at the checkpoint for the last ten minutes and watched Martinson pull out. Just as he reached the last house in town, a village dog ran out to bark at his team. Despite his shouts and curses, his whole line of ten dogs swung to the right to chase the challenger. Several people ran to help stop them but, by the time this was accomplished, half his dogs were tangled in their traces, requiring assistance. The village dog had disappeared.

Martinson, still swearing heatedly, was working hard at getting them back in line when Jessie passed him and drove out of town.

She had to laugh. Then she glanced back at the tangle, relieved. It could just as easily have been hers.

But she was off cleanly and running for the fifty-five miles of Topkok Hills between White Mountain and Safety. She checked the team chugging away in front of her. She had left two dogs and was now down to eight, her best and fastest. All of them were pulling well and smoothly, keeping the lines tight. Tank ran lead as if he knew they were on the last leg of this long trip.

Suddenly it dawned on her. For the first time in the race, or any Iditarod, she was leading the whole field, with no one between her and the finish line. It was a heady feeling, but not one to get attached to. Martinson wouldn't be more than a few minutes behind her, coming strong. For the moment she enjoyed her lead.

All the way to the hills, she ran first. Once into them, the going grew harder. The wind had swept the slopes to smooth, icy patches, making it difficult to keep the sled from sliding downhill on long traverses. Mile after mile, she struggled with the sled, all but lifting it back to the trail behind the dogs. Like a roller coaster, it was slow going up and frustratingly slippery coming down. The brake made little difference, and she had to watch carefully to keep the sled from hitting her wheel dogs.

She stopped the team for a rest and snack in the shelter of a couple of short spruces in a frozen creek bed. She swung her arms to get rid of the ache across her shoulders. Falling back across the sled bag, she waited for the dogs to finish eating.

Just as she was ready to leave, she heard a yell. Martinson appeared above her on the hill and came sideslipping down it.

"Thought I'd never catch you," he called as he went by. "See you in Nome."

You'll see me before that if I have anything to say about it, she thought, calling to her team to follow in his tracks.

What a strange guy, she thought as she watched him pull away. How odd for him to be so antisocial most of the race and then suddenly offer coffee and well-meaning advice in one blow. She frowned, considering it.

Why should he be so friendly now? she wondered. What if I had drunk his coffee? He had time to put something in it. I gave him my cup, like an idiot. If Alice hadn't brought hot chocolate, I would have. Did he look funny when I poured it out?

"Damn," she said aloud. "I'm getting paranoid!"

Tank pricked up his ears and turned to look back at her.

Suspicious of everyone. And Bomber, carrying two guns? Why would he have two? Oh, God. Maybe one of them's mine.

The thought made her catch her breath, and for a minute she couldn't think.

She hadn't really seen the one he stuffed in the bag. Could it be hers? She knew Alex suspected him, but he suspected almost everybody, didn't he? No: he was focusing on Bomber, Martinson, and a few others, maybe.

Think, Jessie, she told herself Could it really be yours? He had plenty of opportunity before McGrath.

How about the rest of the things that had happened? George's death? Ginny and Steve? He was there, too. Racing ahead of them toward Takotna, he could have run the moose into her and Ryan. Had lost enough time to do it, according to the checker's record, if he'd moved the snow machine the night before when he went home. Was he also responsible for Martinson's trail mail being in Harvey's sled? He could have done it at Eagle Island, when they were all stormed in.

She realized that Martinson couldn't have hurt Harvey; he had been sleeping in the shelter with her and Schuller when that happened. But Bomber was unaccounted for. If it is him, he doesn't know I have another gun, she thought. Patting her parka, she felt the reassuring bulk of the weapon beneath it. I mustn't let him catch up with me. And I must get to Alex as fast as I can. I could call him from Safety.

Could I catch Tim and tell him? I can try. But although she saw him in the distance off and on for the rest of the way to the checkpoint, she couldn't catch him.

She glimpsed Martinson for the last time when they reached the final summit and began the long descent to the coast. She figured that she wouldn't have time at the checkpoint to explain it all to either Jensen or Martinson, or Cranshaw would catch her. The wind picked up, but sunlight filled the afternoon sky for the first time in days. By six o'clock, she was traveling along the beach, with Safety little more than an hour away and Martinson nowhere in sight.

Looking behind her, she could see two tiny figures on sleds following her tracks along the shoreline.

32

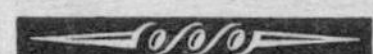

Date: Wednesday, March 13
Race Day: Twelve
Place: Nome and Safety checkpoints
Weather: Clear skies, light wind
Temperature: High −13°F, low −19°F
Time: Early afternoon

MATT HOLMAN FINALLY MADE IT TO NOME JUST AFter noon on the last day of the race. With much on his mind, he went immediately to find Jensen.

He found the three troopers waiting for him at Iditarod headquarters. They moved to a far comer of the big room where they could talk without being overheard.

"You find out anything else?" he asked, hiking himself up on the edge of the auditorium stage. There he perched, working on a cup of coffee. He looked at Alex expectantly.

"Damned less than we'd like and not enough. You?"

"Same. Harvey's okay. Still doesn't remember a thing."

"Well, if we assume Harvey's injury *was* an accident, that still tells us nothing."

"Any word on Jessie's gun?" Holman asked.

"Still missing," Jensen answered.

"Anyone could have had it," Caswell said. "If they got rid of it on the trail between here and McGrath, it's gone for good. Seven hundred and fifty miles of wilderness trail. It might be on the river ice, which turns to water in a couple of months."

Holman nodded.

"I feel inclined to talk to some of these people again," Jensen told him.

"Well, you can't right now. Leaders are out of White Mountain and on their way to Safety. They'll only stop long enough in Safety to drop dogs and gear for the last twenty-two-mile sprint."

"What exactly do they leave in Safety besides dogs?"

"Everything that isn't required. It all goes out, to lighten the sled and give the dogs as little as possible to pull."

"In that case, one thing we could do is go through it all one more time. Maybe our man will get careless."

"Looking for what?"

"I don't know. Anything to connect anyone to this mess in some way. A sort of know-it-when-you-see-it thing. I don't know what else to do, and I'm goddamned tired of sitting in Nome."

"If you find anything and break up the race in Safety, there'll be a lot of angry people, not just mushers. You won't be able to get answers from anyone until they get here and finish the race."

The leaders were getting to Nome as fast as they could. All four of them had stopped to feed their dogs before they reached Safety. There would be no more real rests for anyone, only the long path.

Martinson went through Safety, hardly bothering to slow down. It took him just seven minutes to check in, drop two dogs, throw all but his required gear out of his sled, and check out. The checker made him stand still long enough to put on the numbered bib he had worn out of Anchorage on the first day of the race.

Ten minutes later, at seven twenty-five, it was Jessie's turn. Not dropping any dogs, she accomplished the stop in five, gaining two precious minutes on him.

Eight and ten minutes after her arrival, Cranshaw and Schuller went through, having made up a half-hour between the two checkpoints. They were in and out in six and seven minutes, respectively. The checkpoint, surrounded by planes, snow machines, and people watching the action, now retained a pile of abandoned gear and six dogs, with more on the way.

The heat was on. It was anybody's race, even with twenty minutes between Martinson and Schuller. It was a margin that had been overcome in the past. Nobody's dogs had refused to pass Safety.

The short trip from Nome to Safety in Caswell's plane brought the troopers in just before the arrival of Cranshaw and Schuller. Holman had driven them to the airport late in the afternoon, then gone to continue his duties as race marshall.

They stood near the Safety checker and watched as Bomber stopped his dogs and began to rearrange his team. He pulled one dog from the middle of the line, leaving him with eleven for the run to Nome. Schuller came in while this was taking place and took three of his out of harness. He was now down to nine.

Alex watched in amazement as both men then began to unload everything they could possibly leave behind. The checker tabulated the mandatory gear as they put it back in the sled: sleeping bag, ax, snowshoes, one day's food for each dog, a day's food for the musher, dog booties, and the plastic container of trail mail. They left a confusion of clothes, cookers, flashlights, food, batteries, extra boots, medicine, tools, harness, and personal items, dumped into trash bags.

When they had gone, Jensen stepped up to the checker and held out a hand. "Hamilton, right?" he asked. "What are you doing here? You were in Finger Lake."

"That's right. When they'd all gone through, Holman sent me up here to man another checkpoint. A lot of the volunteers do double duty at times. The ham operator here was in Rainy Pass. There are several trailbreakers helping set up the finish in Nome."

Glad to see someone he knew, Jensen told Hamilton why he was there and asked for an estimate of when the next six or seven racers would come through.

"It'll be at least three hours before Solomon gets here. He's passed Murray again and seems to be pulling out in front to stay. They're both over halfway from White Mountain, but Murray will probably be an extra twenty minutes to a half-hour getting in. I expect Solomon at about ten-thirty, Murray about eleven."

Knowing the race would be over in less than three hours, Alex knew they couldn't stay that long.

"I want you to bag everything the next twelve mushers leave here from their sled bags," he told the checker. "If there is a place, lock it up; if not, have someone watch to make sure it isn't disturbed. Don't release it until you have permission from me."

"Hey, no one will touch it. I guarantee it. You want me to start with this?" He indicated the pile of gear by the door.

"Anyone touch that?"

"Nope. I've been right here."

"We'll go through it first. Then you can keep it with the rest."

Inside the checkpoint building, away from prying eyes, they went through everything left by the first four mushers, moving items one at a time into new bags. No drugs stronger than cold remedies were found. When he came across Martinson's rifle and ammunition, Jensen decided to impound any guns and take them to Nome.

In the middle of Cranshaw's belongings, Caswell found the musher's gun, in a holster with the initials B.C. tooled into the leather. Wrapped into a down vest next to it were two boxes of ammunition, one of which rattled, half-full. Jensen broke off searching Martinson's gear and went to look.

Opening the rattling box, he checked the shells it contained and started to close it up, when an anomaly at the bottom caught his eye. One of the shells was different from the others. Picking it out of the box, he inspected it carefully and frowned.

"What?" Caswell questioned.

"Look." He held it out. "This won't fit Cranshaw's gun. It's a forty-four shell. What's it doing in here?"

They looked at each other, catching Becker's attention. He came over to see.

"Jessie's?" Becker asked.

"That would explain it," Cas nodded.

"And Cranshaw is . . ."

"Unreachable, till he makes Nome," Jensen finished. "The son of a bitch is right behind her. And, if he left his gun, he may still have hers. Let's get out of here."

In an hour from the time they arrived, they were in the air, headed back to Nome.

33

Date: Wednesday, March 13
Race Day: Twelve
Place: Nome checkpoint
Weather: Clear skies, light wind
Temperature: High −13°F, low −19°F
Time: Midevening

THE LAST TWENTY-TWO MILES OF THE IDITAROD Trail lie along the sea ice around Cape Nome, an extension of land to the east of town. In the 1880s, when maps were made of this area, the cartographer could find no designation for the cape. Next to it on the rough draft he scrawled "Name?" meaning someone should find out what it was called. Later, when the map was published, it showed up as Cape Nome. The name stuck and eventually became the name of the gold-rush town that grew up on its beaches.

A little more than two and a half hours after the leaders left the Safety checkpoint, at ten-fourteen, the siren in Nome went off, sending its wail across the town to tell the waiting fans that the winning musher had passed the Fort Davis Roadhouse, two miles out of Nome, was in sight and about to come up over the snow-covered sea wall onto Front Street.

In the dark, no one watching at the edge of town could tell who was behind the bobbing light of the driver's headlamp. But the first musher was coming in, and they would know soon enough.

Over the noise of the crowd in the Breakers Bar, no one was aware that the siren had sounded until the door flew open and an excited voice shouted, "Musher coming in!" It took only minutes for over a hundred people to empty out onto the street. The same was true in homes, restaurants, and hotels all over town.

"Who is it? Who's coming in?"

They could see the light on the police escort car that waited for the musher at the other end of Front Street. They all watched for the racer to come off the ice into the lights of the long, two-lane street, then into the brighter lights around the Iditarod arch at the finish line. The next few minutes seemed to take forever for those who had been waiting for days. Some climbed to the top of trucks and cars parked along the street. Others had staked out positions on the roofs of nearby buildings. Everyone pushed forward to the best possible vantage point. A thousand voices speculated on the results of the race.

Jensen, Becker, and Caswell stood anxiously beside the race marshall inside the snow fence by the arch, watching the crowd quickly grow by hundreds to line the street, forming a solid wall of people around the chute. The entrance was guarded by a public safety officer and two husky trailbreakers, who would swing away a section of the fence to give the musher access to the finish line. They would then swing it back to keep the crowd from following, give the press room for interviews and pictures, and let the checker do his job of confirming that the mandatory items were on the sled.

The press was everywhere. Video cameramen turned on their glaring lights, making the area bright as day. One television crew was raised high overhead on the lift of a utility truck. Others waited with a dozen microphones near the finish line.

Jensen felt his own excitement rise with everyone else's. It was contagious, Iditarod fever, but did not obscure his primary objective. He still had to contend with Cranshaw.

He had wanted to go out after the musher, but Holman had begged him not to interrupt the race at the last minute.

"What if you're wrong? If you make him lose his place and he's not the one, there'll be holy hell to pay. Please. Just wait till he hits the line, that's all."

Against his better judgment, Alex had reluctantly agreed to wait that long. He didn't think Cranshaw would try anything so close to Nome, with so many potential witnesses. There were dozens of snow-machine riders speeding back and forth along the trail, plus spectators who had driven out to the Davis Roadhouse. Frustrated or not, he would accommodate Holman and do it his way. But only until Bomber crossed the line.

Every time he reviewed the desperate actions he was now convinced Bomber had committed, he felt angry and sick. Jessie was out there, alone, racing against him, and there was no way to reach her quickly.

He glanced around for Becker and found the younger trooper standing on a barrel that supported the snow fence, peering over the crowd. The police escort was now halfway down the street in front of the grocery store, moving steadily. Running beside it, on the west side of the street, Alex could make out the figure of a musher. As they passed under a street-light, he got his first good look. At the same time, the crowd at the gate began to shout, "Martinson! It's Tim Martinson. Yeah, Tim. Welcome to Nome."

There was no mistaking the tall, powerful man by the sled. If he had been gloomy and hostile on the trail, it was gone now. A wide grin broadcast his pleasure in the trip down Front Street. He waved as he saw friends in the crowd and encouraged his dogs.

"Hike, Josie. Okay, Butch. Go, gee. Gee. Whoa, now. Whoa."

Nearing the end of the chute, he directed the leader toward it and stopped his team. At the front of the team, he grabbed the harness to guide his lead dog between the two rows of cheering race fans and up the slight incline to the arch. Only the nose of the leader of the team had to cross the finish line to win. As they crossed it together, the media closed in. A hundred flash explosions lit up the night.

"Congratulations, Tim," the familiar sound of the announcer's voice boomed from the speakers. "You did it again. How does it feel to be in Nome?"

"Pretty good," Martinson answered. "Pretty damn good. I'm tired." And for the next five minutes he answered questions and posed with his dogs for pictures.

As it became more crowded around the finish line, Jensen found himself, with Caswell, moving closer in order to see around the reporters. Martinson saw him and a slight frown passed over his face.

Damn, thought Alex. He's still mad.

But the big musher raised a hand and motioned him closer. When the crowd prevented this, he left the spotlight, stepped between two journalists, and leaned over a third to be heard.

"Cranshaw and Arnold aren't far behind me," he said. "You better go make sure she's okay. I could see their lights most of the way but lost them maybe four miles out. Something's fuckin' weird with Cranshaw. He's determined not to let her beat him and he's acting real funny. He gets mean when he's mad."

Jensen whirled, caught Caswell by one arm, and half-dragged him around the outside of the arch next to the snow fence.

"Becker!" he barked at the trooper on the observation barrel.

The authority and immediacy in his voice, a tone Becker seldom heard, brought the younger man quickly to the ground.

"What did he say to you, Alex?" Caswell asked as Jensen pushed forward through the crowd toward the entrance to the chute.

"Cranshaw's after Jessie. I'm not waiting any longer."

"What?"

At that moment Holman stopped him. Standing beside him was a panting runner from Iditarod headquarters,

"Phone call from the Davis Roadhouse says they spotted two more mushers, but something's wrong out there. After the roadhouse they run into no-man's-land, where they can pass each other anytime, but the one in front doesn't have to move over. But it looked from the headlamps like they ran into each other. Then the lights went out, and a few minutes later they caught a team without a driver as it headed for town. Say there was a shot. Want to know should they go out."

"Whose team was it? Damn it man, whose?"

"They don't know."

Becker was headed for the police escort car, but Jensen knew he couldn't get out on the trail with it.

"Snow machines!"

Several of the iron dogs were parked, idling, near the finish lines. They had been driven up the street during the excitement, accompanying Martinson to the line. Alex and Caswell sprinted to commandeer the closest two, all but dumping startled riders from their seats. One after the other they took off down the street toward the seawall, leaving Holman and Becker in the process of liberating another pair to follow them.

"Damn it. Damn it. Get out of the way. Move. Move!" Alex shouted as people scattered from the street in front of him. Swerving around a pickup, double-parked in front of the Board of Trade, he gave the machine as much gas as it would handle. Another snow machine whipped out of a side street ahead. As the driver fought to avoid collision the machine rolled, throwing him into a snowbank.

Then the buildings ended and Alex was free of most of the traffic. Slowing before he turned down the ramp from the seawall to the ice, he heard the whine of Caswell's machine coming up behind him. The headlight of his snow machine began to pick up the slat and tripod trail markers with their flutter of pink tape. He cranked the accelerator as high as he could on the uneven ice and snow of the trail.

Three miles out, hurt, angry, and determined, Jessie crouched behind a snow-covered block of sea ice and tried to force herself to think and listen carefully in the face of panic.

When he left Safety nine minutes behind her, Cranshaw had driven his dogs relentlessly, a man obsessed. Gradually, he gained until he could see her ahead of him. Just as gradually, Schuller had dropped behind him until, finally, his light disappeared.

Halfway to Nome, when Jessie noticed the light gaining on her, there was never a question in her mind who it was. Schuller would never push his dogs so hard and risk burning them out so close to the finish. The fanaticism of it shook her. She pushed her team as fast as she dared, a sliver of fear cold in her throat.

Five miles from town, he was so close she could hear him swearing obscenities at his dogs. Then she became the target.

"Get out of the way, Jessie. Goddamn you, move over and let me by. Fucking woman. Get the hell off the trail like you're supposed to. Goddamn it. I said give way, bitch."

The litany of abuse went on. Terrified, she refused to let him pass, knowing how close he would come to her if she did. She couldn't see his face in the dark, only the anonymous beam of the headlamp. But she couldn't miss his harsh voice.

"Fucking, selfish bitch."

"Mush, Tank. Go boy. Hike," she called as the team slowed slightly. They picked the pace back up at the sound of her voice. Luckily, her leader had never liked to run behind another team and required little encouragement to strain to stay in front, where he felt he belonged. A couple of the team dogs were beginning to tire, not quite keeping the lines taut. Soon they would pull the speed down, and she could only hope Bomber's dogs would suffer first, having been pushed hard longer.

"Get those mutts off the trail, damn it. Fucking pull over."

If I can reach the roadhouse, she thought, where people can see us. Get to the roadhouse. Hold on and get there.

They came to a relatively flat area, which, for a way, drew away from the ice blocks and into rolling swells. Jessie heard a snap and realized Cranshaw was whipping his dogs with a piece of line. Barely long enough to reach the first few, it nevertheless had its intended effect on dogs familiar with the sound and threat of punishment. To her left a blur of motion in the dark told her he had driven off the trail to force his team by hers. His leader and first two team dogs were even with her sled. Bit by bit the rest of the dogs moved past, until she could see his sled bow.

"Get off, Jessie. I'm warning you."

Ahead she could see the white bulk of more ice blocks looming out of the dark.

"I'll run you into the ice. Fucking pull over."

As the blocks came nearer, he began to run closer, ready to force her off the trail.

"I mean it, bitch. You've cost me too much."

With a crunch, his sled banged into hers and rebounded. Her sled shuddered but, miraculously, clung to the ruts left in the trail by Martinson's team.

Until that moment, Jessie hadn't answered Bomber's shouts of demand and threat. Suddenly her temper took over, along with her fear.

"Get the hell away from me, Bomber. You may have got mine, but I've got another gun and I'll use it."

She dared not let go of the handle of the speeding sled to pull Holman's gun from its holster, but she doubted he could get his either.

For a moment there was silence, then a roar of anger from Cranshaw. He threw his weight violently to the right, driving his sled toward hers again. But his dogs suddenly slowed, causing him to almost miss as the sled fell back. The bow of his sled caught the back of hers, throwing them both. Jessie felt the handle jerk from her hands, and she fell backward as her team dashed away from her. Cranshaw, his team stopped dead by the block of ice rising to the left of the trail, clutched at his sled and regained his balance without falling.

As she rolled and clambered to her knees, Jessie saw him pull at the bag on the back of his sled. Metal gleamed in the pale reflection from snow and ice. Throwing herself to the right, she tried to crawl behind another block, but the crack of the gun was followed by a burning sensation in her right shoulder. Her arm went out from under her.

The sound of the shot startled Cranshaw's dogs into motion, and they followed Jessie's team around the ice. The sudden jerk of the sled accomplished what the collision had not, yanking him off balance, toppling him into the snow before he could fire again.

While he was down she snatched her headlamp and shut it off. With her shoulder still on fire, she crawled one-handed into the shelter of the ice, where she drew herself into a crouch and fumbled for the gun under her parka. Her right hand was numb and wouldn't work. Awkwardly she unzipped her coat with her left hand and reached across her body to get the gun. If she could brace it, maybe she could aim it well enough when he came.

"Jessie? Goddamn it. I'll get you. You hear me? So help me God, I'll get you."

Carefully she braced the gun on a shelf of ice and

aimed it at the sound of his voice. A flare of pain took her breath as she bumped her injured shoulder, and she bit back a yelp of agony. Silently she waited, listening for the sound of Cranshaw moving, trying to guess the direction from which he would come.

34

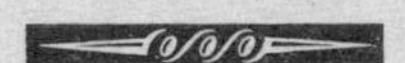

Date: Sunday, March 17
Race Day: Twelve; and four days later
Place: Nome checkpoint
Weather: Clear skies, light wind
Temperature: High −6°F, low −8°F
Time: Late evening

HOLMAN, FIVE MINUTES BEHIND JENSEN AND CASwell, caught Jessie's team as it trotted toward town. Anchoring it securely to an ice block, he continued toward the erratic snow-machine lights he could see in the distance.

Jensen's first indication of trouble came as a bullet hit the windscreen of his snow machine, missing him by inches. He whipped around beside the trail and retreated to the protection of an ice block, catching Caswell and dragging him into shelter. Shutting down both machines, they listened, but heard nothing.

"Jessie!" Alex shouted. "Are you okay?"

Another shot cracked a chunk of the ice over their heads into fragments.

"Alex? Thank God you're here."

The call came from across the trail. It was followed

by another shot from the same direction.

"Goddamn you, Jensen. Stay back or I'll fuckin' kill her. I know where she is and I'm closer than you are." To emphasize it, another shot hit the block on their side of the trail. "Cranshaw. We've got you. Give it up. Come on out."

A string of obscenities spewed from the mad musher.

"You can't get away. There's nowhere to go. Give it up."

"Come and get me, bastard. I'll get her before you get me."

Caswell gestured around the ice. Pointing to himself, he whispered to Alex. "I'll go that way and try to get behind him. You go across and work your way up to Jessie. Okay?"

Alex nodded and Cas went on. "I won't fire unless I get a clear shot at him, but if you hear him move, fire high to keep him back."

They moved. The dry snow crunched and squeaked under their boots, giving away their progress. Pausing, Jensen could hear Cranshaw moving toward the position of Jessie's voice.

"Jess, don't say anything. Keep quiet."

She didn't answer.

Good, he thought. He moved swiftly, keeping behind the ice, crossed the trail, and continued, slipping from one block to the other. Pausing to listen, he could hear Caswell on the other side. The sound of Cranshaw's progress now came from Jessie's side of the trail. Slowly, Jensen advanced until he was within two blocks of where he estimated her to be. He crouched behind the block, peered around the edge, and waited. Silent.

Against the pale white of the next block, he hardly

saw the shadow in the dark, but heard the giveaway sound of the snow as Bomber closed in on Jessie.

A flash, the crack of a gun, and Cranshaw's howl filled the cold air. The musher clutched at his arm. His gun flew spinning into the dark.

"Bitch. Fucking bitch, you shot me."

Raising his eyes, Alex saw the dark shape of Jessie on the ice block where she had waited for Bomber to come hunting.

He reached Cranshaw just as Caswell arrived from the other direction to take charge of the musher.

"Come down, Jess," Alex said as he reached up to her.

"He got me in the shoulder," she warned holding her right arm across her chest as she slid down into his arms. She kissed him fiercely, then held on tight, shaking and gulping big breaths of cold air.

"You don't shoot too bad left-handed, lady."

"I was scared to death."

They heard Becker and Holman pull up on snow machines and shout. Caswell, with Cranshaw handcuffed, wounded forearm and all, called them in.

"Let's get a look at that shoulder," Alex told Jessie, pulling her into the beam of a snow machine's headlight.

"It hurts. Where's my team?"

"Got them tied down about half a mile on," the race marshall told her. "Don't worry. They're okay."

"I'm not worried. I knew they were out of it. But as soon as Alex puts some kind of temporary patch on me, I want them so I can finish this thing."

"Jess, you can't."

"The hell I can't." She took a furious step toward Cranshaw. "Let him get away with this? I'll finish it for George, and Ginny, and Steve, and for me. And I want him to see me do it."

Do it she did. With an escort of snow machines, she completed the race. Driving one-handed, her shoulder packed with snow and gauze from her first aid kit, right arm bound tightly against her body to minimize the jolts of the rough trail, she talked Tank and the rest of her team up the seawall and into Nome, as the siren howled its welcome.

Schuller caught up with her before she reached town, but somehow, as he later related it, straight-faced, to the sympathetic, cheering crowd, "I really thought I had her, but gunshot wound and all, she beat me."

All the way up the long street, she smiled a thank-you she couldn't wave to the folks on the street who gave her an enthusiastic welcome at the finish line. She walked Tank under the arch and stood smiling while the checker accounted for her required gear. She spoke for a few minutes with the press and hugged her leader with one arm while the press snapped pictures. Tim Martinson stood grinning in the background.

Alex and Becker stayed close. Caswell, standing with the reluctant Cranshaw by the police squad car, made sure Jessie got what she had asked for. He made Cranshaw watch it all.

Then, when she had petted each one of her dogs, she let Alex take her to the hospital.

Although it was late, they all sat in the Gold Dust Saloon at the Nugget Inn: Becker, Caswell, Holman, Alex, Jessie, Martinson, Schuller, and Ryan. Beer and popcorn had replaced the first round of champagne, ordered, as promised, by Jessie. Alex contentedly filled the air with pipe smoke.

The awards banquet had taken up the major part of the evening. Now they enjoyed one another's company, not wanting the celebration to end. Two-thirds of the racers had crossed the finish line in the four days since the race had been won. Only a few were left on the trail approaching Nome. Already, mushers were discussing strategy for next year's competition.

Since all entrants were required to be at the post-race celebration, most had stayed on. Martinson spent the time in Nome, where no bar in town would allow him to buy his own drinks. Jessie, after two days in the hospital, had been released just the day before, her arm immobilized in a sling.

Cranshaw remained in the Nome correctional facility, but he would later be transferred to Anchorage. Everybody agreed he couldn't get a fair trial in Iditarod City. Jensen, Becker, and Caswell had gone to Anchorage to report and work out the immediate details of the case, then returned for the banquet at the request of Matt Holman.

It had been an exciting and satisfying evening for them all. Packed full, the gym in which the event was held rang with laughter and applause for hours, as trophies were presented and tales of the race shared. There had also been sadness and a sense of loss for the three mushers who had died on the trail, as well as those who had been injured. That both Harvey and Ryan were in Nome for the dinner and festivities was a lift to everyone, glad to see them healing. Pollitt was still in the hospital in Anchorage recovering from surgery, but he sent a telegram.

The IAMS dog food company's sportsmanship award was given to two people: Solomon for staying in the burn with Pollitt until he could be airlifted out, and Murray and Solomon for taking T.J. Harvey back to Shaktoolik through the storm.

Martinson and Jessie had picked up their first- and second-place trophies, to enthusiastic applause and the flash of many cameras.

Midway through the evening, Holman had called the three troopers to the front, where he thanked them for their dedicated perseverance in solving the case. He presented them with patches, usually given only to mushers who complete the race, because, hc said, "They worked as hard as anyone on the trail."

When it was over, the group had walked back to the hotel's saloon.

"You've got to explain a few things to me, Jensen." Jim Ryan leaned across the table. "I missed the last half. When did you know it was Bomber?"

"I was suspicious from McGrath," Alex told him. "But I wasn't sure until much later."

"You did think it could have been me though, didn't you?" Martinson asked.

"Suspected is a better word," Alex answered. "Because you were such a bad ass and could have gone back to McGrath from beyond Takotna to run that moose. And when the trapper described the guy he saw on the snow machine, I did think it might be you for a while."

"Tim," Jessie teased, "you were a pain. I could have kicked you a few times, and I wasn't alone. But you're a pretty nice guy for a winner."

The big musher blushed bright red.

"Yeah," he grinned amid hoots of friendly laughter. "You're okay, too."

Alex watched him, marveling at how his hostility

had disappeared in the pleasure of winning. There was something boyish in him now.

Jessie turned serious. "I still don't understand why Bomber would do those things."

"Well, he talked a lot after he watched you finish. He told Cas that he *needed* to win. That isn't all, of course, but it's what started it. He was about to lose his only sponsor if he didn't make a good showing this year, and he thought he wouldn't be able to race next year. He blames his failures on other people. He has so little self-confidence he had to make up for it by putting competitors out of the race.

"The idea wasn't to kill anyone to begin with. He didn't know Ginny was doing George a favor by filling his thermos at the same time she filled her own. He slipped dope into the thermos marked G.K., thinking it was hers, and was as shocked as anyone when Koptak died, because he really respected George. It upset him badly and changed the equation. He began to panic, caught between doing well in the race and being found out. Afraid Ginny would figure it out, he tried again at Finger Lake and killed her too. Then he doped Smith's dogs when the opportunity presented itself in Rainy Pass.

"The rest of his anger kicked in because of jealousy. He doesn't think women should be allowed to race. You thought he was over that, Jess, but he just didn't let it show until he was angry and scared. He was jealous of you because he was interested in you and got turned down. He let it work on him."

"How the hell did he get the PCP bottle down to Rohn before he poisoned Steve's dogs?" asked Ryan.

Becker, who sat next to him, answered that question. "Like we thought. He poured the stuff into a plastic bag and stashed the bottle on Gail Murray's sled before she left Rainy Pass. It worked loose on the way down, fell off, and Schuller picked it up."

"What about Pollitt and Harvey?"

"They were both accidents," Alex told him. "They confused the issue because all the others looked like accidents to begin with."

"Sure kept us going for a while."

They all started to talk at once, and for the next half-hour, his arm across the back of Jessie's chair, Alex watched and enjoyed the gathering. Caswell said his usual little, but grinned a lot. Holman was already looking forward to the next year's race, making plans and figuring angles.

"Hey, you and Jessie look pretty comfy there, Alex," Becker kidded. "Better watch it. She's a tough act to follow."

"Are we going to have to see much of this motor-mouth?" Jessie asked Jensen with a grin.

" 'Fraid so. But he grows on you, if you only listen to half what he says."

Becker clutched his heart and rolled his eyes at the ceiling.

Alex got to his feet. "Well, guys. It's late."

Reaching across, he took Jessie's good hand to help her up.

"Walk you home, ma'am?"

"Sure, trooper. Yours or mine?"

"Mine. Yours has too many dogs in it."

Here is a thrilling excerpt from another Sue Henry Alaska Mystery as Jessie Arnold returns to the dog racing world for the first time since her award-winning debut in *Murder on the Iditarod Trail* . . .

Murder on the Yukon Quest

An Avon hardcover available at bookstores everywhere

DAWSON CITY WAS LOCATED AT THE CONFLUENCE of the Yukon and Klondike. The added water of the smaller river increased the flow and created rough and rugged winter ice, with huge blocks that had jumbled up the freezing and refreezing—blocks as big as boxcars or small houses that the mushers were forced to run between on a winding track laid down by the trail breakers on their snowmachines.

People from Dawson had worked hard with chain saws, sledge hammers, and axes to clear the way through this silent city of ice, making it as safe as possible for the dogs and drivers. But after a mile or so of twists and turns, Jessie found herself once again forced off the ice for three or four portages onto the historic freight and mail route that had been used by mushers in the old days. It took complete concentration and quick reactions to avoid crashes as she ran the team back and forth between this trail and the river track below it.

"Take a left, Tank—go gee. Up now, onto the bank. Good boy. Haw—go haw now. That's it. Good dogs."

Her leader gave her a glance over his shoulder that

told her she needn't have bothered with instructions, that he *was* totally capable of negotiating the obstacle course on his own, as he moved with experienced confidence up the riverbank and along the trail.

After this demanding section, Jessie noticed that the land around the river had begun to widen, allowing its banks to spread farther apart, and the slowing of the current had made smoother ice as it froze in the fall. Because of this, and also due to the many small rivers and creeks that poured into it during the warmer months of the year, the broadening Yukon showed the first signs of becoming a really big river.

Through the night she ran alone, neither passing, nor being passed by, another musher. Once she thought she heard dogs barking a long way behind her, and going around a bend in the river more than two hours after leaving Dawson, saw a flash of light that might have been a musher's headlamp, but it did not reappear. For the first time in several years of mushing, she felt very much alone and vulnerable. It reminded her of the fear she had experienced during one Iditarod race, when she had known there was a killer on the trail somewhere. Tension tightened her neck and shoulder muscles, and kept her awake and alert, on the lookout for anything unusual.

The temperature had dropped a little more and the sky was overcast, allowing no light from moon or aurora borealis to add definition to the trail with soft light and deep shadows. The dogs kept up a good pace, well rested and eager to run as they always were when starting a new race. After the long layover in Dawson, this seemed like a new race, but she knew that the feeling was also because her objective in running had decidedly shifted. Now it was much more a race to deliver the ransom and less a race to Fairbanks. It no longer mattered so much to her where, or even if, she placed well in the Yukon Quest.

Where and when, she wondered, would she find out how to drop the money she carried? Who would pick it up? How would they contact her? Was anyone keeping track of her progress? It would be difficult for anyone to come near her on the trail without her knowledge. But they could certainly find out where she was at a couple of unofficial stopping places along the river between Dawson and Eagle.

A stiff and chilly breeze had come up, swirling dry grains of snow across the ice in ripples and waves, moaning enough to make it difficult for anyone at a distance to hear the scraping sounds of her runners over the ice and her infrequent commands to her dogs, though her headlamp would be a bright, moving point of light in the darkness. Her vision was limited to what fell within the circle of light from that lamp, so she saw very little of what she was passing.

Mushers, intent on winning a race, trying to keep other racers from knowing how fast they were traveling, or exactly where they were, sometimes turned off their headlamps and ran in the dark trusting their lead dog to keep the team on a trail other dogs had passed over before them. This could be misleading if the front runner took a wrong turn and it was not unheard of for several racers to wind up lost together and retracing their own trail.

It was pleasant to run dark when the northern lights were putting on a show overhead, but in the inky blackness of this overcast, Jessie had no inclination to switch off her headlamp, for she found that even the single, narrow beam was a comfort compared to the immensity of the wilderness that surrounded her. This was a foreign feeling, for she often found it more comfortable to be out with her dogs in the wide, welcoming, open spaces of the north than holed up inside walls and behind closed doors. Now she was constantly aware that anything, or anyone, could be out there, unseen. She felt observed, as if some threatening watcher knew exactly where she was and followed her every move from some hidden location. The feeling made her swallow hard and glance often behind her, though there was never anything to see, and if there had been, she could hardly have seen it anyway, light-blind as she was.

At one long curve of the river, high on a west bank that Jessie felt was there, but could not make out, a figure *was* watching as she steadily moved past on the ice below. The bluff was not so high as that on the Takhini a few days earlier in the race, but it was farther from the track the racers followed, for the river here was much wider and the trail breakers had found the smoothest ice near the center of it.

Secreted in the black silence of the night, a lone individual stood beside the snowmachine that had carried him to the spot an hour earlier. There he had waited, frequently moving to make sure his feet were warm in their insulated boots, swinging his arms and tucking his hands in their heavy mitts into his armpits a time or two—not because they were cold, but because it seemed that they should be, with the temperature hovering at less than twenty below. As the bobbing beam of Jessie's headlamp fell onto the scarlet bag of gear in her sled, it illuminated the white letters of the name painted on the side, *Arnold Kennels*, and from his lookout the watcher knew this was indeed the musher for whom he had waited. He stood without moving near one of the trees that lined the banks of the river and waited until the dancing light disappeared around the next bend. Then he waited a while longer and, twenty minutes later, was rewarded by the appearance of another light following the same track.

He did not bother to ascertain the identity of this racer, wanting only to know how closely Jessie was being followed by the next team, but did not start up the engine of the snowmachine until this light had also vanished around the bend. Then the machine roared to life, shattering the peaceful stillness.

Another musher, still out of sight, heard it and raised her head from the standing doze she had fallen into on the runners of her sled, wondering what on earth anyone could be doing out along an uninhabited section of the Yukon in the frozen dark. The sound was faint however, and had ended by the time she rounded a curve and approached the location where the watcher had stood, so she shrugged it off and continued toward Forty Mile.

Running on the ice of a river, though tough at times, was always essentially the same—flat. Washing in broad bends through a sweeping expanse of country following the path of least resistance, rivers lack sharp curves, and do not give mushers and sleds the up and down motion of a trail on solid ground. Adding to the sameness was an odd feeling that Jessie was making no headway at all in the total dark, that the forward motion of the team was an illusion and she was remaining in the same place—like a jogger on a treadmill.

Clouds overhead reflect light back to the earth, when there is light to be reflected. In the enormous almost deserted wilderness between Canada and

Alaska there is seldom any light at all and what there is comes only from the tiny fire a musher may build for warmth or food, or the glow from a cabin's window that barely reaches the snow-covered ground outside. Such slight gleams are easily snatched and swallowed up by the encroaching dark.

Traveling through the blackness on ice over water often gave Jessie a sensation of being somehow suspended, that she was floating, not really touching the earth, though the surface, in most places frozen several feet deep, was more than substantial. She had noticed the same feeling close to the end of the Iditarod as she traveled across the sea ice of North Sound near Nome.

Sometime before midnight she pulled up the bank and stopped for a short rest at a tiny wilderness cabin that belonged to a former Quest racer, then continued for another hour and took a long one in a spot on the riverbank where she found Ryan bedding down his own team, cooker already alight under a kettle of melting snow.

"Hey," he greeted her quietly, careful not to disturb the team that was resting close to his, another musher soundly sleeping on a pile of straw near his dogs.

"Who's that?"

"Gail Murray. Glad you made it. Everything okay?"

"Just fine. It's pretty black out there, though. I didn't get to see much of the country."

"Like running in a tunnel, isn't it? I've made a daylight run through here before, going the other direction, and you didn't miss much but riverbank and miles of ice. The wind's picking up—it'll be howling down the channel soon. Guess you were right about the weather changing. We're supposed to catch some more snow on the summit."

"At least we'll be going over most of that in the daylight. I think I'd rather be blinded by snow than only be able to see what my headlamp hits and have to imagine the rest."

"Yeah, me, too. Still, it could be a real struggle. This summit doesn't have a lot of switchbanks, just a couple of quick ones. It just goes up and up—straight up the mountain at an angle so steep you'll be pushing your sled to help the dogs keep it moving, when it's just about all you can do to move yourself. You think it's never going to end, then it goes on some more, and that's in good weather. In bad weather it can be a real bitch. There're always teams that quit and refuse to go on until they've rested and made up their minds to it, and there's no place to rest that's out of the wind and blowing snow."

"Sounds just peachy. I can hardly wait."

"I'm not fooling, Jessie. Be ready for it."

"I know. I will be. But right now I'm more concerned with getting these guys and myself fed. Then I'll crash until about six. There's still the rest of the run to Forty Mile and up that river before I have to start climbing."

Jessie did not sleep well; she woke up several times at small sounds in the dark that made her take long looks around their camp, finding nothing untoward. She was glad to be resting with someone else, but wondered if she should have found a solitary spot. What if the kidnappers had intended to approach her when she stopped, not as she had been expecting, while she was traveling. Well, she decided, too late now. If that had been their plan, they'd just have to wait. They can't expect me to begin to think the way they do. Though maybe I already have, she thought and hated the idea that her racing strategy was being influenced.

When she woke to the sound of her alarm, Gail Murray, the sleeping musher, had already departed with her team and Ryan was harnessing his dogs.

"Coffee's over there by the fire," he told her as she rose from the sleeping bag she had placed atop her sled, stretched and stomped around to help get her circulation going. "There's hot water in my cooker, if you want some before I mix it with kibble to take along for the dogs."

Jessie used some of it to wash her face, then poured coffee over powdered hot chocolate in her insulated mug, to which she added two heaping, calorie-loaded spoonfuls of sugar. As Ryan packed the rest of his gear, she moved a skillet from her sled bag onto the fire, tossed in a dozen frozen sausages and a handful of snow. They would steam themselves thawed and hot, then brown when the water evaporated. While she drank the hot chocolate and waited for her breakfast and water for dog food to heat, she watched Ryan finish his preparations.

"Those sure smell good. Sure you don't want me to wait a bit?" he questioned, turning to her when he was ready to go.

She laughed. "Yes, if you mean you want more breakfast. There's enough, with some powdered eggs. Otherwise, no. I'll be okay by myself, Jim. You go on and make good time. Maybe I'll see you at Forty Mile for another break."

"If not, I'll be watching in Eagle to be sure you come in."

She gave him part of an hour before putting her own team back on the Yukon River ice, taking even more seriously the instruction that she must run alone. After this, she would make sure she camped alone, too, unless the unofficial checkpoints came at times when the team needed to rest.

Damned if I let these guys destroy my whole race for me, she thought, heading down the steep bank to the ice again.

The cabins at the tiny site of Forty Mile are the farthest west buildings in Canada. Built even before the Klondike gold rush at a place where the Forty Mile River meets the Yukon, it was believed to be forty miles from a trading post, Fort Reliance, near where Dawson City would later be established. In reality, it was closer to fifty miles between the two.

Jessie was perhaps five miles from the Forty Mile River, when she was passed by a racer she had not encountered before in the front runners. Slowly, he pulled up behind her with a team of eleven dogs, called for the trail, and went by as she pulled her dogs to one side of the track.

"Thanks," he called out, bringing a mitten to the band of a bright orange stocking cap in a jaunty salute as he passed.

She encouraged the team back into its normal seven to eight mile an hour trot, then slowed them slightly, ignoring Tank's tendency to try to race after anyone who got in front of him, talking him into a trot of about seven miles an hour. The ice was quite smooth and slick, easy running, so they cruised along, watching the distance slowly grow between them and the orange-capped musher, who seemed in a hurry to reach the next stop. He was still in sight, however, when he reached the place where the Forty Mile River ran into the Yukon.

The churning water at the meeting of the two rivers had resulted in rougher ice, with thick and thin spots that must be carefully negotiated, a dangerous situation for those traveling the frozen highway with heavy sleds. Jessie was just close enough to be able to see a large hole in the ice by the left hand bank, where someone had broken through sometime earlier, when she heard a shout, accompanied by an ominous cracking, and the other driver was suddenly waist deep in icy water, his sled rapidly sinking; the wheel dogs and two more on the line were being yanked in with it.

Calling her team to a lope, Jessie quickly drove a wide circle to the right to be sure she was on solid ice, stopped the dogs, threw down the hook, which refused to dig into the hard surface, and ran across to grab at the team leaders of the sinking sled, trusting Tank to keep the dogs where she had left them. The driver was now completely wet and struggling with the sled, which was partially afloat with air trapped in its bag. Still on firm ice, the dogs at the front of the other team were scrabbling, toenails scraping frantically to find a purchase on the slick surface, but being inexorably drawn back toward the hole by the weight of the team and sled. Jessie threw herself down and added her body weight to the front of the line, which helped stabilize their slow, steady, backward slide toward the freezing water.

Someone on the bank was shouting in the dark and she had the impression of a light, but couldn't turn to see if help was coming without loosening her tenuous hold on the line. In the water the racer, headlamp still burning and in jerking motion, was gasping with the shock of the sudden cold, but kicking hard, trying to shove the sled onto the shelf of solid ice, which continued to break off in chunks. Finally, after long moments that resulted in burning pain to her arms and shoulders as Jessie pulled with all her strength and felt that she was getting nowhere, the tension on the line eased a little and two of the drenched dogs managed to clamber out onto unbroken ice. Immediately, she helped the rest of the team take up any slack and prayed the ice wouldn't break again. It held long enough for the wheel dogs to climb out as well, but she was distrustful, almost certain it would crack under the burden of the fully loaded sled, its weight increased with water and becoming more saturated by the second.

"Hup, boys. Pull, Silver," the half drowned and frozen musher was calling through clinched teeth to his leader, the dog pulling beside Jessie's right shoulder.

With almost super-human strength, he managed a strong kick and gave the sled a giant shove that, along with the efforts of the whole team of dogs and Jessie, tipped it up and far enough onto the solid ice to keep it from sliding back. Remarkably, the ice still held. Scrambling to her feet, still holding tightly to the line, she carefully moved the dogs forward, giving thanks that most mushers have strong upper bodies from sled wrestling and weight training.

"Come, Silver . . . keep them coming," she encouraged the dog, talking her forward.

As the obedient leader threw her shoulders against the harness with all her weight and will, slowly the soaked figure of the musher was dragged out of the hole behind the sled, clinging desperately to a rear stanchion, dripping water that immediately began to freeze his clothing to the ice on which he collapsed, gasping. As he let go, rolled, and struggled to regain his footing, Jessie kept his team in motion until she had moved it away from any thin ice, closer to her own and in no danger. Leaving it, she went quickly back to do what she could for the musher, knowing the man was now in more danger than the dogs, though they would need help, too, or they could freeze; their undercoats were clearly sodden.

Three men from the tiny settlement, watching for approaching mushers on the river, had seen the accident, climbed down the bank, and were hurrying across the ice, flashlight beams joggling as they ran. They carried a rope, which was now unnecessary, and a blanket, which was.

"Th-th-a-anks," the dripping racer, so cold he could hardly speak, managed to sputter at Jessie, as he was cocooned in the blanket and forcefully propelled toward the bank by one of his three would-be rescuers. "My t-t-team."

"Don't worry about it," he was told. "We'll take care of them. He's the vet." A hand was waved in the direction of the other two, one of whom was already getting set to drive the team toward some buildings Jessie could just make out on the edge of the dark river. "Let's get you inside, where it's warm, and out of those wet clothes."

"You okay?" one of them asked her.

"Yes, fine."

"That was a good job you did. We'll see you up there then." And they were off, hastening to find life-giving warmth for the man and his dogs.

He was lucky to have gone through the ice in a place with assistance and a fire handy. Soaked and shivering mushers who had fallen through the ice far from any shelter were forced to build their own quick fires and hope for dry clothes to change into, stripping off their wet ones as fast as possible, sometimes hopping from one bare foot to the other in the snow. Most carried a complete set of extra clothing and outwear carefully sealed in plastic for just such an emergency. Boots, even with felt liners, could be emptied of water and put back on, for their cold-repelling insulation worked the other way as well and kept feet warm even when they were damp. The dogs had to be rubbed as dry as possible, then kept near the fire like their driver.

Glad the accident had not resulted in serious problems, Jessie went back to her own team, which had remained standing where she left them.

"Good, dogs. Oh, you are the very best dogs in the whole world," she told them, giving each one a pat or two.

When she looked back at the frightening hole in the ice, her headlamp caught the bright orange of the musher's hat, floating gently in water that had already developed a thin skin of ice. Leaving it to its fate, she drove on into the historic site of Forty Mile.

"I couldn't have got out without you," the musher, warm and dry, though still suffering a periodic shiver, told her later.

"You'd have done the same, if I'd gone through," Jessie told him honestly. "Hey, do you have a name?"

He grinned. "You want to know who you're responsible for, now that you saved my life?"

"Nope, just want to be able to tell about it," she teased. "Can't tell credible tales without names. Besides, you saved your own skin. I was just an anchor."

"I'm John," he told her, holding out a hand. "John Noble."

His grip conveyed the temperature of the mug of

hot soup he had been using as a handwarmer between swallows.

"Oh, you're the guy your handlers were bragging about in Dawson, on their way to Gerdes. You're a very good musher, from what I was told."

"Terry, right? And Hank? Had to be the night they went out to party."

"Might have been just a bit sloshed, as I remember it," she grinned.

"And who are you?"

"Jessie Arnold."

"Yeah? Hey, wait a minute. I've got something for you."

He turned to the gear that was spread out to dry around the small trapper's cabin that a hundred years earlier had been a gold rush store and dug into the wet pocket of the parka he had been wearing when he took his unexpected bath.

"Here," he said, handing her a soggy, folded envelope. "Sorry about the baptism, but it's probably still readable."

Stomach tightening as she recognized the squarely penciled letters that formed her name on the outside, Jessie sincerely hoped so.